CHICAGO NOIR

CHICAGO NOIR

EDITED BY NEAL POLLACK

AKASHIC BOOKS
NEW YORK

This collection is comprised of works of fiction. All names, characters, places, and incidents are the product of the authors' imaginations. Any resemblance to real events or persons, living or dead, is entirely coincidental.

Series concept by Tim McLoughlin and Johnny Temple

Published by Akashic Books
©2005 Akashic Books
Chicago map by Sohrab Habibion

ISBN-13: 978-1-888451-89-4
ISBN-10: 1-888451-89-0
Library of Congress Control Number: 2005925468
All rights reserved
Second printing
Printed in Canada

Akashic Books
PO Box 1456
New York, NY 10009
Akashic7@aol.com
www.akashicbooks.com

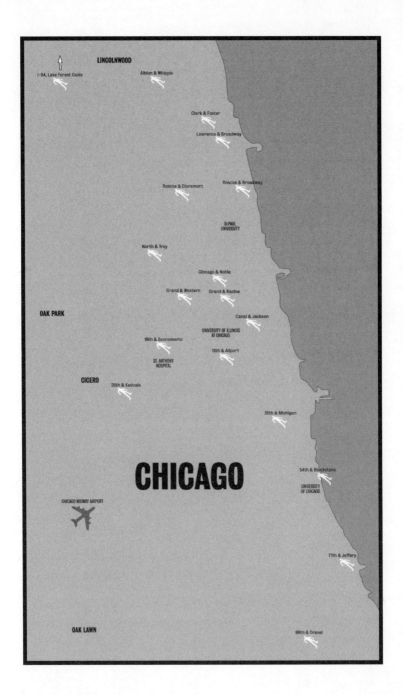

Now I'm walkin' on the sidewalks of Chicago
If I buy the bread I can't afford the wine
Now I'm walkin' on the sidewalks of Chicago
Wishin' I had lived some other time
—Merle Haggard

TABLE OF CONTENTS

INTRODUCTION
ONCE THERE WAS A CITY

While I was working as a reporter in Chicago, from 1993 to 2000, the city changed. Very profound, you say. *Of course* the city changed in seven years; that's what cities do. True enough, but cities change during certain periods more than others. In the '90s, Chicago changed *a lot*, and it's changed even more, and more quickly, in the years since I've left.

It's very possible to visit Chicago these days and see no more grit than you would in, say, Indianapolis. During his nearly twenty-year reign over the city, Richard M. Daley has overseen a studied program of urban renewal, civic booster-ism, and tourist pleasing. His Chicago shines with a well-buffed gloss. One by one, the weird old bars and restaurants, the bizarre little museums, the hardware stores that never had any customers disappeared, some in blatant land-grabs, others subtly, almost imperceptibly, like construction dust blown out to the lake. In their place stand condos and fresh-brick branch libraries, a Frank Gehry bandshell, and a spaceship in the middle of Soldier Field. In many ways, it's a better city than the one Mayor Daley inherited, but it's a far less interesting one, and it certainly makes for less interesting stories.

Chicago's literature, with a brief detour into the world of Saul Bellow and occasional forays by Theodore Dreiser, has rarely concerned itself with the vagaries of the upper and upper-middle classes. The city's best writers—Nelson

Algren, James Farrell, Studs Terkel, Richard Wright, and so on—have traditionally used working people as their palette. They accurately captured the rough streets and random cruelty of urban life, but for people living in Chicago, their stories meant something more. They shaped the way Chicagoans think about themselves, and about Chicago.

The excellent new stories I've collected in this volume try to fill the gap between how the world sees Chicago and how Chicago sees itself. Many of the stories take nostalgia as a theme. Some have a yellowing snapshot feel, as though they're trying to archive a city that's just about gone. Adam Langer looks wistfully back at neighborhood life in the 1970s. C.J. Sullivan's protagonist, long past whatever sad prime he once had, also remembers the '70s as a golden age. Peter Orner drifts even further back, to the 1950s, while inhabiting the mind of one of Chicago's most sinister criminals, and Claire Zulkey visits the city 100 years ago, when people were strange and their crimes even stranger. Now *that* was a city worth writing about.

This is a *noir* book, so it features a little police procedural and lots of gory violence. It contains the full range of urban types, from jazzmen to slam poets, cab drivers to shop-owners, barflies, waitresses, petty thieves, lovelorn husbands, and sexual predators both gay and straight. But Chicago noir, to me, has a special quality of nostalgia, an extra dimension that makes nearly every story seem like an epitaph for a city now gone.

A classic Chicago joke goes, "What are the three Chicago streets that rhyme with vagina?" The answer, "Malvina, Paulina, and Lunt."

For those of you who haven't now slammed the book down in disgust, I'm using that joke to illustrate something. Chicago's neighborhoods have totemic value to those who treasure them, but even more important are its street names. Every intersection runs thick with meaning, and every one has its own personality. So I've organized the book by intersection, moving from the Southeast Side, with its view of the smokestacks of Gary, Indiana, to the verdant Wisconsin border in the north. Along the way, many faces of Chicago appear, and the truth of the city's segregation reveals itself. The first part of the book, the South Side part, is mostly black, with occasional glimpses of the Jews who used to rule that part of town. Then, as we move to mid-South, the book takes on a distinctly Hispanic impression: Mexican, Cuban, and Puerto Rican concerns rule the day, with a paprika sprinkle of Eastern Europe. Once you hit downtown, things turn Anglo pretty fast, with plenty of down-and-out types, but very little variation in skin tone. There's a brief detour into the melting-pot diversity of the far North Side, and we end up in the northern suburbs, the domain of the WASP ruling class. It's a journey as old as the city itself, though none of the stories take place on Malvina, Paulina, or Lunt.

Now, with your permission, I'd like to dedicate this book to some of the places I knew in a Chicago that no longer exist. Don's Coffee Club, Weeds, Rest-n-Pieces, Bucket O' Suds, Ronny's Steak Palace, Sharon's Hillbilly Heaven. The names alone invoke a city that's more dream than reality. But those places were real, and I knew them well. They, along with so many other spots now gone, comprised the Chicago I loved. Hopefully with this book, and with the help of these excellent writers, I can put a small piece of that city back. I hope you enjoy these stories as much as I do.

Neal Pollack
Austin, Texas
May 2005

GOODNIGHT CHICAGO AND AMEN

BY LUCIANO GUERRIERO

99th & Drexel

Never know how you gonna end up. Or when and where. Or why, for that matter. You just know you will. You will end up somehow, somewhere, sometime. That something to think about. It is now, anyway.

I always been an all-purpose guy, game for pretty much whatever you got, long's it bring me what I want or what I need. I'm mostly known as a robber, stickups and like I help jack an armored truck once, and hold up a whole bunch of stores and shit. But I also commit arson for some guy over insurance money, deliver heavy weight of drugs plenty times. Etc. and so on. Never knock over no bank yet—I always seen myself doing that, but it don't seem likely now.

I done murders too. Three, to be exact. Usually I do murders for five heavy, my rate. I done one for half price once, as a favor to somebody. But five is my rate for murder, less there's extra risk or something else hairy about it. Then it take more.

Back starting out, I never think I be doing hits. But my twenties they behind me and I'm trying to branch out. Since this here new hit job's a cop, one of them "something else hairy" murders, this one takes five up front and *another five* behind.

Yeah, Katrina's paying me ten large for this one and I'm

happy about that. Plus, doing a cop puts me on a whole new level far as future work goes. Not every hitter will take on a cop job, and for good reason—the reaction is stone fierce, man. Still, set up for this one nice, seems sane enough to me, so it's perfect, suits my needs.

Specially now, I need the boost. See, a week ago I got out of Joliet after four and a half on a five-to-ten for an armed robbery that went bad. Nobody inside got in my shit though cuz word spread that I'm connected, so I did my time clean and walked early.

I get connected cuz after the heist my car gets slammed by a mail truck and it break up my leg pretty good, so I get nabbed. I go deaf and dumb right away, take the whole weight of it on myself, cop myself a plea for a reduced sentence and no trial, no further investigation. Kind of guy I am. So on my taking the bust, my partner on the heist, gangsta man named Blue who's driving the other car, he stay free and clear.

Blue one capable guy. His operation gets even bigger since I go in. Blue naturally is grateful to me, which you can understand, sends word in to his boys that I should do easy time. The brothers make sure the time I do is easy as pie. Or as easy as any time can get in prison, which sucks any way you look at it. But it could be a lot worse, is what I'm saying, cuz I'm one stand-up guy about the whole thing.

Second I hit free air outside the Joliet walls, Blue has a car there to ride me back to town. Driver tells me Blue wants me at his new bar next night, Blue's setting me up for a sweet little payday. That's what this cop hit is all about, far as I'm concerned. Little reward.

Yeah, okay, I know it ain't too swift to go on parole for armed robbery and right away do some cop murder. But this ten grand gets me set up again, like a human being, not some brain-dead rodent ex-con sweeping supermarket floors. I'm sending Blue a Christmas card this year, though he never send me one inside. Kind of guy I am.

Some shit happens during the week, and seven days later, here we go, we on the job, me and this uncle named Hector in coveralls, shovels in hand. Katrina is watching us dig. Soil in this yard is good and black, smelling like rotten leaves and earthworms. Gonna turn a body to compost in, like, two seconds.

Look, she cocking her head now, listening for out-of-the-ordinary sounds that might float their way back here through the evening air. Katrina's sharp. Hector, the guy digging with me, he got no idea how sharp she is. He gonna find out, though.

This a good spot, the edge of Blue's turf in the 8th Ward. We digging behind some apartment houses on Drexel north of 99th Street. People in this nabe know not to get too nosy, even if they do see something. They better off look the other way, and that's what they do. I just can't picture nobody calling cops about the suspicious earth turned near the tree in the backyard.

I'm making like I ain't looking at Katrina, cuz I'm s'posed to be cool. But I do see she almost topples back when them stiletto heels sink down in the wet sod. Lord, her thigh muscles flex really nice when she bends her knees and shifts her weight to the balls of her feet, sliding them heels free.

I should look away, though, before Hector notices me checking out her legs. But shit, why not look? Not only do Katrina got bitchin' legs, but that fine piece a ass knows it too. Yeah, I take myself a decent look. Long as we keep digging, what she gonna say? This ain't church.

Damn, it's getting cold, though. October breeze down out of Canada, gusting off the lake. Every so often the hem on Katrina's thin little mini goes up and I can see every bit of them Tina Turner thighs. Yeah, and look, she know she distracting us, which I can tell by how she folds her arms across her chest, hiding them nips like we ain't already been checking them out too. It's her way of trying to get this here business done, not cuz she some prude. Katrina definitely *not* no prude.

Every so often a shovel clangs against a stone and we all freeze and look around the backyard. I can understand their feelings. Digging somebody's grave some serious business. But if I'm thinking at all, it ain't about a shovel hitting a rock. I'm thinking mostly about this ghost watching us.

Katrina tells me before we come here ghost all taken care of, nothing to worry about, so we do this thing tonight and nobody gonna step in early. Now, though, Katrina's playing the whole thing straight, making like she don't know about no ghost, I guess to keep Hector's head in the right place. I'm playing along, freezing when she do, giving nobody reason to squint their eyes at me later. I can just picture Katrina later, telling everybody in the bar how I'm one hell of an actor, which I'm gonna love. She look down now and see me smiling at that, which I can see she don't understand.

Katrina breaks up the freeze with a nod toward the hole we standing in waist deep. Me and Hector start digging again, making the pile to one side. Way she look at Hector, I can tell she expect my boy to say something stupid, and my boy don't disappoint.

"Ain't this goddamn hole deep enough yet?" he whispers loud.

"Dig it my way, Hector, head-deep," she spits back, eyes

flashing all serious. "No more static, now, you dig."

Hector give a pause looking at her like he don't like her tone. On cue, she repeats herself, even more serious, "Just dig."

I smack him on the arm and he get digging again. Hector can't tell, but I see Katrina worried about his attitude. She wants this thing to go smooth and if he's all belligerent and shit, could be trouble. Guess she don't know I'm here to take care of any and all business tonight, no matter what. S'okay. This my first job with her. If seeing's believing, she find out good what she got in me, and soon enough.

Can't help thinking while I dig, though, my mind moving around. Thinking about the night after I get out of Joliet, hanging around Blue's bar when Katrina comes in. Place is on Dobson Avenue right near to 95th Street. Busy spot, but not too busy. Neighborhood place, mostly people Blue know coming in.

"Don't make that much money, but it's just like I like it," Blue say to me, cranking the music. Always great music playing in Blue's place, just like his crib.

They call the man Blue cuz his skin so black they say it looks blue, which all I see is dark brown, but then I don't care about that shit. Always funny to me how the brothers and sisters always got their skin tone in mind, like it matter somehow, while a white boy like me don't give it no real thought. I never understand that.

Katrina goes back in the office with Blue that first night and right quick they send word out I should come back. Blue introduces us and right off she flirtatious. I look at Blue and he laughs with Katrina coming off all mad hot for me, which is all the okay I need. This, you know, like, especially being inside Joliet for that amount of time, kinda gets my attention.

You also have to understand one thing, I'm impressed as hell with the fact Blue and Katrina bringing me in this way, me being white and all. Hardly ever works that way in Chicago, or anywhere that I know. But I tell myself they smart, cuz all they interested in, and all they should be interested in, is talent. That and loyalty, which I proved to Blue some years back.

So I'm thinking right away in the bar this Katrina chick's got a thing for me, partly cuz of what I am to Blue, and I'm real happy about that. Right off, I'm taking my time sucking in air and eyeing her up and down, like some kind of real stud, which let's face it is a stretch for somebody look like me. But 'tude always counts for a lot with chicks and I got plenty a dat, so in half a snap Katrina has me in a cab back to her hotel and I'm already thinking I da man.

We get in the room and things don't quite go like I think. I mean, Katrina lets this inner tigress out to play. This stone freak Amazon lady is surprising the hell outta me, all pure aggressiveness and shit, and I'm thinking, hell, not what I'm used to but this gonna be good. She pulls out this box of toys, and I'm like, okay, fine, she must be one of them electro-magnetized robo-chicks who gets off on modern technology, plenty of those around. But then she announces the toys are for me, not her, and now I'm in way too deep to refuse.

Let's just say we go at it real good, till we both like totally wrung out. And I'm thinking later she uses me maybe like some prison daddy might, only I don't give a shit what she do to me, it being a long, long time for me.

After all that, she figures I'll do whatever she wants— even dig a grave. For her. And even though I see that clear enough, she right about it anyway. I mean, I take the job for the money alone, but she show me some personal interest and it's just what the doctor ordered. I leave that room sure she got a thing for white boys, sure she wants me to be her Chicago man for a while. Cuz all the signs are there. And I need 'em all to be true.

Next night, things with me all arranged, she comes back to the bar and Blue puts her in touch with Hector. Blue got some mad blues playing on the system and I'm watching them from a stool down the other end, sipping drinks while Blue's driver goes on about how Blue got some big-ass moves in the works. I want to see how Katrina plays it with Hector, see if last night's jag was for me alone or if she do that with just anybody.

Katrina start doing the flirt thing with Hector and he's real funny, man. He's like drooling at *hello*, and right away she know he so totally into her she don't even need to toss him a tumble like she did me. She just shoot him some hot looks, and tease him with a little dirty dance in the middle of the floor. Seems like the dance leaves him half-unconscious with desire. And that is that. Deal is sealed. She tells me later in her room that Hector even buys her excuse why they can't go somewhere and do it tonight, so I figure Katrina really plays that macho muchacho hands down, bitch is something else.

After that, though, when Katrina tells me Hector's the goddamned uncle we gotta take care of, you could push me over with a fingertip. I would *never* make that guy as an undercover cop. She tells me they find out he the one sours a whole bunch of gigs they got going on while I'm in the joint, tells me it's Hector put some of Blue's key guys in jail, and now they gotta put an end to it. That's when I'm thinking maybe Hector *allows* Katrina to play him that way in the bar that night, cuz cops ain't supposed to get it on with the women they working to put away.

Probably both are true—Katrina *is* truly hot enough to get Hector thinking with the little head, but also Hector made it easy for her to seal the deal without having to seduce him cuz he a goddamn *cop*. Hell, this crazy game's all good to me. One way or another don't change a thing. Just pay me and point the way and I am there.

But like I say, once Katrina lets me in on the job details, one question keeps nagging at me, all night: What's going on with Hector's ghost? These uncle guys almost never work undercover without some other cop keep an eye on them from the shadows. Some cop watching me do away with his partner puts me in mind that this job could toss me in the deepest of shit in a freakin' heartbeat. And nobody do short *or* easy time off a cop murder, cuz they make sure every single minute you do inside is a living hell.

Katrina quick. She see my concern, tries to calm my nerves by telling how she and Blue have this sweet arrangement with Hector's ghost, this old cop Eddie.

"Eddie?" I say, that name perking me right up. "Eddie McClusky?"

"Yeah, you know him?" she say.

"Bad-ass mother," I say. "Eddie's an Unknown Chicago Legend."

"What d'ya mean, unknown?" she say.

"To the public," I say. "But not to half the population of Joliet. I even hear about Bad-ass Eddie Mac when I'm on the street before I do my stretch. How you so sure Eddie ain't playing y'all?"

"Don't you worry," she say. "Me and Blue don't do this if it ain't all in place."

"Do me favor," I say. "Lay it out for me and I decide if I should worry or not."

I see she pissed at my question, but I guess she decides it's fair to ask, so she gives me the respect I deserve and answers me. "First off, Eddie played ball with Blue plenty in the past."

"Wait a sec, you saying Eddie Mac ain't righteous?" I say. "That ain't the word I hear. How about all them arrests he bring down?"

"When it suits Eddie to play straight, he bring arrests down," she say. "When it don't, he don't. That big Irish gang bust over in Bridgeport? Believe me, Blue helped Eddie out with that. It don't happen if Blue don't come through big."

I'm laughing now. "You saying Blue helping Eddie Mac lock up the bad guys?"

"Blue and Eddie only do deals when they *both* get something out of it. If they don't, they enemies again."

"Okay, so what's Eddie getting out of knocking off this uncle Hector?" I say.

"Hector knows Eddie play both sides of the street, Eddie don't trust him to be cool. We do this for Eddie, Eddie do something else for Blue," she say. "But I don't know what, cuz that's 'tween Blue and Eddie, and it don't matter to me."

I see it do matter to Katrina, but I leave it right there, cuz I can also see she knows Eddie'll be cool when it all goes down and that's what really matters to me.

"Heavy duty, baby," I say, smiling again. "That's the real deal."

She puts her hand flat on my chest, all sincere and tender.

"We gonna have to lay real low after the job, though," she say. "Think maybe you and me go somewhere and enjoy the quiet life for a little bit?"

"Sounds good," I say, cuz it do sound good.

"I got a place in Costa Rica."

"Gotta get around my parole thing here, baby, but you singing my song."

"Good, Zane," she say. "You gonna like it down there."

I want to ask her about how she first get involved with Blue's business, but I leave that for some other time. Maybe when we in Costa Rica. And I'm wondering how I got this lucky all of a sudden, money in my pocket, beautiful woman all into me. All this shit going through my brain as me and Hector are digging the hole toward head-deep, like Katrina orders us to do, and I keep on thinking and thinking and thinking like this. Wondering what I know.

I know what Katrina say about Eddie, about Blue and Eddie, that's what. And I know Blue owe me. And knowing Blue and Katrina got my back is good enough for me, or I wouldn't be here. But I still can't help coming back around to Eddie Mac, Hector's ghost, lurking out there in the dark watching his partner dig his own grave. I know I should be scared out of my skin over this job, but now that Katrina and Blue lay it out for me, I'm cool. Except for the sweat soaking through my dark green coveralls, about ten percent fear sweat and the rest shoveling sweat, even in the chilly night air.

All this digging is boring now, and I'm sneaking peeks at Katrina checking her watch. We been working this pit a good while, breathing heavy, and my eyes are level with her toes. Hector's head don't even reach up to the grass, he being one short Puerto Rican. Got dirt in my coveralls, dirt on my face, dirt soiling my brand new White Sox cap, dirt in my boots, blisters on my hands, but from this angle I ain't thinking of none a that, cuz I can see right up under that miniskirt, right to Katrina's white thong against her smooth coffee skin, and what a heavenly sight that is. I want to just pull her down and get us both really dirty right here in this black soil.

But she surprise me.

"Good enough," she say. "Zane, use your shovel to get out first."

Show Time is at hand. I prop the shovel against the end of the grave, spade end down on a rock, and use it as a step to boost myself up. My heart's racing now cuz I been thinking about everything else but the big moment.

Katrina back off a step or two as I climb out. Like me and Katrina plan, I hold my hand down to Hector and say, "Don't leave it behind," and he hands me his shovel.

Then he looks down to step on my spade end, his hands grabbing at the sod above, ready to boost himself out of the grave. He still looking down as his head comes up, and I take a full swing with his shovel right down hard on his head. Only it don't hit quite square and the edge of the shovel scoop off a hunk of Hector's scalp and skull bone, which goes flipping onto the grass at Katrina's feet like a bloody tea saucer.

You could even see some of Hector's brain sitting in it like some freaky *Fear Factor* stunt. Sight gross me out, man, don't know why cuz I seen that before. Lying back in that grave, Hector give out this puny little cry and his body start in on some serious shaking.

Can't say I feel nothing much as I watch Hector shiver and bleed out the top his skull, 'cept maybe tired and dirty, just want to finish and go clean off this dirt. So I lean down and grab my shovel up out of the pit, and just when I straighten up—*BAM*—this explosion slams the inside of my head—and everything goes queer and too slow—and then I'm coming out of this blackness and I find myself looking up from inside that pit, Hector underneath me trying to shake even with my weight on top of him.

After I don't know how long, I'm coming out of another darkness and I see Eddie Mac and Katrina looking down at me. Eddie Mac holds a nine with a silencer on it. Then things go black again.

Next time I come back from the dark, I'm half covered with dirt. I can't hardly see cuz dirt's on part of my face and some in my mouth and I can't lift my head to shake it off. I try to call out to Katrina, but can't make no words. I try to get up but my body don't care what I try, it won't budge.

With my one eye that can see, I see that Eddie Mac's busy shoving dirt down from the pile, working at the end where my feet are. I can hear him pant cuz the old guy's working hard. I can move my left arm and I try to bring it up and take the dirt off my face. On the way up my stomach, I feel my strap under the coverall, hanging just under my arm. Real slow, inch at a time, I crawl my hand in and slip my nine out. They don't see me move cuz . . . well, I don't know why, I guess it's too dark or they think I'm already dead.

I ain't thinking about what happened or why. It don't matter to me now if Katrina done me dirty this way, or Eddie, or even Blue, though all of them must have, I'm sure now. It plain this is where I'm gonna be for, like, ever. I don't even give that much of a damn, really. Never know how you gonna end up. Or when and where. Or why, for that matter. You just know you will. Somehow, somewhere, sometime. That, and how'd you use your time? Those all some things to think about. Now, anyway. My line of work, I always figured I have something like this shit coming.

I coulda finished high school, coulda fixed cars. I could say I shoulda done all that. But this is what I want, so this is what I do, and this is what I get, no big deal.

They say before you leave the world you see your life flash before your eyes like some kind of big movie, which amounts to making some kind of sense of things. Nothing big and grand like that happening for me right here and now, probably cuz my life never make much sense anyway.

So I can't even say why I'm looking up with my one free eye, lifting my nine out from under the dirt and pointing it at Eddie Mac. I can't exactly say why it makes sense for me to put two quick slugs in him and then turn my wrist and put another two in Katrina. But as soon as I do, it feels okay.

Eddie Mac, he falls on top of that dirt pile and I can see his legs shaking bad as they stick down over the edge of the grave. More and more dirt slips in and I know it's only a matter of time till his body slides down here.

Meantime, sweet Katrina, she down to her knees on the other edge, gurgling and gasping as she holds herself, red spreading across that blouse, down onto that cute little mini. She look so beautiful to me. And so sad. She cries a little bit, but I guess the pain cuts into that, and then she loses her balance and she fall right in on top of me.

Time short now. I can't see nothing. I guess that's Katrina's blood making my face wet. I like the warm feeling. I like it's her blood, not some stranger. She making it hard for me to breathe, which is just as well, I don't mind. The kind of guy I am.

Just before the dark closes in on me again, I'm laughing on the inside, cuz we all four ended up in this pit here, all four headed underground no matter what other plans they had. And I'm also laughing cuz when anybody, Blue maybe, come looking to find one uncle, one ghost, and two gangstas, all they gonna find themselves is four ghosts, surprise surprise. Like to see them try to figure this one out.

Still can't form no words, but in my mind I'm saying, *Don't you worry, Blue, you be in here soon enough.*

And now that I finish thinking all these last thoughts, weak as I ever been in my whole idiot life, heading into the darkness again, all I can think to add is four more silent little words in my grave in the big, bad Southside, not one mile from the place where I was born: *Goodnight, Chicago, and amen.*

THE GOSPEL OF MORAL ENDS

BY BAYO OJIKUTU

77th & Jeffery

S wear I'm trying to keep up with Reverend this morning. Ain't so easy, not with the black angels crooning at his back, *alleluia,* and these *amens* rising in flocks from the Mount's bloody red carpet and gleaming pews, and the Payless heels square stomping up above my head until Calvary's balcony rocks in rhythm with the charcoal drum sergeant's skins. Seems the flock understands his sermon mighty fine, else why would they make all such noise in Mount Calvary? It's me then. I am the lost.

"Today is a good day, Church. Ain't it, Church? Always a good day for fellowshipping in the community of the Lord God, ain't it?"

The woman leaning on her walking stick across the aisle echoes loud as the speaker box boom.

"Amen!"

"We come in here on this good day looking for the righteous way to serve Him to bring manifest—y'all like that word, Church, that's a good word—let me say it again. We come in here to bring *man-i-fest* His glory in a world gone wicked, Church. We got this here fine church built on a mount—and we call it Calvary, like that hilltop where the Lord God sent His One Son to hang from a cross for us and save us from sin, deliver us from black death, Church. Make me so happy when I talk bout how the Savior came to this world to sacrifice His life for us, so happy, Church, all so we could come back here to the hilltop and build up a palace that'd shine bright in His city, so all would know. But all still ain't here celebrating the Good News, Church—no matter how loud I speak it, y'all sing it, and no matter the blazing beauty of this here Mount Calvary. City's wicked, Church, so wicked; we got folk look like us, talk like us, breath like us out here. But them folk is confused, Church, lost out in concrete Gomorrah. Y'all know too much about that place already. That's right, the wicked place right outside the oak doors to our Mount Calvary. Right down there on 79th Street, where sin whirls among folk blind to the Good News."

Maybe my trouble understanding Reverend Jack comes from these tiny ears, a quarter of the space the Good Lord carved on either side of my head for hearing. Or maybe confusion comes from eyes gone pus-yellow driving Sunday sunrise fares out to the good places north, south, and west; far, far from the wicked, whirling city and never back into concrete Gomorrah a moment before 7 o'clock the following Saturday night.

Or maybe I'm carrying the soul of a Black Jew up inside me. Not like the one-eyed Candy Man, or the musty shysters on the corner of State and Madison, their nappy heads hid underneath unraveling crochet hats. Sammy Davis was a happy half-monkey/half-rat, and the zero corner hustlers call themselves "Ethiopian Hebrews," selling their stinky incense sticks. I know I ain't no chimp dancing on a music box or no rat running into corners, or no shyster either. Ain't looking to get down with no big-boned Swedish honeys or start no funky sweet revolution. Just getting hold of this preacher's babble before salvation passes me by, trying to—Black Jews, you see, don't sing or dance God or shout *alleluia* in the temple. We read holy script in quiet. That way, we understand what the rabbi's spewing. We Black Jews get to know what the sermon means, Church.

My religion would explain this Scandinavian wanderer's nose misplaced on my Down-Deep-in-the-field face. I smell from it plenty good, better had what with this crooked beak jabbing from my head, stabbing and jabbing at the rearview mirror reflection as I pull on seeing holes to explore my rot. The nose's tip hooks down like those of the old olive diamond hawks underneath the tracks on Wabash Avenue, except that nostrils gape wide and jungle-black where cheeks meet. I breathe the stank of the Lord Jesus' celebration: this funk of salt, Walgreens makeup counter product, relaxer lye, and air panted from deep in guts filled with only starvation and desperation. Smelling lets my beak know something's ill in the reverend's Sunday spiel, and that knowledge means trouble on the Mount.

"But why's the world still so wicked if the Lord God sent His One Son down here to die and save us from sin? Let the Reverend explain the mystery to you—"

Reverend Jack's Satan changes every first and third Sunday. God is always the father, Jesus is his namesake son, and the Holy Ghost is that daytime creeping soul who slips inside the good Calvary Baptist lady in the satin dress, takes hold of her up in row ten after the reverend drops the sermon's main point. Twists her skull at the base of the neck, bends her in half, then snaps her holy rock-head front to back with the drum sergeant's beat; until the Ghost is done with her and he tosses the top half of this lady free so the end of her spine slams into wood pew.

She never cries or screams in pain as the Holy Ghost works her fierce like so; saved lady just shouts in this thrusting rhythm, "Praise you in me, Holy Ghost. Stay up in me, Holy

Ghost. Deep up in me, Holy Ghost. *Glory*. Praise you in me, Holy Ghost," and then again, before she hops into the aisle, mist rising from cocoa forehead, arms and legs flapping against each other while her neck snaps backwards without wood to interrupt the flow of ecstasy. There she goes with that sancti-fied chicken jig, same dance every other Sunday of the month.

Mount Calvary Missionary Baptist has sat just west of 77th and Jeffery Boulevard since the real Jews first let dark folks on these blocks fifty years back. Deep Down wanderers brought the Mount with them from Mobile County, Alabama, or some such burning place, so this is really Mount Calvary Second Baptist, too many words to get in before crooning an *alleluia* and interrupting the mission. The church used to be a rickety wood frame worship-shack blending in perfect with the houses leaned sideways by lake wind, siding smudged orange-brown by the burn of the wicked city's July sun, same as the Rothschild Liquor store across from the church parking lot. That old mud-weed lot where the Cadillac hearses parked whenever one of the Section C heads who sit under haber-dashery and Easter brims passed on from this world to that better place prepared for them in the Kingdom.

But that old Deep Tuscaloosa–style shack didn't shine sufficient for the Good News. So Reverend sent me to the alderwoman's main ward office in the old Gold Medallion cab, carrying five large from Calvary's tithe right after Mayor Harold died. Handed the flock loot over to that elected bag lady in exchange for imminent domain over half the row of homes just east of Jeffery, and the mud-weed lot too. City crashed down them shacks that used to line 77th long before they swore in Gomorrah's new king. Then the church board started passing around a second collection pot on the second and fourth Sundays. They called it "the building reserve special blessing fund."

"Give what you can, Church," Reverend told the flock then. "Know times is rough for folk round here right round now, but sacrifice is remembered eternal—and remember, you sacrificing for the One who gave the greatest sacrifice, who made that path into Glory with His own blood. If you can't give to build up a new place for celebrating Him, there's still gon be a place for you on the Path, Church. I promise it. Still gon be a place for you in His new house. Somebody say *amen*."

Before hardhats started pouring foundation to the new temple, Reverend had to payout six weeks worth of bingo proceeds to the bag lady, just so she'd change the title to this block of 77th Street into his name. Original paperwork claimed the Lord, or the Mount itself, or the flock, as the new church land's owner. "Naw, that ain't right," Reverend moaned back then. "All deeds got a price, Moral." Then he pointed me toward the bags of bingo gold, and watched as I piled them into my cab's trunk.

So the Church got to building its shining palace on the north side of 77th Street, foundation laid by the sacrifice of the flock, bricks stacked by the real big-time loot kicked back from D.C. in '93, after the reverend sent us around in the bingo vans and the hearse to collect all the living and dead souls, bring them on back to the rickety old shack to cast rightful vote for our good brother, slick Willie C. That honorary deacon on the Mount never would have sat on his high throne not for the tireless work we put in here in the city, and the new church never could've afforded its masonry not for the deacon's big payback.

Like the reverend say, "Rejoice and be exceedingly glad: for great is our reward in the Kingdom. That's from the Good

News, Church." No trouble understanding that sermon, not even in my dwarf ears.

Today the wood pews in the Mount shine with fine finish, and you can't hear the high heels clicking as the Section C women prance about the vestibule cause this plush red carpet stretches front door to black angel choir bandstand to swallow the sharpest points. Drywall towers above us, spackled to match the floor, with stereo speakers built behind and up into the ceilings, too, so no matter whether you're sitting in row J on the second balcony or downstairs in the toilet stall, you hear his sermon in surround sound. My sweet Lord Jesus, don't forget those holy shining basement bowls below the Mount, porcelain from Taiwan with the automatic power flush, and the perfume shooting from vents as stall doors open and close. Just enough mist let loose so you never smell your own shit, no matter gaping nose holes.

Even if you arrive late to the 11:30 and find the Mount packed through to the balconies with blue-black city souls, and you end up sitting in the last row of main floor pews—even then, you still see the reverend's pockmarked skin turn orange as he spews the Good News in front of a thousand furs and brims and palms and heels stomping. Last summer, Reverend had me install this camera here over the back row, lens set to beam him to the four movie screens at each corner of the service. Lens don't leave the podium until Reverend Jack's calligraphy-mustached grill crackles from his microphone as he dances one of his glory circles and drops the main point. I strung the camera chord up to stretch past the Mount's balconies and the rafters, just like he told me, and now this wire carries the sermon and the sight of its pinstriped deliverer out for broadcast someplace way beyond the flock.

"What we doing on this good day here on Mount Calvary?"

"*Celebratin'!*"

"All right then, y'all hearing me. Only one thing that word could mean after how I just told it to you—'I celebrate man.' You celebrating the Lord God sending His One Son in man form just to sacrifice that human life so that the souls of we men would be forever saved. If you bring manifest, Church, then you celebrating the Good News. See how warm that makes you, just saying it. I know it makes me warm. Say it with me together, Church, and feel the shower of His Glory. Celebrate the Good News . . . Celebrate the Good News . . ."

"*Celebrate the Good News!*"

"Well all right then, Church. You been hearing about this fellow Teddy Mann all about the streets, ain't you? If you ain't heard, Church, then best time you listened in close. You come in here on Sunday morning and you feel *sanctified* bout the way of your souls, sacrificing your time for the One—"

"*Amen,*" the church sister squeals short-throated on her cane.

"Yes siree, Reverend—" the drummer boy in his clean green fatigues answers before he two-stick slaps his cymbals.

"*Amen,*" some Low End woman in the first balcony says before stomping square heels together.

"Sing his name on high now, Church. But the minute you step back outside them oak church doors, we ain't on the Mount no more. You back in the world, Church, and it ain't so warm. Not with that icy wind whipping up from the concrete. Even your Mah-shall Fields wool ain't fine enough to keep you covered out there. Ain't nobody praying to Him at the liquor store counter, no sweet virgin voices humming hymns by the lotto machine. Ain't no Good Book studying in the battlefield, out there as one man spills his brother's blood over the wages of sin, Church. No Reverend Jack preaching the Word over the rivers of pain and lakes of broken glass. Them folk don't even know the Good Lord out there in the concrete world, do they, Church?"

"No sir," Deacon Nate responds. "They don't *even* know."

"Or maybe they got the facts all switched up. Cause out there, I hear children who look just like your good children talking about Teddy Mann like he himself is the Lord God Almighty. Say Teddy be making rainwater fall out the sky; Teddy, he feeds us with the warmth of his crack glory. He brings smiles to faces flush of ashy worry and worn wrinkles. Teddy do so it, cause he's the king of 79th Street, that concrete path. Folk swear they see him walking on top of the pond down by the Highlands. Strutting with the ducks just before he goes and turns that same water into wine, multiplies the fishes and loaves, cures the leper, and raises the dead. Breaks my heart to hear folk talking like so, Church, but I go on and listen to them desecrate and blaspheme Jesus' holy name. These are my people, even when they lost in their confusion. I know this place, don't I, Church?"

"*Amen!*"

All the flock, they did say *alleluia-amen* together, as Lucifer is a black angel fallen down from the choir, never the church board folk in Section C.

The Calvary ushers appear at the service hall's front door with their fake gold sashes draping right shoulder to left hip. "Mount Calvary Missionary" is scripted in sparkling letters along the diagonal of their chests, and they cradle collection pots between stomachs and clasped hands. Ushers always start with the back row. Such is the price for coming late to the 11:30. So I reach into my left pocket, palm brushing against the Good News just slightly, but find nothing save for lint and receipts from my weekend fares. The church sister on her cane stands and stares at me crooked-eyed, no matter that it was me who carted her to the Mount. Because of her, I was late this morning.

I left all my spare cash locked in the yellow cab's glove compartment, parked out in the new paved lot. Been leaving cash locked up since I accidentally dropped a hundred spot into the pot; that c-note earned carrying the serpent Teddy Mann from Cornell Avenue all the way out to O'Hare to catch his red-eye to the islands one Sunday morning. Tried to explain it to the usher, that longtime fellow flock member, how I'd made a mistake that good Sunday, tried to get my tip back from him. Missionary sash-wearing muthafucka just looked at me crooked-eyed as the church lady on her walking stick and strutted on to row twenty-four to continue collection rounds.

Ain't got nothing for them on this good day then, nothing but my Good News message. So I climb over the legs of the other late folk and dash for the service's corner door, holding onto my crotch like I've gotta go bad. Old church sister still stares at me though, I see her, and so does the reverend in the fourth corner movie screen, gray-black eyes beaming down. But I do make it to the red carpet stairs, and I let go of myself only as I touch the banister. I walk up along the thick fiber instead of down to the basement toilet. Got plenty of time before the collectors make it up top. Takes them twenty minutes to finish rounding up the fellowship loot from Section C. Don't feel or hear a damn thing as I step into the blackness separating staircase from square stomp in the Payless balcony aisles. Nothing except for this Good

News rubbing steel against my side and the reverend panting heavy into his podium mic.

Teddy Mann's got the finest honey mamma ever seen on the Mount. Kind so fine you want to call her "mamma" just so you can go on pretending like you remember sliding headfirst from her in the beginning. And maybe you would've held on to that joy somewhere had you been the one so blessed; sure know if you were born from between there, Church, you wouldn't need Reverend Jack to tell you a thing about Galilee.

Honey mamma looks to be some righteous mix of Humboldt Park Spaniard, Howard Street Jamaican rum, Magnificent Mile skyrising, and 95th Street sanctifying. Got slanted eyes, cold as Eskimo soles, and a fish-hook nose. Not a beak hook like mine, no, hers is curved upwards just so funk's gotta climb to seep into her. Her skin's the same color sand used to be on top of Rainbow Beach when I was little, but clean sand—only thing that shows against her smooth face is the peach fuzz barely sprouting from her pores. You only notice it if you're blessed enough to catch yourself daring to stare her way; of course, you're only so brave because Teddy Mann's never to be found in these balcony pews.

Her smile is just slightly yellowed from all the sugar breathed from bubblegum lips. She's tall, not so tall to cast shadow over that sly serpent Teddy; but she stands high and regal like the queens who ruled history's pale make-believe lands. So fine and upright that when honey mamma reaches down to tap your shoulder, you know you're a hero just short of the gods in heaven.

Teddy must have claimed honey mamma after he turned to evildoing. Serpent served some 26th and California time after he first started playing with that dope—Burglary,

Assault with Intent, some desperate something—and hooked up with the old-time concrete kings from Blackstone Avenue behind those bars. Vestibule says after his bid, Teddy returned to 79th Street and proved his soul in flowing blood and cash rolls, and before long the kings turned Sodom, Gomorrah, old Babylon Lounge off Stony Island, and the Zanzibar on the Isle, over to him. Almost twenty years later, he's still the king with all the paper ends and crooked angles covered. Must be the game that won her over, that same street player's game that lets the congregation know sly Teddy is the king on Reverend's sin throne this third Sunday.

There his honey mamma goes, celebrating in Row D first balcony. The sweet mother of Jesus, halfway smiling in that faded yellow gleam, halfway smiling and halfway weeping, sharp bones jabbing through hands patted together soft in Reverend Jack's pauses. Purple shame just now fades from her cheeks and these slant eyes cut into slices so her pupils hide from the good day sermon. Reverend just told the Mount all about her man, like they ain't already heard the concrete tales. Yet honey mamma's still gotta go through these sermon motions. She may have lost Paradise and fallen down from the Mount, taken by Teddy Mann's sly way, but the fact that she's here seeking to celebrate His Good News only goes to prove Reverend Jack's main point about the iniquity of that black serpent, evildoing Satan.

Teddy told me this story about his lady while we rode out north to O'Hare. Her name is Eva, with the "a" from the reverend's "feast" tacked on for the sake of the celebration. Back in the beginning of their thing, baritone Deacon Nate, who was Teddy's cousin just up from Mississippi, long before he came about his saved seat in Row Two, he arrived in concrete Gomorrah and tried to convince the serpent how this heifer couldn't be about nothing special, how she'd bring him down from his throne like all them other fake-ass mixed-nut tricks be doing a nigga trying to get his money right. Spewing hatred's spittle, that's how Deacon Nate talked before he came to know Jesus.

Or maybe Nate was such a hater until Teddy took him for a ride along 79th Street in the purple custom Jaguar. They kept riding the strip until they found Eva, then they rolled half a block behind, following her sweet strides. The Jag's passenger seat and Teddy's cousin's Mississippi gabardines were all wet with shame, and Nate was babbling off at the mouth in baritone tongues as the light turned red at King Drive, praising the glory of His name and the wonder of His deeds. Then he begged the serpent for explanation.

"That's what this life in the game is all about, brother . . . What's your name?" Teddy's black eyes reached over the cab's sliding glass protector, burned into my dashboard ID card. "Moral? *Hah.* That's a good black man's name. That's what I tried to tell my bumblefuckin cousin sitting there all stiff-nutted staring at my lady; a black man goes and gets into this game, right, and sets himself up proper, I told the fool. Get hold of as much knowledge here, as much cash as a nigga can on this earth. Not cause being a smart nigga means a god-damn thing, Moral, or cause calling your black ass rich is worth shit in the end. Black man follows the path to treasure so he can get himself something beautiful in this life. Get him something so fine he knows he's alive cause his limbs is stir-ring with fresh blood. So fine, he believes there's a god some-where, one who is good cause he gives life this purpose. A true god, not this quarter-wit bullshit they got ill pimps like Reverend Jack preaching up high on the Mount about, that bastard. Him and his cockamamie god standing on high with the kings, getting paid off lost souls. Ain't talking about no lie to make niggas feel good about the chitlins down deep in their guts and the stupidity sky high in their minds; a true and real god who creates sweet, beautiful things for human beings. That god leaves you humble with his mighty eye for making beauty, humble but proud at the same time to be alive. Can't help humble pride walking down 79th Street next to a living creation that fine, brother. Hear me? You gotta get that god knowledge so you grasp how to appreciate it. Gotta get that man's paper so you can afford her, cause the god rule say she costs. That's all we're in this cockamamie quarter-assed game for, Moral. Told my cousin this as he sat next to me—know what that buzzard went and did right afterwards? Country fuck went and got religion on the Mount with the pimp. Deacon's nuts ain't got stiff since. Punk-ass plantation retard. But *you* hear what I'm saying to you, don't you, Moral?"

"I hear you."

Sly Teddy reached his hairy black hand through the protection shield and dropped that Ben Franklin note into my lap, then he used the orange palm to slick down goatee waves on either side of his lips. He stared into the cab's rearview mirror all the while, checking me for doubt, fear, or worship, burning into these rot holes in search of my soul. But there wasn't no rhyme or revolution in me that good Sunday morning, Church. I wasn't but a gypsy cabbie, sore eyes running off into the Good Lord's purple sunrise.

Serpent squeezed my shoulder blade just a bit before pointing shaped nails at the fare meter: $48.50, the red bulbs blinked. I dug down in my pockets for change to return to him, without glancing in the rearview.

"Ain't got nothing smaller?" I asked. But before I could look up, he'd patted me on the left shoulder and propped open his back door as a United jet roared over my "For Hire" sign—couldn't even shake the serpent's hand cause I was busy unraveling the torn dollar bills from my pockets.

"What a friend we have in Jesus, hey Moral?" Teddy crooned in funky gospel rhythm as his steppers tapped against O'Hare's tar street. "You take it slow and easy and keep your eyes peeled ahead on that path riding home, will you?"

Sly serpent left the rest of his message in my backseat. Not another c-note, no, that there lump sitting snug up under the Saturday edition of the *Chicago Tribune* Metro section (y'all know sly Teddy's bout the only soul you'll still see round here reading the *Trib*, Church). I brushed the thin paper sheets to the floor, and there was his black steel, same one he wears underneath the flaps of his snakeskin leather as he slithers about the city, a cold killer .357 piece, chromed to shine in its camel pouch. Tried to call out the window to let him know he left it, I did, but that driver's-side glass wouldn't roll down. Swear, Church.

Been riding round the Mount three weeks now with this message and its thick holster right next to the spare cash in my glove compartment. The Metro section, I threw that away long before making it back to 79th Street for Reverend Jack's early service.

For as I passed by and beheld your devotions, I found an altar with this inscription: TO THE UNKNOWN GOD. *Whom therefore ye ignorantly worship, him declare I unto you. God that made the world all things therein, seeing that He is Lord of Heaven and Earth, dwelleth not in temples made with hands.*

This is what their Bible book says proper. I snatch the soft cover from the Row A pew before this crusty-lipped child hops about and screams with the Good News at the end of our days. Heist this scripture from the cross-eyed and the stu-pid to read the words of Acts as written by old dark fellow Hebrews. I've freed the bound holy book and tucked it into the chest pocket of my driving shirt. Because I need the word kept close to life, as I ain't one of these just-up-from-the-Down-Deep flock, bouncing mad about the Mount's pews and aisles as the reverend preaches his sermon.

"Am I my brother's keeper, Church? Y'all come on, come on and tell me now—"

"Yes, siree, Reverend," Deacon Nate replies, "that's what it say."

"*Well.* Somebody been coming to Bible study like they suppose to." Reverend Jack's gray-blacks cut to the choir bandstand. "Yes, Church, Good Book tell us we're our brother's keeper, indeed. Repeat it with me: *indeed.* It's on us to certify he ain't strayed from Paradise or off the Mount. Book don't tell us something though, Church—cause back there in Paradise, the answer was obvious. But today we've got to ask the question. Need to get some kind of resolution before we go out and *proselytize* in His holy name. Uh-oh, Reverend . . . y'all like the sound of that fancy word now, don't you? I'll break it down for you next week—y'all remind me, Church. What I got to know now before I send y'all out to do the good works, is who is 'my brother,' Church? *Hah.* Who is my brother?"

The drum sergeant lets cymbals quake as his foot pounds the bass drum pedal to cover the church's silence—yes, finally, silence from the flock—raining down from both bal-conies. Reverend Jack's eyes switch about holes in the movie screen pictures as he wipes the ballpoint end of his nose.

"We gotta know who our brother is if He expects us to be keeping him, don't we, Church? You gotta answer soon if You expect me to look out for him on our way to Your bosom. I'm gon listen to what You tell me, whatever it might be, Lord, but You gotta tell me something soon. We had a talk, me and the Lord. Know how I tell y'all bout getting down on humble knees and praying to the Most High for guidance, and mercy, and deliverance for the wicked? This time I got down to pray and asked Him for an answer, Church. Understanding's what I was after. Do y'all hear me?"

"Amen, Reverend," the first balcony shouts, honey mamma Eva louder than all the rest, purple shame gone from her now. *"We hear ya. Go head on."*

"But Church, in His benevolent wisdom, I'm still waiting out an explanation from on High, Church. It's one of them mysteries; Lord puts um down here for us sometimes, in this maze of concrete and glass. Lays rhyming riddles in the cracks of our lives. Like when He sent His son into the shadow of darkness to withstand the temptation of Beelzebub, Church—y'all remember that? Why'd He put His One Son through such tribulation? He don't never give us no questions we can't handle though, Church. Never an answer that'll break us."

"Glory, *ah-ley-lu-ya*," the woman says down below before hobbling into her pew.

"He left me to think on it, amidst all this wicked darkness in the city Gomorrah. I sought for understanding, and I waited patient, Church. Is my brother the hustlers and the pimps and whores and crooks and killers scampering about like dark rats—is my brother Teddy Mann? Jesus the Son Himself kept even the most vile sinner close to Him as He spread the word of His coming. But that was back before Satan took over the living earth and the minds of the lost. Lord didn't have to think on pandemic pestilence and Tech-

Nines and poison powders in the mail and flaming terror wielded by the lost. Them Romans overran Judah long before Satan swallowed the minds of the wicked, you see. Not like now—we gotta be cautious on the Mount today. It's a good day for fellowshipping, yes it is, long as we stay cautious, Church. Y'all still with me?"

"*Amen!*"

Reverend Jack snatches the microphone from its stand and slides his wiggling Stacey Adams from the podium to spin inside the microphone chord's electric circle, and my camera follows him just below us, broadcasting Reverend's jig to the four corners and up above, too. The crusty-faced boy jumps wood pew to not-so-plush balcony carpet, and sweet Eva's face turns sun-kissed as she applauds, and the balcony folk praise him on high. I try to listen still. I'm patient as the flock, as the reverend beseeches us to be. No matter I may be one of those gypsy cab Jews with loss and confusion beating against my stolen holy book. Patient, because if Jesus came now I know he'd be a gold-medallion cabbie; taking folk where they asked to go because that's the job script, just waiting for his chance to save them from their requested destination. Church, don't you know that gypsy-cabbie Jesus would catch the lost way switching about those passengers' eye holes long before the ride's end?

"It's time for a cleansing, Church—a rapture—time for us to start preparing the path. As He prepped the way for us into His Father's Kingdom by shedding His own blood. We, brothers and sisters, must shed *wickedness*, so the city is purified for His coming. He's riding in on that pearl white horse of His, come again to destroy the most Wicked One and deliver His peace unto the chosen. *Well.* Y'all know I got mercy in me, Church, y'all know it—we gon go out there and give the wicked and the lost their fair chance with the two-step test. Those that pass, we gon keep them and wait for Him to ride on to the Mount and deliver us together. The rest of them, Church? Old preachers used to talk about for-saking immoral means on the way to righteousness. But when the ends we preparing for is His return, Church, I can't think of no means that qualify as *immoral*. Slick-tongued serpent lives a long, lavish life, if y'all let him do it. But it's time for us to go bout changing this city, getting it ready, Church. Time for lies and false righteousness and double-dealing and back-sliding and all such wickedness to be cast down from the Mount and out of the city, so we can start to make a way for salvation. Y'all hear me?"

"I hear you," I say, as Reverend's come to his main point in these tiny ears of mine. The answer rains with the heel stomping and the skin-pounding drum sergeant's celebration. Honey mamma Eva sings *alleluia* and jumps on the red carpet like the child in Row A, and she claps those pretty hands together, more than going through motions now.

The Reverend steps further left of the podium in the big movie screens, spinning and sliding and whirling without ever touching the chord that connects him to sound. He chants into the mic as clean sweat pours free along his brow, and the black angels sing with him. *"Celebrate the Good News. Celebrate the Good News."* Mount Calvary shakes with the power of His glory, and I know the path, Church.

Celebrate the Good News.

I walk toward the balcony ledge once, twice, until my waist bounces against drywall and the Good News' steel does feel so very mighty. Reverend Jack tells the truth about this, so very mighty, this message gripped in the left hand. Put it between his gray-black eyes, and the Mount is silent once again. Miracles do abound. Flock's quiet enough even for the reading of the Word hidden against my chest. Save for this bouncing boy screaming out because he ain't ready for the News like he thought he was gonna be when it was delivered all funked up in charcoal and war fatigue drummer skins and rhythm guitar strum, and those sweet black angel hymns. When it comes in silence, the Good News tears righteousness from the child until his eyes fill with yellow rot like mine. He is as lost as I was lost.

Underneath this obnoxious fear, the sound of pearl hooves sound near. *Klump. Ku-lump.* Since the drum sergeant must've lost his sticks, let the Good Lord's pony keep the rhythm for you. These boys is just scared is all, Church—don't pay them mind. Just ain't used to Good News without screaming in exaltation, *alleluia;* so feel their trepidation, *amen.*

I want to look over my shoulder at Eva, feast upon her glory one last time. Finest thing to ever set foot on Mount Calvary since they strung Him to that tree and drove in the spikes. Since the Lord called imminent domain over our salvation for the price of His Own Son's blood. Can't look back there though, for Teddy Mann's black steel has got me—and it's throbbing in its hot might, shining and reflecting the gray in Reverend Jack's movie screen eyes. I've never seen a yellow testifier with pupils this color; bet they never seen a Black Jew with eyes rotted yellow neither. *Wicked City.*

I let go the Good News' truth blasts, one, two, three times. For Father, Son, and Holy Ghost, though my real religion tells me to only believe in the First. Church, you hear this boy screaming wild still?

All the black angels run down from the bandstand. One of them, the curly headed Alabama queer who bit into thick lips as Reverend damned the sodomites last month, he dashes to the podium in time to catch Reverend before his head's fallen from the circle, and this black angel cries as sacred life spills to turn the choir robe a darker red than Mount Calvary's carpet. Purple-crimson sea to swallow the main point in whole.

Celebrate the Good News, and hold on to it tight, Church, cause the wicked will make one last stand on this good day for fellowshipping, stand against the Mount until He comes to vanquish them. Yes, they must. Says so at the end of their holy book.

Before Eva turns away from the two-step test, I swear she shines that sugar-stained smile down my way. Still no shame in her glorious face. Honey mamma smiles and runs off to the darkness before the steps, going through glorious motions again with most of the rest. She runs quivering hips from me, Church, and my Down Deep gabardines soak wet at the crotch. The church has fallen from the Mount, and the mighty temple rises once more.

"Quit your screaming now, boy," I say. "Wanna hear the hooves coming near. That's the Holy Ghost almost in me."

Deacon Nate's baritone sounds down in Row Two. "It's him, that black Satan, Moral," he yells. "Good Lord of Mercy, Church, put him down now!"

The wicked do come for me, just like in their Book. But they ain't swift as the Holy Ghost or this blazing white horse riding in from Galilee.

I leap into their path. "Praise you in me, all up in me. You in me real good." I sing and dance my chicken dance, arms and legs and Good News flapping all about in the first balcony aisle. "Stay up in me. You my salvation, *Glory.* Praise you in me."

DEAR MR. KLEZCKA

BY PETER ORNER

54th & Blackstone

Castaner, Puerto Rico (Associated Press, April 7, 1958):
Nathan Leopold is learning the technique of his ten-dollar-a-month laboratory job in the hospital here and using most of his spare time to answer his voluminous mail. One hospital official said the paroled Chicago slayer has received 2,800 letters in the three weeks he has been here . . . He has expressed his intention to answer every letter.

The room is not as bare as you might imagine. In fact, it is crowded. A distant relative in the furniture business shipped a load of overstock from the Merchandise Mart. Sofas, love seats, end tables, floor lamps, a pool table. It took three trucks to deliver it all from San Juan.

Nathan, home from work, sits squeezed behind a large oak desk, big as a banker's, and takes off his shoes. He rubs his sore feet awhile. He watches his birds. The canaries are, for a change, silent. He leaves their cage door open. He likes to watch them sleep, their heads up, their eyes vaguely open as if on a whim they could fly in their dreams.

He takes the next letter from the stack and sets it in front of him. He puts on his glasses. He reads.

When he's finished, he brings his hand to his face and gently rests his index finger on the tip of his nose. He thinks.

The room has a single window that looks out upon the village and beyond it, a small mountain. When he first arrived here this view was heaven. The spell, though, was short-lived. He no longer feels the urge to walk cross the village to the mountain and climb it.

Dear Mr. Kleczka,

I received your correspondence two weeks ago. Please accept my sincere apologies. I receive a great many letters and am doing my best to reply to them with a reasonable degree of promptness. Also, please understand that the mail delivery service here in the hills outside San Juan leaves a bit to be desired, although of course I am the last to complain. Among other things, Mr. Kleczka, you call me God's revulsion and express the wish that I choke on my own poisonous froth. You write that my employment in a hospital is the ghastliest joke Satan ever played and, as veteran of Hitler's war, you know from whence you speak.

I do not doubt you, Mr. Kleczka. You write from what you describe as "the old neighborhood." You say your father even knew me when. Let's not indulge ourselves. I will not attempt here to defend the role I played in the death of Bobby Franks. Nor am I going to tell you of the thirty-three years I spent as convict 9306 in Joliet. I want you to know that I believe— this is something even we can agree on—that I am the luckiest man in the world. I am free and nothing you could conjure is more delirious. Yet delirium, I might add, always gives way to a fog that never lifts. This said, allow me to describe a bit of my work at the hospital. I met a woman today. She is dying of a rare disease. It is not pancreatic cancer but something far more uncommon. The disease is untreatable and the most that can be done for this woman is to prescribe painkillers and ensure a constant supply of nutrients because, apparently, this is the way I understand it, her body rejects those fluids necessary for the survival of her vital organs. In other words, her life leaks—from every available orifice. Her name is Maya de Hostas and she has two children, Javier and Theresa. There is no husband to speak of.

Maya de Hostas is dying, but it is a slow process. The doctor says it could take six months or perhaps a year. Do you scoff? Do you tear at this paper? Do your hands flutter with rage? Nathan Leopold is telling a story! Nathan Leopold, a story of suffering! Because as you hold this paper that my hands have touched, I am your symbol. You need a symbol, don't you? You think of my youthful arrogance like it was yesterday. All the brains they said I had. All the languages they said I spoke. Russian, Greek, Sanskrit! My famous attorney glibly talking away the rope . . . *The easy thing and the popular thing to do is to hang my clients. I know it. Men and women who do not think will applaud. The cruel and thoughtless will approve. It will be easy today; but in Chicago, and reaching out over the length and breadth of the land* . . .

This very yesterday. It's men like you, Mr. Kleczka, men with long memories, that make your city great. You sweep the streets of scum. Rich sons-of-bitches like me. This is no defense, Mr. Kleczka of 5383 South Blackstone, but allow me to tell you I love you. To tell you I love you for keeping the torch lit, for sitting down to write me. I am deadly serious, Mr. Kleczka, oh deadly deadly serious, and as I sit here—the waning moments of day purple the mountains—I imagine you. I imagine you reading of my parole with such beautiful fury. You wanted to come here yourself and mete out justice. Didn't you want to get on a plane and come and murder me with your own bare hands? No gloves for such a fiend. You wanted to feel my death in your own glorious pulsing veins. And then take a vacation. Why not? Bring the wife and kids. It's Puerto Rico.

But your wife said an eye for an eye wouldn't help anybody or make a dime's bit of difference to Bobby Franks. It wouldn't bring that angel back and they'd only throw away the key on you. (Though of course your defense would have much to say by way of mitigation.) But the monster, you cried. Beast! Your wife is a wise woman, Mr. Kleczka, but you, sir, are wiser. And should you come here, know that my door is always open. I have done away with the notion of locks. I live in a two-room flat. If I'm absent at my employ, please await me. Make yourself at home. Don't mind the canaries. I feed them in the morning. I keep whiskey, though the conditions of my parole forbid spirits, in my third desk drawer. Why not pour yourself a glass? I'll be home soon. And know that as you strangle me or slit my throat or simply blow my head off, I'll love you. As I bleed on this upswept floor (the maid comes only on Tuesdays), I'll love you, Mr. Felix Kleczka of the old neighborhood. What else can I say to you? Do not for a moment think I say any of this slyly. I have been waiting with open eyes and open arms for the last thirty-three years, prepared to die the same death as Dickie Loeb, whose rank flesh is only less tainted than mine for being murdered sooner. Well, I am here. I will never hide from you.

I get a great deal of mail, Mr. Kleczka, as I said. Much of it is supportive of my new life. This week alone I received three marriage proposals. Your letter reminded me very starkly of who and what I am. Even so, I must ask you: Are there still old neighborhoods? Are there still fathers who knew us when? And should you decide not to come and take up the knife against me for reasons other than your wife's wise Christian counsel, know that I think no less of you. Your cowardice, Mr. Kleczka, more than anything this I understand. Once a young man bludgeoned a child with a chisel. To make certain, I stuffed my fist in his mouth. My hands are rather plump now. Still, even now I recognize them some days.

Yours Truly,
N. *Leopold*

The dark outside the window now. He's lived so long craving it. It was the light, all that light. He thinks now that he—
Now that he what?
He flicks on the lamp for comfort. He watches his face in the window. His laugh begins slowly, like a murmur. Eventually it's loud enough to wake the birds.

THE NEAR REMOTE

BY JEFFERY RENARD ALLEN

35th & Michigan

T he Police Superintendent sat bent forward at his sturdy mahogany desk, a big man in a big leather armchair, framed by a floor-to-ceiling window looking out onto the vast and vicious wonders of the city. He was reading a file, which lay flat upon the leather-topped surface of the desk.

Ward slammed the door shut.

The Police Superintendent raised his eyes from the file and saw menace, tall and bony, standing in his office. If he was surprised that someone had been watching him, he didn't let on. He wet his thumb against the blotter of his tongue, picked up the file between wet thumb and dry forefinger, and placed it on top of a stack of papers at the corner of the desk. He curled his small and enormously pink lips into a smile, placed both palms against the desk edge, and scooted his chair backwards. Then he gripped the padded armrests, rose up from the seat, and came around the desk, carpet muffling the sound of his white cordovans shined with a high polish, and came over to where Ward stood, with a hand extended in welcome.

"Ward," he said. "You've decided to come."

"I had to see you for myself," Ward said.

"Pleased to have you with us."

Ward stuck a finger inside his nose and worked it

around. Only then did he offer to shake hands. The Police Superintendent looked at the finger, looked Ward straight in the face. Ward seized one cuff of the Police Superintendent's white linen shirt—so out of season, the thinnest fabric in the coldest weather—and cleaned the finger on the sleeve.

To Ward's regret, the Police Superintendent slowly raised his line of sight, offering a face lacking any signs of anger or distress or revulsion, a face betraying no emotion other than authority and duty. He spoke to Ward in polite, even tones, asking that he be seated, motioning to a leather armchair directly in front of his desk. Cautiously Ward settled into the chair. The Police Superintendent walked over to a second picture window and stood looking out, dust drifting like unmoored astronauts in two smoky shafts of sunlight on either side of him.

"A damn nice secretary you have," Ward said.

The Police Superintendent seemed to be looking off at a skyscraper surprisingly small and dull in the afternoon sun. He was a heavy man, so heavy that he might at any moment sink through the floor and plunge forever downward.

"'Go right in.' Damn nice. It can't be easy for her."

The Police Superintendent made slow steps away from the window, then sat down leisurely in his big leather armchair, eyes trained on the desk, giving Ward time to study the lumpy mass of his head. Light from the window gave the desk a liquid glow. The Police Superintendent joined the fingers of both hands into a meaty cup. He cleared his throat.

"Might we get to it." He lifted his eyes to Ward's face. "I cannot stress enough"—gesturing with his hands—"how important it is that we follow our plan to the letter"—his palm held upward in supplication. "Unless you can adduce any legitimate grounds for some fresh course of action." He locked his fingers before him on the desk.

Ward watched him in silence.

"I am sorry. Profoundly sorry," the Police Superintendent said. "Every one of us should be entitled to a private corner in the garden." He shook his head, weary, defeated. "Alas—" He parted his hands, nothing to offer. "If your associates had been more careful in their actions, perhaps we could—"

"My associates?"

"Yes. Speaking plainly."

"Let me ask you a question. Did you spend your lunch hour bobbing for turds?"

Just like that. He began unbuttoning his black overcoat.

The Police Superintendent watched the unbuttoning without comment, blinking each time a button snapped free. He stirred heavily in his seat, then pushed himself up from his chair and walked to a third massive window. He extended his arm stiffly out in front of him as if preparing to bend it in salute, caught the soiled shirt cuff between the thumb and forefinger of his other hand, unsnapped the button, and rolled the sleeve to the elbow, revealing dense wiry hair on his wrist and forearm. He did the same with the other sleeve. Stood still a moment with his arms hanging at his sides. He brought both hands to his chest and pulled violently at his shirt, buttons catapulting into air, like some high-story flasher exhibiting himself to the world. He twisted backwards and began freeing himself of the shirt, tilting his torso to one side then the other until both sleeves were free. That done, he crumpled up the shirt between both hands, his violent belly hanging like a mound of descending lava over his belt, and moved forward, the sausage rolls of his sides quivering with each step and the shirt trailing along the carpet behind him.

He dropped the garment into a wicker wastebasket and resumed his station behind his desk, hands folded in his lap, watching Ward with murderous hate. His chest rising and falling. He cupped his hands underneath his belly and began rocking in the chair. Continued:

"As you know, in this suspect we are dealing with a man who has been fortunate enough to travel in some of our most distinguished circles, not to mention the access he has . . ."

"I've been thinking," Ward said. "Would you take my hand in marriage?"

The Police Superintendent grabbed the edges of the desk and leaned in close. "Look! I am appealing to your—"

"Don't refuse me."

"—better nature." His nostrils blew hot air onto Ward's face. "A selfless act. Lives in the balance. After all, you gain as well. Your time to shine."

"So thoughtful of you. Such abundance of caution and concern."

The Police Superintendent glared at Ward and remained poised over his desk like some indecisive highwire acrobat.

It was cold where Ward lay. The yellowed glow of streetlamps seeping under and around the edges of the window shade, frail wisps of light spinning like ballet dancers in the dark. A reserved wind tapped modest applause against the paned glass. He shut his eyes and let the world spin free. The next thing he knew he had spun out of orbit, his brain ricocheting off the black walls of his skull. He opened his eyes and found darkness in slow dissolution.

"Everything all right in there?"

A hand pounded muffled words into the door.

Ward turned his face in the direction of the sound. No

visual evidence that the door even existed, but he knew it was there. Shadowy crabs crawling in the strip of light under its frame.

He listened to the wet whine of the rusty radiator.

"Hey!"

"Just relax."

"The Police Superintendent will be here soon."

"Just relax."

He turned back the bedcovers. Shivered to a cold greeting of air. Kicked his feet from under the sheets. Sat upright in the bed, a cot really, a narrow iron frame small and set low. The lax springs sagging under his insignificant weight. He placed his feet on the cold wooden floor. Bent forward and fingered the shade, which snapped back upon its roller, allowing morning light to rush like gate-crashers into the room. He shut his eyes.

"Hey!"

"Relax. I'll be right out." Ward placed a blanket across his shoulders.

Hands shoved in his pockets, a young officer who had spent the entire night outside Ward's door sat slumped over on a stool wearing his department-issued cap and jacket, the side of his young face barely visible in sixty-watt gloom. He turned his head and peered up at Ward, one corner of his mouth twisted as if he were biting down on something. The sight of Ward changed the look in his eyes, the angle of his chin, the red polish of his cheeks. He pulled his hands from his pockets, sat as straight as he possibly could on the stool, and redirected his gaze to a neutral wall.

Ward pulled one side of the blanket tighter about his shoulders. "Fine job," he said.

The young officer remained perfectly still, like someone sitting for a photograph, though Ward detected faint suggestions of some forbidden emotion rising to the surface of his face.

Some time later, Ward returned from his shower and was dismayed to find the Police Superintendent stretched out on the cot, arms folded pretzel-like behind his head, not unlike how Ward himself might have been positioned in times past, less somber days. The mattress sagging under him, its white bottom almost touching the dark floor. The Superintendent's breathing did not come easy, a labored wheezing and blowing, some beached sea creature. He made several slight shifts and turns of the body, incremental adjustments of arms, torso, legs, a model responding to a painter's instructions. The bedsprings strained and squeaked. It was only then that Ward saw a white derby adorning his windowsill, drawing attention like some ill-placed trophy.

Ward stood there, astounded. "Glad you see fit," he said.

The Police Superintendent turned his head and looked Ward up and down in disgust, an action of such surprising force that Ward's lips parted.

"Have a seat."

Ward collapsed into the chair beside the bed.

"Crazy damn hours."

"Don't blame me."

"No, I won't. I can send your friend a note of thanks and—"

"He's not my friend."

"Oh no, then how would you describe him?"

Ward sat there watching his other.

"Please, hold nothing back. I wish to make every effort to understand."

Ward shrugged the shawl from his shoulders onto the chair back and bent forward, his plastic-lined shoes at his feet. "There's nothing to understand."

"No?"

"No." Ward tugged and pulled at the tongue of one shoe, as he began to squeeze and wiggle and stomp his foot inside it.

"Indeed. Not surprising, your curious—"

"Why don't we just go?"

"—range of reasoning."

"Kindly spare me the sermon."

"Certainly. They don't pay me to preach. What would you care to hear? You would care to hear that—"

"We have someplace to go." Ward squeezed in the second foot and stood.

"No? Perhaps if I kneeled down and—"

"You wallow!"

The Police Superintendent popped upright on the bed. "Nothing could wallow like you." He sat there on the bed staring at Ward.

"Are we going to sit here all day?"

"May you rot."

"Take comfort in the thought."

Ward lifted his overcoat from its closet hook and slipped inside it, his body mockingly insubstantial, the padded wrapping loose on his frame like a hospital gown. But the Police Superintendent made no effort to move, anchored to stubborn place, unable to pull his hate back inside him, link by link.

"Why don't I meet you downstairs," Ward said.

These words might have gone unheard, escaped comprehension. It was only when Ward started for the door that the

Police Superintendent took to his feet and blocked his exit. He smacked his palms against his trouser legs to rid them of lint, shook the lapels of his overcoat, and brushed his hair flat with the sides of his hands. Then he eased around Ward, lifted his white derby from the windowsill, and fitted it on his head. He pulled the door open, without hurry, and motioned for Ward to go through.

The winter sky was high and clear above short snow-banked streets. Pancake-like flakes falling in rapid succession and blowing aloft again in fierce gusts. A car waited, idling. The hard-of-muscle young officer tugged harder at Ward's elbow. Ward bent into the car and settled back onto the rear passenger seat. The officer slammed his door tight against the wind and cold. At the same moment, the front passenger door hinged open, snow rushing in with malicious intentions of beating the Police Superintendent to his seat. Only when his door slammed shut did he thoroughly examine his white derby for damage. The young officer seated himself next to Ward and shut the door. He turned his face to the glass, a full yard of leathered space between their bodies.

A second uniformed officer positioned himself behind the steering wheel and eased the smooth running car forward. "Coldest day of the year," he said, black-gloved fingers drumming on the wheel.

Ward brushed snow from his coat, removed his own gloves, and blew hot air into the well of his joined hands. The wipers switched back and forth across the windshield. A second car moved ahead of them, venting smoke. A third car behind.

"Coldest so far."

"You're a genius," Ward said. "Now turn up the goddamn heat."

"What?" The driver craned his neck to look back over the seat. Perhaps he would steer the car with one hand and shoot Ward with the other. "You want to repeat that?"

"You heard me."

"Officer," the Police Superintendent said. "Do the honor. Turn up the heat."

The driver shot a quick unprotesting glance at his superior and clicked on the blower.

"Thanks, you cocksucker."

The Police Superintendent looked at Ward's reflection in the rearview mirror. "Take a moment or two, if you must."

Ward offered no reply, only sat rubbing his palms together. The blower roaring like an untamed beast.

"That warm enough for you?" the driver asked.

"No. Have your mother send up a faggot or two from hell."

The driver began rocking from side to side in his seat, his fingers tapping anxious rhythms on the steering wheel. The Police Superintendent gave him a sharp look and he pressed his shoulders into his seat.

"Kiss him once for me, would you?" Ward said to the Police Superintendent.

The Police Superintendent turned around in his seat and gave Ward his familiar look of disgust. He shook his head slowly. "Who would have ever thought," he said.

"Certainly not you," Ward said.

The ride was otherwise uneventful, the streets specked with people, black forms silhouetted against the snow.

"Here." The Police Superintendent dropped a ring of keys into Ward's lap, letting them fall from his hand with the highest form of disregard. "The keys to the city."

"You're so thoughtful."

Ward quickly deposited the keys into an inside pocket of

his coat. He looked over and saw that the young officer who had kept vigil outside his door was snickering into his upturned jacket collar. When they made it to their destination, this same officer pulled Ward from the car and rudely bumped and shoved him into the snow, but in such a way as to make the action seem accidental, an inadvertent trip over the curb. Ward regained his feet, brushed snow from his clothes, retrieved his scattered thoughts, and checked his pockets to make sure the keys were still there. His outer garments were thoroughly soaked through.

The Police Superintendent took a firm hold of Ward's gloved hand and led him forward like a child on the first day of school. They walked some fifty paces. Ward's breath coming a little harder as they went. The Police Superintendent stopped as if on cue and spun Ward in front of him like a practiced dance partner. "Please sign, here and here."

Ward did as instructed. The Police Superintendent slipped the damp paper into his jacket and stood before Ward under his white derby, the hat tiny on his massive head like some ghastly baby bonnet. "I would be lying if I said it has been a pleasure," he said.

"Spare me."

The Police Superintendent turned and headed back for his car and left Ward to the snow and wind. Ward vowed to take away with him some memory of the man. However, the weather being what is was, he was already having trouble remembering exactly how the man's features fit together. So much so that Ward considered calling out to him and requesting a quick but comprehensive physical inventory, fully aware that, in all likelihood, the Police Superintendent would not even rebuff him with an insulting refusal. So he looked through the neutral and colorless distance and saw an old five-story walk-up building slanting away from the ground at a precarious angle, snow swirling around the leaning structure as if to lasso it upright. His appointed destination. What was keeping it standing? He turned for a final look at the Police Superintendent, who was now leaning against the car, white derby snugly atop his head. The two young officers were huddled over sharing a cigarette while uniformed men from supporting vehicles worked to cordon off the street with brass barricades they took from the trunks of their own cars.

Ward reached into his coat pocket for the ring of keys but fumbled them against his chest into the snow. At once he dropped to his knees, biting at the ends of his gloved fingers until his hands were free of the leather. He stuck his bare fists into the snow and began clawing about, reacting to the cold in an almost clinical way. The snow both surprising and mundane. He scooped up two fistfuls and weighed them in each palm. Snow was actually rising up from the street and fleeing into the heavens, but the domed sky would allow no escape. That thought took hold of him while he was kneeling at the very center of the world, its cold icy navel. He trembled to shake himself free.

No sooner had he done so than he noticed twenty feet ahead a familiar figure trudging through the snow toward him. He stuck his hands back into the slushy mounds and worked more frantically after the keys. Heard the snow-crunching approach of the two young officers behind him. Looked up and turned his head to see them bobbing forward with pistols drawn. He thought about shouting, *"The keys! I dropped the keys!"* Instead, he burrowed down, trenched in this place that had already started to corrode beneath him, to melt and puddle around his knees.

DESTINY RETURNS

BY ACHY OBEJAS

26th & Kedvale

Destiny scratched the back of her neck with her left hand, the glistening pink nail on her index finger digging into the skin until it almost hurt. With the other hand she held a short, slim, and brown Romeo y Julieta to her thick, rubbery lips and breathed in. The tobacco indulged her, sweet and vaguely spicy, and she rocked for a moment, savoring her refuge from the freezing Chicago winds outside her window.

The tiny coffee maker, stout and metallic, hissed, cradled by fire on the stove. Destiny shot up from her kitchen table to extinguish the blue and orange flames before the crude sprayed all over. No one at the bodega where she'd bought it would ever consider it was anything other than Cuban, certainly not provident from the island but from Cuba nonetheless: diasporic, exiled, absolutely imaginary. Using an oven mitt to hold the hourglass-shaped coffee maker, she poured herself an exact thumbful in a wee cup that sported a raised pink and green floral pattern. Destiny lifted the cup to her lips and let the heat rise like a wet, gentle fog around her mouth. She stuck her tongue out, a marsupial peeking from its pouch, then tucked it back in a flash.

"Fuck Cuba," she said aloud, in shamelessly accented English. She paused to regard the coffee's approachability. Fuck fucking Cuba—and Mexico too.

Then in one cranelike swoop, she snatched up the demi-tasse, opened her wide mouth even wider, and tossed the scorching black bracer down her throat.

It had been twenty-five years since Destiny, a/k/a Dagoberto Fors Arias, a/k/a Dago Fors, had landed on American shores. He arrived in South Florida from Cuba on a blistering summer day in 1980 in a small yacht named *San Dimas* which carried a beneficent Catholic dissident to Key West and was piloted by the meanest-looking priest Dago had ever seen, a bulldog of a guy named Mariano Delgado. It had been a lifetime since that journey and Destiny was in no mood to look back. But the Mariel boat lift had been both historic and controversial and, on its twenty-fifth anniversary, she was one of its stranger success stories.

Now a newspaper reporter, a young Cuban-American dyke with misplaced nostalgia and a predisposition to all things Cuban, had tracked her down and wanted an interview. Destiny had tried to demur but the girl was insistent. She'd seen her on TV, an intense but pretty tomboy, disarming in a way but with the ferocity of those small dogs who clamp on and never let go. Somehow, she'd gotten Destiny to agree to the interview; somehow, she'd gotten Destiny to agree to meet her at the one place in all of Chicago Destiny had vowed never to return, La Caverna Club on 26th and Kedvale, so deep in the heart of the Mexican barrio that it seemed, but for the cruel cover of snow, that it wasn't in a northern enclave at all but at the very center of some lawless border town.

Destiny sighed and ground out the Romeo y Julieta on an ashtray in the shape of the island, a long pink caiman, hollow inside.

* * *

Dago Fors had gotten out of Cuba because in 1980 Cuban authorities let open the island's borders, causing a gush of refugees to force their way north on anything that would float. Almost immediately, hundreds of exiles had begun racing boats south to pick up their seafaring relatives. When the avalanche of refugees was so great that it embarrassed the socialist government, the Cubans emptied their jails and mental hospitals and forced the exiles to take along former inmates and other undesirables. It was their "lacra social," their catch-all category. Indeed, the snarling priest who'd brought Dago to safety had been promised the release of the Catholic dissident, who was his brother-in-law, as it turned out, only if he agreed to take a bunch of fairies back with him on his roomy boat.

Dago Fors, café au lait, pouty-lipped, a catlike twenty-four-year-old drag queen, was doing his best to be one of them. When word got out about the goings on, he put on the trashiest orange blouse he could find, the tightest, most worn jeans (with nothing underneath, naturally), and immediately set himself to slapping his flip-flops up and down the Malecón in the hopes of getting arrested. Within twenty-four hours, he found himself with an itchy crust of salt from the sea spray on his skin but at last standing in an official line of so-called "social scum."

By his own calculations, Dago knew it might be days, if he got out at all, unless the official system was interrupted in some way. A bribe was impossible for him, with a life's fortune of less than forty pesos in his pocket. So Dago screeched, his back arching each time. And the more he began to loudly comment on this or that part of the guards' anatomies, the more irritated they became, and the more anxious they were to get rid of him. When Mariano the priest pulled up, the guards figured they could exact a double price: rid the revolution of the insufferable fag and make him pay for his unrelentingly bad behavior by sticking him with somebody big and mean and morally imposing.

To their surprise, Mariano sternly shook his head and touched his clerical collar every time one of the Cubans signaled for him to let Dago on his boat, but the brother-in-law, already on the deck and perhaps delirious from his prison trials, beckoned otherwise with his hand. That's about when Mariano threw open the throttle, sans scum aboard.

Immediately, the guards started swearing, shouting and waving frantically, the dissident brother-in-law began to scream at the taciturn priest, and in the confusion Dago Fors gritted his teeth and threw himself, or was pushed by one of the guards (it was hard to say), into the froth, his fingers urgently gripping one of the yacht's dangling ropes. At that, the brother-in-law whooped with joy and began to reel him in, Mariano now gunning the yacht's engines as it roared its way out of Cuban waters.

It had been a surprisingly quick trip north, Destiny reminisced so many years later. But it wasn't Mariano, as the Cuban guards had hoped, but the brother-in-law who gave him a lesson in catechism, going out of his way to explain Saint Dimas, for whom the yacht had been named.

"He was the good thief," he said, "died on a cross just like Jesus, on the same day, with him. Patron saint of criminals. Bet you didn't know criminals had a patron saint, huh? Well, Saint Dimas repented at the last minute, surrendered, and so Jesus said he'd take him to Paradise. It's what we Catholics call baptism by desire."

Sitting in her kitchen now, Destiny remembered the hel-ter skelter arrival in Key West and the resettlement unex-pectedly negotiated for him by the gruff Mariano. In a matter of weeks, Dago Fors found himself sponsored through a church in Chicago's trendy Lake View neighborhood, living in a spare room belonging to an elderly white gay man who practically licked his lips at the sight of him.

Mariano was assigned to a small but thriving parish in a South Side Mexican barrio. As soon as he left, the elderly white man immediately took Dago by the hand around the apartment, explaining exactly how he expected each room to be cleaned and with what products. He lingered lovingly over an antique bureau and demonstrated the gentle rubbing action to be employed with the special cloth and lemon oil. He also seemed to think that Dago's penis should be grateful enough to stand on command and insert accordingly.

"He thinks he hit the lottery!" Dago complained to Mariano that night, whispering into the kitchen phone now that the elderly man was asleep. "Somebody to clean his toi-let and fuck him too. This isn't my idea of freedom!"

Mariano showed up the next day, accepting a cup of cof-fee from the elderly man, who nodded enthusiastically as he explained that these were difficult days of transition. The old man was aghast as Mariano delivered his sermon, with Dago prim and still across from the two of them at the kitchen table. The elderly man, his hand shaking, assured them both that his largesse had been lost in translation. On his way out, Mariano gave Dago a stern, annoyed look.

That night the elderly man made himself a scrumptious beef brisket, heaping mounds of creamy mashed potatoes doused in butter beside it. It was not by any stretch a gourmet meal, though it was a particularly hearty one. Dago watched him devour it, his mouth flooding, his own plate empty. When Dago reached for a roll, the elderly man slapped his hand, surprisingly hard, and suggested that if he wanted a roll, if he wanted anything at all, Dago could clean the mess in the kitchen, bloody cutting boards and green stems, peelings and greasy foil scattered all over the counters. Later, in the privacy of the spare room, a determined Dago took a shoelace from a boot he'd found in the hall closet and tied the tightest, most arduous knot he could in its very center. He did this over and over, until it was hard as a pebble.

"Saint Dimas," he whispered in the dark, remembering the prayer that Mariano's dissident brother-in-law had taught him on the yacht, "I will not undo this knot from around your balls until you return to me my way, my path, my fate."

The reporter—her name was Zoe Pino, an understandable reduction, Destiny would find out later, from Zozima Castro Pino—already knew most of his arrival story. She'd drawn its outline in an email that made the jaunt across the waters seem considerably more adventurous, yet abbreviated it into one solid paragraph. Destiny knew that what Zoe wanted now was the story of how Dago Fors had transformed himself from a little nobody Cuban wetback to something of an international drag legend. But she didn't just want a recitation of facts, of this-happened-then-this-happened. She already knew about all the pageants Destiny had won, she could list all her titles and claims to fame. She had Destiny's lines memorized from her cameo appearances in *The Garden at Midnight*, a film based on a murder mystery that ended up getting much greater box office than anyone could have suspected. Destiny had turned that into a flurry of talk show appearances, in English and Spanish, and even set up a website that sold DVDs of her performances, a beauty booklet she'd penned, and assorted Destiny accessories, like T-shirts and lunch boxes.

Zoe had immersed herself so completely in the minutiae of something so incredibly niched that she'd said, as casually as if she were asking a waiter for a tall drink of water, "Destiny, I think you're even bigger than David de Alba," who was really the greatest of them all and who, like Destiny, was a Cuban who had gotten his professional start in Chicago. Of course, David had never been to La Caverna; David, who could pass as Judy Garland's reflection, would have never in his life set foot in La Caverna.

Dago Fors had always been very, very good at one thing: being a drag queen. He wasn't a cross-dresser, he wasn't a female impersonator; he wasn't confused. He was a marvelously talented performer, an impressive six feet tall, with style and imagination and just enough restraint to give off an air of enduring elegance. No bookkeeping or waiting tables for him, this was all he knew how to do, all that he'd ever done.

In Havana he'd gotten to practice his skills due to uncommon good luck. Sure, there were tons of underground drag shows, something pieced together at somebody's apartment until an intolerant neighbor turned them in. But his real showcase had been a lunchtime show, performed completely under the auspices of the local Committee for the Defense of the Revolution. It was conveniently chaired by a friend's aunt, whose husband was a high-ranking military officer blackmailed to okay the whole thing. It turned out that Dago's friend's aunt had found out her husband was having an affair with the wife of an even higher-ranking officer and was now using the info to get him to do pretty much whatever she wanted, including lending his official imprimatur to the lunchtime drag extravaganza. As a result, for two years Dago had been free to be himself—or whomever he wanted to be—for ninety minutes every Monday to Friday.

The show took place at a worker's cafeteria across the street from the Presidential Palace, right in the middle of the city, accessible to anyone who had the time and inclination to come. There was no stage per se, just a space opened up by pushing the long lunchroom tables together. This discouraged complicated choreography but really put the premium on presence. Moreover, without stage lights, and with the light of day pouring in unfiltered, the queens really had to be extraordinary to make magic in so naked a place. For Dago, it was a grueling but exuberant apprenticeship. Nothing would ever be as hard again. Nothing would ever require so much of his psyche and heart.

In Havana back then, all the girls loved to do Celia Cruz, the exiled queen of salsa. It was not that Celia was particularly beautiful, because she wasn't at all, but her music was saucy and her costumes, even then, interplanetary. Lots of queens also liked Garland, of course, and Barbra Streisand and Marilyn Monroe. But the girls of color tended to go for Celeste Mendoza, who wore towering African wraps on her head and rivaled Celia for sheer rhythmic audacity, or Juana Bacallao, who had a nice ghetto thing going and was a lot of fun.

For Dago there really was only one choice: Moraima Secada, also known as La Mora. A gorgeous mulatta, a little richer in color than Dago, she'd begun as a member of a famous quartet but went off on her own to record a style known in Cuba as *filin*, a kind of over-the-top ballad in which both lyric and melody worked from simple melancholia to unfettered tragedy in about three and a half minutes.

Her style was *sui generis:* She sang with a stern face, as if she were incandescent with rage. She would tilt her head up, press her lips together, and raise her arm, fist clenched. But as she brought up her trembling limb, her fingers would slowly open, almost against her will, as if all fortune could take flight. La Mora was so intense that after her husband was killed in the terrorist bombing of a Cuban airline on its way back from Panama, she still kept her nightclub engagement that night in Havana, the only crack in her otherwise militant façade a suppressed sob, like a hiccup.

Of course, in Chicago no one knew anything about La Mora. When Dago finally found himself covered by the honeyed lights of a real stage, there wasn't a soul in the audience who had a clue about his inspiration. In the long run, it was just as good that way—Dago was able to inhabit her, to fold and tuck and invent without worry. After a while, he came to believe he'd conjured her whole, except for the aching sadness left by the turbulence of love suddenly and unexpectedly lost. That was real, real for both of them, real and terrifying too.

The phone rang. Destiny didn't need to glance at the caller ID to know it was Zoe Pino. There was just enough of a yap to give her away.

"Destiny, babes," the girl said into the answering machine, "I'm just calling to confirm our date tonight. You say the first show doesn't start until 1 a.m., right? I was thinking then we could meet a little earlier, for a late dinner or drinks or whatever, you know, and just talk. I really wanna get as much of the background on this as possible. Call or text me, okay? See you later, *corazon*."

Destiny knew what Zoe wanted from her: a story about the good queen, the queen that against all odds found the liberty and success that was the inspiration for so many Marielitos. But in her few informal talks with Zoe, Destiny had already experienced a certain discomfort: Was Zoe trying to get her to say her dreams had all come true? They hadn't, but would admitting that be some sort of betrayal? Or would going along with the story of awe be what was treasonous? If she had been able to accomplish what she had, was she inadvertently passing judgment on those who'd had a hard time?

In fact, what Destiny feared was that Zoe might have a secret angle: that Dago Fors had come to town, learned the ropes at La Caverna, then forsaken his Latino brethren forever to become a huge hit uptown and around the world. After he'd crossed north of Fullerton Avenue, not once had Destiny ever set foot in a Mexican club, or anywhere near anything even vaguely Mexican, for that matter.

Initially, Dago had actually gone in search of La Caverna, although he didn't know that then. The day after Mariano's visit to the elderly gay man's, Dago got up, borrowed a coat from the hall closet, and walked out. But as soon as he opened the door, he was stung by the bite of Chicago's autumn and he hugged the coat closer to him as he headed east on Barry Street to Broadway. He had no idea then he had aimed for the very heart of Chicago's gay male world.

He'd vaguely imagined he could sleep in a park if he had to but that had been before he'd tested the temperatures, which were to him the equivalent of a Havana winter. The sky was gray; the streets were shiny from a predawn shower.

He turned south on Broadway, unaware of direction, and

peeked in the large window of a diner right on the corner. It was well lit and clean and no sooner had he slid into a booth, a slender Mexican man with cobalt hair and a caterpillar mustache was deftly and deferentially wiping clean his table. Dago surveyed the room. It took him all of a second to real-ize the busboys were Latinos, square-shouldered youth who walked with a slight side-to-side sway, their heads tilted for-ward whether they were carrying trays or wet towels or sim-ply disappearing between the two rubber-mat doors that slapped into the kitchen.

Dago waited patiently, then focused on the boy who'd cleaned his table. He was a little shorter than the others, a little boxier and compact, with more of a macho strut per-haps, although—Dago knew instantly—gay as a goose. Dago also knew that it was only a matter of throwing him a slightly bewildered smile, a vaguely helpless sigh, and the boy would find a reason to come back.

Quique Lopez proved a better connection than Dago could have ever guessed. He was, as Dago had hoped, Guatemalan, but with fake papers that said he was Mexican, fluent in Spanish but also perfectly capable of communicating in English. And he'd been in Chicago long enough so that, once Dago explained his plight, Quique knew immediately what to do.

"La Caverna, that's where you need to go," he said, "but all I can do is take you. The people I know there, I don't even know their real names, you understand? There are American places, a couple around here, some downtown. One on the South Side, I think, but that's a black thing. Maybe you could pass but . . . without English, I just don't know."

After his shift, Quique took Dago to the red line on

Belmont, paid for his fare, and, various line changes and
nearly an hour later, led him off a bus from 26th and Ashland
to a nondescript building a few blocks away. There, in a stu-
dio apartment with six mattresses, they napped platonically,
ate a modest meal of *carnitas* and rice, and watched TV until
about 10 o'clock, when Quique again led him to the bus stop,
this ride straight west, until they were deposited just steps
from La Caverna, a club so notorious it didn't boast any kind
of sign. Instead, it had a huge metal door with black lettering
stenciled across it, unintelligible to Dago at the time, but
warning customers not just about IDs but also about its ban
on handguns.

There wasn't much of a crowd inside at that hour. A gaggle of queens who doubled as waitresses stared as Dago and
Quique strolled in, waved through by the cross-eyed bouncer.
Dago was amazed: There was a man dressed in black, replete
with black boots, black bolo, and black cowboy hat at the bar.
A stern looking middle-aged Mexican man served drinks.
Quique led Dago to a corner table where a tiny elderly
woman with reading glasses was going through a ledger. A
glass of lemonade accompanied her.

The woman—Virginia was her name—didn't say much
during the conversation. Dago was never sure if she ever
believed that he was, in fact, one of Cuba's most popular drag
attractions, as he described himself. He talked nonstop for
ten minutes. Then a man walked in, utterly dashing, maybe
thirty years old, about 5'9", cinnamon-colored and princely,
bearing a boyish grin. He wore denim pants with a huge
buckle in the shape of what looked like Cuba if somebody
had tried to take the hump out of it. Later, Dago would learn
it was Sinaloa, a Mexican province notorious for its drug run-
ners. The man whispered in Virginia's ear. He looked at Dago

only once, and only long enough to wink in his direction before disappearing again.

Dago had drinks on the house that night and watched the show, a parade of queens trying their best on Third World budgets to create First World fantasies. The next day at noon sharp, he was given a tour by Virginia of the storage closet that served as the queens' dressing room (they shared the bathroom with the customers, male and female), and offered a look at the DJ's collection to pick out his debut song. There was no La Mora. There was no Celeste Mendoza or Juana Bacallao, though plenty of Lola Beltran and Veronica Castro. Dago sent the resourceful Quique off with twenty dollars and a list of possibilities. He came back with Olga Guillot's greatest hits in pristine condition.

That night, Dago was introduced to the overflow Saturday night crowd as La Mora, covered in a simple blue chiffon dress with black pumps, his naps under a towering black hive of a wig, his jewelry accidentally tasteful by virtue of its simplicity. After hours of rancheras and accordion-laced banda music, La Mora came out defiantly, her supple lips shaping the words to Guillot's "La Mentira," a slow-burning torch song that entrusts the lying lover to God's judgement.

Dago faltered only once, and it was only for a split second: To her astonishment, there was Father Mariano, sitting expressionless next to the man with the Sinaloa buckle from the night before. By now Dago knew the man was Beto Chavez, Virginia's straight, married, drug-dealing son, a rascal who flirted with every queen at La Caverna but had never been caught with his pants down except with natural born women. Quique didn't know anyone but he certainly knew everything. Beto Chavez winked again and lifted a can of Tecate in Dago's direction.

When a shaken La Mora finished, her eyes downcast, chest heaving, there was a silent pause, then Dago heard the applause like a rolling wave gathering force as it neared the shore, finally crashing in shouts of "bravo!" and "viva la mulata!" and general whistling. As she exited the floor, La Mora turned for an instant. Beto Chavez was clapping, but slowly, looking after her with a distant melancholia.

"Did you love Beto Chavez?" Zoe Pino asked, her leonine hair straying into her line of vision as she positioned her pen on a blank page of her reporter's notebook. She shook her hair back with a shrug. They were two hours into dinner, well into a second bottle of wine, and had long put all of Zoe's questions about Cuba-this and Cuba-that to rest.

"Did I . . . did I love Beto Chavez?" Destiny repeated, aghast. "What gives you the idea I . . . I mean, what are you getting at?"

"C'mon, Destiny . . . I know."

"You know what?"

"About you and Beto."

"Well, I don't know what you're talking about." Destiny began to gather her lighter and the pack of Romeo y Julietas she'd dropped on the table.

"Look, I'll close my notebook." Zoe flipped it shut. "Off the record, I swear. I'll never use it. I certainly have no need to for these Mariel profiles. But please, I've heard so many rumors about you and Beto . . ."

"And you listen to rumors?"

"I'm a reporter, yeah . . ."

"They're just rumors, that's all."

There was silence. Zoe reached across the table to Destiny's hand. "It's a great love story. One of the greatest, if it's true."

Destiny shook her head and turned away. There was no need for Zoe Pino to see her tears.

It was Beto Chavez who'd created the opportunity for her at La Caverna, immediately realizing the young queen talking to his mother had to be the same one he'd heard about earlier from Mariano. It was also Beto Chavez who named her Destiny. "It was fate," he said to her after her first show. "Destiny, pure destiny."

After the performance, Mariano and Dago stared, dumbfounded by the other's appearance in this most unlikely of places. Mariano would learn Dago's trajectory to La Caverna that very night but it would take Dago a bit longer, more than a year, to understand that Mariano was actually a defrocked priest, a pre–Vatican II follower, who offered Latin masses in a former Lutheran church, now converted and supported by Beto Chavez and an entire community of narco-traffickers.

It had been Beto's boat, the *San Dimas*, that the priest had taken to Mariel to snatch up his brother-in-law, a boat normally used to ferry between Florida and the bleached islets of corrupt coral that served as hideouts for smugglers. Beto Chavez was a Dimas devotee, and he showed Dago the cross on the chain that hung around his neck.

"Not Christ, no. Look: no crown of thorns, no nails, just rope," he explained, as Dago examined the little crucified man and breathed in Beto's cologne. "Dimas, Dimas the good thief."

Beto Chavez was beautiful: his eyes wet with sadness but his smile a beacon. Dago fingered the knot in the shoelace he'd tied before, the tight little vise he'd placed on the saint's venerable testicles, now securely tucked into his handbag.

"Destiny . . ." Beto said, this time in a whisper, his lips grazing Dago's ear.

It was not lightning between Destiny and Beto Chavez. That Beto flirted surprised no one. That he was chivalrous was the norm. At least that's what Quique Lopez kept telling Destiny so she wouldn't have any illusions.

But what few people realized at first—including his mother Virginia—was that, within weeks of her debut, Beto Chavez had set up Destiny with her own apartment above a barbershop in Pilsen, far enough from La Caverna that he could pretend no one knew of his visits, but only ten minutes southeast of his family's home on Kedvale, around the corner from the club in La Villita that served to launder so much of his profits.

It is unlikely that anyone would have believed that Beto Chavez was not fucking Destiny by then. It was clear he was utterly bewitched by her, by the way she walked, by the smell and feel of her hair, by the silky arousal her hands on him provoked. But when Beto had explained that he had no intention of touching or being touched by Destiny's manhood, he got quite the surprise.

"I'm no fag," he said, grinning.

"All of me or none of me," Destiny said in refusal, flatly turning down the handsome, powerful drug lord, the one whom the sorority back at La Caverna yearned for precisely because he'd never, ever been known to betray the slightest interest in a queen.

Beto tried once, and only once, to force himself on Destiny. But he was stunned to discover how strong and limber she was, how easily the much taller and felid Destiny flipped him over, tying his hands with his Sinaloa belt, her knee jabbing Saint Dimas into his neck. She swore that if he tried it again, she wouldn't hesitate to kill him, no matter what happened to her afterwards.

"I have nothing," she whispered fiercely, "so I have nothing to lose."

"How'd you get so . . . so strong?" Beto asked, coughing, not afraid but even more in awe.

"Cutting cane, forced 'volunteer' work in my country," Destiny said, massaging Beto's neck and shoulders as he leaned back on her, both of them still on the floor. "You'd be amazed by what I can do with a machete. Or a knife."

Six months later, six months of Beto pleading and threatening to cut her off or have her fired, six months of Destiny shouting back that she'd tell the whole neighborhood how she'd thrown him on the floor, six months of Beto getting used to recognizing the pulse of Destiny's desire against his leg or belly, of kissing and feeling her everywhere but there, Beto Chavez showed up one rainy April dawn at the apartment and let himself in with his key. He lifted the blanket from Destiny's sleeping body, lowered himself to his knees and put his hungry mouth to her triumph.

Zoe Pino stroked Destiny's hand gently. "I know some things," she said. "I know you were, in some ways, almost married for a few years . . ."

Destiny winced. "I wouldn't ever say that. He was married, you know, really married, to a woman."

Destiny had seen her only once and had been surprised. Beto's wife was not a roly-poly demure woman, older than her years by virtue of the stress that Beto engendered with his lifestyle. Staring at her across Mariano's church, Destiny found she was nothing like she'd expected: at least as tall as Beto, a pale skinned Mexican woman with reddish hair, strong and dignified. If Virginia hadn't been right by her side, Destiny might have doubted it was her.

"A sort of second wife then . . ." Zoe said.

"You mean a mistress," Destiny clarified.

"Was that it then? You were his mistress? You know, they say mistresses are often the big love of men's lives . . ."

"Don't patronize me, Zoe, please."

Had she been Beto Chavez's true love?

That apartment above the barbershop on 18th Street had been a cozy little nest for many years. After work, when Destiny got home as the skies cleared for morning, Beto would come over for breakfast and the sweet exhaustion of their play. They'd spoon together for what seemed hours but which Destiny knew must have been only a little while, until she was asleep. Then he'd tiptoe out, back to his world of mystery and violence.

It was not unusual for him to come home hurt, to have sprained an ankle running, to have his face torn apart in a fight, to take a bullet in the flesh of his arm. He'd always come to her first, he'd always come to be cured by her hands and to sleep off the doubt and fatigue in her bed.

He brought her the usual romantic offerings of chocolate and flowers but also books and records, including an import of Moraima Secada singing *filin*, which could always make her cry. Instead of cocaine, he brought her what seemed an interminable supply of hormones; these made her smoother and curvier, her muscles softer though she was no less formidable.

Sometimes, on her days off, he'd show up in the early evening and they'd watch a movie and make dinner together.

Destiny realized she'd never seen him anywhere outside of the club or her apartment, a place she kept warm, ready, but barred to all other visitors out of respect for Beto. Except for that last time . . .

At some point, of course, Virginia knew, the other queens knew, everyone knew. But it was so startling that even as time passed and all the little clues accumulated to create a rather convincing circumstantial case, doubt nagged even the most vociferous gossips; insecurity, and perhaps fear too, because Beto Chavez wasn't anyone to trifle with, dogged even the most convinced.

Could it be real?

If things hadn't changed so dramatically, if everything hadn't ended so abruptly, if her world hadn't collapsed so utterly, Destiny wondered how long they could have gone on like that . . . Back then she would have said forever, she would have wanted forever, would have believed in it.

But now, even as she sometimes touched the loosened shoelace on her own homemade altar to Saint Dimas, she knew that everything Zoe Pino would write about her—the pageants, the titles, the movie, her sanctified role in the most prestigious drag show in all of Chicago, the ridiculously profitable website (Quique, now her manager, had come up with it), the sensation she caused on returning to Havana for a millennium appearance captured by CNN (for 2001, not 2000, because the Cubans did not agree with the rest of the world on the new century's commencement)—none of it would have happened if she and Beto had continued their journey together.

Catastrophe happened on an early and placid Tuesday evening in late summer. Destiny's windows were open and she heard Beto's voice downstairs greeting the barber, who'd stepped outside to take in the wild palette of sunset descending west on 18th Street. She leaned out eagerly, imagining herself like Juliet for a moment, ready to hear promises from her Romeo, when she suddenly caught sight of a pickup truck inching its way down the street, a couple of black-garbed men, not cowboys but more like ninjas, leaning over the cab, the stout barrels of their automatics slowly taking aim.

Destiny's mouth opened. In her head, she screamed, as loud and precise as a missile. But the only sound heard for blocks and blocks was the explosive *rat-a-tat* of machine-gun fire as Beto Chavez danced like a marionette on the cracked Pilsen sidewalk, his arms reaching out to the barber who fell beneath him. Within seconds, the pickup truck was an eastbound blur, a cloud of smoke and black powder slowly settling in its wake.

Destiny raced downstairs, her throat still incapable of noise. She pulled Beto off the barber, onto his bloodied back, only to find the bullets had made tripe of his chest and belly. Her hands went to keep him together, to keep him whole. The barber's wife was now on the ground beside him, the light disappearing as people gathered, leaning in. Someone tried to pull Destiny off Beto but she cuffed him so hard he fell back and no one else dared get near her.

"Go . . ." Beto whispered. "Get out of here . . ."

She tried to protest but the words were still struggling to exit, impossible to form. She noticed his chain with the Saint Dimas cross on the ground and picked it up, letting the light glint off of it so he could see she'd saved it.

He licked his lips. "See you in paradise . . . okay?"

Zoe Pino cocked an eyebrow in Destiny's direction. "C'mon, he didn't really say that."

"I swear."

Destiny lit another Romeo y Julieta. She'd lost count. The bitch had gotten her to tell the whole damn story and now she didn't believe her?

"'I'll see you in paradise'? I mean, that's . . ."

"I know, I know," Destiny interrupted. "How do you think it made me feel? And how do you think it makes me feel now to know I can never tell that story because nobody will ever fucking believe me?"

"No, no, I believe you," Zoe insisted. "It's just, well, unbelievable. I mean, it's . . . Look . . . you know what I'm trying to say."

Destiny nodded.

"So that's when you left Pilsen?"

"I had to."

"What do you mean you had to?"

"I had to! Before the ambulance had even arrived, another car drove up, this one full of Mexican cowboys with their pistols drawn. One guy, a little skinny guy, his eyes all mean, he looked right at me and pointed his gun at Beto and just shot him point blank. I felt like Jackie Kennedy, gathering bits of his brains into my lap. I was screaming—finally!—and crying, and he made this motion with the pistol for me to go, and I did. I just ran and ran, scattering pieces of Beto all the way to Quique's apartment and stayed holed up there, terrified and traumatized, until the day of Beto's funeral."

When she and Quique finally made it back to her apartment, they found the place had been tossed. All of her records and books were on the floor, clothes torn from the bar in the closet, the mattress gutted. The refrigerator leaked a foul smell from a puddle underneath.

Destiny just sobbed and sobbed.

"My god . . . what did they want? Do you know what they wanted? Did Beto keep anything here?" Quique asked, his voice shaky.

She shook her head.

"Are you sure?"

Beto hadn't even kept a change of socks there. Destiny realized all she had of him now and forever was the Saint Dimas cross from around his neck.

Later, at Mariano's church before the family arrived for funeral services, the priest, his stone face wet, opened the casket so she could have a last look. Destiny, wearing a men's suit for the first time in her life, looked down at her lover. Beto was in pieces, like Saint Dimas himself, with a forearm in Jerusalem and a tibula in Istanbul.

A noise from the front of the church revealed Beto's family, a mournful Virginia leading the widow and a gaggle of children. Stern-faced men, no doubt armed, flanked them on both sides. Mariano immediately snapped shut the casket and Destiny stepped back, disappearing into the shadows.

The only other thing she remembered from that day was Mariano's prayer: *Saint Dimas, from great sinner and criminal, a moment of mercy turned you into a great Saint. Remember me, poor sinner like you, and maybe greater sinner than you . . .*

Zoe parked her boxy Nissan in front of a Western-wear store on 26th Street with a garish yellow awning and snakeskin belts draping one of the windows. Across the street was La Caverna, as anonymous as ever.

"You ready?" she asked.

Destiny nodded and pulled the car door open. She could smell the *carnitas* from the corner.

"You've really never come back?"

"Never," Destiny said.

"See, I just don't get that, because you weren't in danger. Unless, of course, somebody thought you knew something . . . ?"

Destiny sprinted ahead, sick of Zoe's baiting. Upon seeing Destiny, the same cross-eyed bouncer from years before grinned and called her by her old name: "La Mora! Doña Mora!" There was a flurry of activity then, with men stepping up to bow and kiss her hand and queens popping out of nowhere, screeching and jumping up and down. Zoe struggled to keep Destiny in sight, though she was easily the tallest person there, her head high and steady.

Inside La Caverna, Destiny saw the same Mexican man, now white-haired, serving drinks. But the place was different: cleaner, painted. There were color posters of all the new queens framed on the wall. She was stunned to see her own face staring back at her from above the bar, in the center of a sort of Wall of Fame of famous queens who'd started at La Caverna.

Destiny clutched her heart, unexpectedly moved. Then she saw that Virginia was still there too, sitting on a stool behind the bar, taking money. The woman, now an old crone, flinched when she saw Destiny. The crowd parted like the Red Sea.

A few feet behind, Zoe battled to keep up. "*Con permiso, con permiso,*" she repeated as the waters closed in on her. Then the crowd crushed around Destiny when she and Virginia hugged across the bar, the old woman shaking from so much emotion.

"Listen, I'm with Destiny, really!" Zoe yelled, reaching so that she caught Destiny's arm with her fingers for a second.

But no one could hear her. The shouting and whistling was thunderous. The DJ immediately injected a battery of percussion into the club, the clattering beginning of a salsa roundup they'd later learn he'd titled "Destiny's Cuban Fiesta Mix."

"Destiny! Destiny!"

Zoe was just about to give up hope of ever reaching her when suddenly a gunshot rang out. Then another and another. She leaped through the mob and yanked Destiny by the arm, pulling and pushing through the masses of sweaty human flesh until they were back outside, breathing the *carnitas*-infused air of 26th Street.

"You've gotta tell me the truth!" Zoe demanded, leaning up on her toes to get in Destiny's face.

"The truth? What the fuck are you talking about?" Destiny asked as she jerked her arm away and straightened her dress. "What the hell do you think you're doing?"

"What the . . . ? Just tell me, okay? What it is? What do you still have of Beto's that made you run, huh? What is it—an address book? The last two digits of a Swiss bank account? The combination of a secret safe? C'mon! What do you have that would make somebody want to kill for it twenty-five years later?"

Destiny grabbed her by the shoulders. "Are you out of your mind?"

"Am I . . . ? What? You didn't hear those shots in there?" Zoe asked, indignantly shaking herself loose.

"Oh, for god's sake, Zoe—it's 4 o'clock in the morning and everybody in there has had three bottles of who-knows-what and they're out of control. It's a crazy, violent bar—that's all!"

"That's all? But you've never been back—that has to be for a reason!"

"Is this what you've really been getting at? Is that what all your interest has been about? This ridiculous *telenovela* scenario where I have some terrible secret that someone wants to avenge? Oh, Zoe, you're so much more Cuban than I ever gave you credit for!"

Destiny started to laugh.

"But . . ."

A crowd was forming again.

"There's got to be a reason . . ."

"There is," she said, and she strolled back into La Caverna.

Hours later, Destiny found herself back home, inhaling another Romeo y Julieta, and sucking on a cup of Cuban coffee with Quique, who'd gone to La Villita to pick her up. The sun was starting to gain power outside her window.

"It was never about what you took from that place . . ." he said.

"But what I left behind," said Destiny.

Destiny ground the thin cigar out on her pink caiman ashtray. She sighed.

"Got it back, though," she said, and patted the place on her chest where her heart beat.

THE GREAT BILLIK

BY CLAIRE ZULKEY

19TH & SACRAMENTO

The new neighbors moved in the winter of 1905 to a small place a few houses down. We'd come by to say hello to Mary, who was frightened and intrigued by the additions to the area. She sat in the front room, peering through the curtains to see if she could monitor the family's activities. She seemed jumpy and skittish as usual, but also excited.

Our poor sour cousin Mary. Ginny and I didn't mean to make fun of her as much as we did. We probably had some leftover resentment from when our mothers told us to look after her when we were younger. It was hard not to mock someone who took herself so seriously. Granted, she didn't have all the opportunities in the world for excitement; she'd been appointed caretaker of the house when her mother died. But she acted like an old maid, so it was hard not to have fun at her expense sometimes, especially as life grew brighter and the city grew more exciting, while she grew more determined to stay away from it. So we tried to stay kind, because without us around, she'd have nobody to talk to other than that old clammed-up father of hers.

"I hear they're Bohemians," she said. "Come from Cleveland."

"Wouldn't they be coming from Bohemia?" asked Ginny, sipping her tea. Mary looked at her sharply.

"Mrs. Vzral says that he's got three kids," Mary continued, "but I haven't seen any yet. Just his wife. She looks like a horrid woman."

We gasped when the neighbors' front door opened, as if the aforementioned wife were going to come out and berate us after somehow hearing what Mary had said. Instead, out came a man. He was stout, with pale skin and short ginger hair, with black eyes that Mary called "piercing." I found them beady and ratlike, but she never listened to me. I preferred blue eyes anyway.

The man stepped out in front of the house, carrying a sign. He took a hammer from his pocket and tacked it onto the front of the house. The sound carried into Mary's front room. The man looked at his sign brusquely, straightened it, and turned and walked back into the house.

"For sale already?" asked Ginny again.

"Shush," Mary said. "I wonder what that really is."

"Well, we can't walk right up right now and look at it," I said, "or else he'll know we've been spying on him. Let's wait and have another cup and then we can walk by." I was just trying to torture Mary. She seemed like she wanted to run out the door. I found her small life irritating. Rushing into the street to see a sign tacked onto a little old house was the highlight of her day.

After about twenty minutes, we got up. Ginny and I pretended to make a great deal about properly putting on our coats to stay warm, even though it was a mild day. Finally, we strolled outside, acting as if we were chatting about the weather.

The sign was painted brown, with neat red and green lettering. It said:

The Great Billik
Card-Reader and Seer

Mary's mouth hung open in a mystified gape.

"Black magic," I said.

"Rubbish," said Ginny.

We tried to keep walking but Mary lingered, stupidly mouthing the words on the sign.

For the next few days, Mary couldn't be budged from her home. She claimed she had housework to do but we knew she was keeping an eye on that strange man's house. I assumed she still believed what they had told us in Sunday School, that black magic was the devil's work, and she would keep the devil locked out of the house.

Ginny rushed over one day. "You won't believe it," she said, and before I had a chance to respond, she told me.

"My second cousin Ruth was downtown yesterday and *she* ran into her friend Sophia, who told her that she heard something unusual from Emma Vzral. Seems like Mary's gentleman friend is even stranger than we thought. Emma's father was delivering the milk to Billik and Billik stops him and gives him a strange look, and then says, 'Your enemy is trying to destroy you.'"

"So the seer has seen something!" I said. "I hope the Vzrals got a good laugh out of it."

"No," said Ginny. "Apparently they're quite frightened. You know how superstitious they are."

"But I didn't think they'd fall for a shyster. I wonder if Mary knows more about this," I said, and we went to her house. When we told her, we realized that she *hadn't* heard the news, and was quite peeved that we'd found out information about him before she did.

She was still infuriated a few days later. "I have walked back and forth in front of that house several times and even said hello, as new neighbors, and I don't know what is wrong with that man or that family," she said. "He won't acknowledge me at all." Apparently she was more intrigued by the magician than afraid.

"So you have no enemy, let alone one that's trying to destroy you?" I asked.

"No," said Mary, ignoring my joke. "But did you smell that foul odor yesterday?"

"Was it Billik?" Ginny asked.

"It was coming from Henry Reynolds's house, I found out. I just followed my nose," she said, proudly. "But do you know what Reynolds does for a living?"

We looked at her blankly.

"He's a milkman. Like Vzral! That's his enemy!"

"So?"

"I asked around, and one of the neighbors said that they saw Billik stride up to the Reynolds's house and pour a pail of some mysterious liquid on the front steps. He was cursing them!"

"Mary, it doesn't seem terribly magical to me. A foul-smelling house is certainly a curse, but I don't think it's a mysterious one. What's wrong with you? I think you're a bit too caught up with this Billik person. Forget about him. Why don't you—"

"No, thank you," Mary cut me off.

A week later, Mary came over, looking smug. "Have you seen Mrs. Vzral lately?"

"No, I haven't," I said, wanting to point out that I had better things to do than keep a watchful eye on all my neighbors.

"Well, she's worn new dresses three days so far this week. And you know what that means."

"Time for laundry?"

"No, it means that the milk business is doing well. And you know why."

"More cows?"

"It was Billik! I told you, that man had powers!"

I stared at Mary. "Have you spoken with this lunatic?"

"Yes, I have," she said firmly. "And he was quite a gentleman. Anyway, he told me he had nothing to say to me."

"So there you have it," I replied. "He's a charlatan, Mary, he's practically admitting it. Why don't you come back to us in the real world? Aren't you concerned at all about his intentions? Maybe this business is just a lure for gullible young women."

Her face reddened and briefly crumpled.

"Are you in *love* with him?"

She was silent.

"Mary, he's married. He's an immigrant. He's old. He's insane. He's *ugly*. Come on. You're almost twenty. Don't you want a man your own age?"

"I have to go, I'm sorry," said Mary.

And Mary didn't speak to us for several months. I'd see her in church, and she'd ignore me, but she'd stare venomously at the Vzral family, who appeared to Mass less and less frequently, looking worse and worse for the wear each time.

Eventually curiosity got the better of me as well, and since Mary wasn't speaking to me, in spring I went up to Emma, the oldest of the Vzral children, after services one day. She and I had been in class together in elementary school, so it wasn't completely inappropriate, even though it was admittedly none of my business.

"Is everything all right?" I asked, trying to seem casual. I couldn't tell if Emma recognized me or not but she looked pale and very thin, very tired.

"My sisters Catherine, Elizabeth, and June are all working for that man," she said bitterly.

"Billik?"

"It's not enough that my parents have paid for his trips, new clothes, but now my sisters are working as *maids* and giving the money to him," she spat out.

"But why?"

"I see your friend creeping around him," she said, ignoring my questions. "You tell her to stay away from him."

"Mary?"

"Tell her to stay away," Emma said, and walked off.

I went straight to Mary's house after Mass. She looked at me coolly when I answered the door but I ignored her expression.

"Mary, have you been talking to Billik?"

"Why do you care?"

"Mary, I spoke with Emma Vzral at church—"

"You did? What did she say? Did she tell you anything about Herman?"

"*Herman?*"

Mary fell silent.

"Mary, what have you been doing?"

"I don't know why he won't talk to me," she said.

"Mary, honestly, are you in love with this man?"

"No!" she shouted, loudly enough to make me jump. "No, I am *not*," she whispered. "I just wanted to know if maybe . . . he could tell me things."

"You don't actually believe—"

"A mystic! I know it's silly but how often do you encounter

something like that? I wanted to see if he could tell me about my future, about my father, about falling in love. . ."

"And?"

"He tells me he has nothing for me. To go away and leave him alone. And I blame the Vzral's, really, I do. They are hogging him all to themselves and I don't know why. They're selfish. He's helped them with their problems and they should just help themselves now."

"You go over to his house often?"

"I just wanted to get to know him better . . . I thought that maybe if he knew more about me, he could tell me things. Or even just tell me about his travels, about his old home and his family. His mother was a witch, you know," she said, so matter-of-factly that I laughed out loud.

"Mary, you're going to be burned for being a heretic. What's next, making offerings to the gods?"

But she gazed out the window, eyes narrowing as she saw Mrs. Vzral hurry down the steps of Billik's house, something in her hand, her breath steaming in the cold April weather. Spring came late in Chicago, and briefly.

"Mary, you are going to come out of town this weekend with Ginny and me," I said firmly.

"What about father?" she asked dreamily, still looking out the window.

"Ask one of the neighbors to take care of him. Ask my mother. No, you know what? Tell him to take care of himself."

Mary let us drag her up to Detroit for the weekend. We stayed in a women's house, went to the theater and even a Tigers game, which was a little frightening but exciting to attend unescorted, although Mary kept wincing every time she heard the crack of the bat. Mary was quiet for the first half of the trip, but on Saturday she brightened and genuinely seemed excited by the city. By the time we returned, she was giddy and chatty, almost like we'd never seen her before.

We returned Sunday night. Monday morning, we heard that Martin Vzral was dead.

Mary was alarmed and unusually remorseful when we told her. It wasn't as if she'd been that familiar with Mr. Vzral. So I was surprised when Mary asked me to attend the funeral with her.

You wouldn't know that it was a funeral if it weren't for the casket. I was surprised by how sparse the ceremony was. The Vzrals did well for themselves, I had thought, yet their clothes looked threadbare, there were no flowers, and the coffin looked as if it were made of plywood. I saw a hint of smugness in Mary's face as she took in the scene.

"I always thought that family put on airs," she whispered to me, as we left the parish.

The weather warmed up, and Mary proposed that we take a trip north to Riverview. Everyone was talking about the new amusement park and Ginny and I were surprised by Mary's proposal. It seemed too frivolous for her, but we attributed it to spring high spirits kicking in. Plus, we were excited to get a look at the new park.

It was a wonderful day, much warmer than usual for May. We ate ice cream and rode around on a giant carousel and screamed down a toboggan ride. Tired, we strolled down the Midway, cheery German music pumping out from one of the tents, when Mary casually asked to stop by one.

Set up under a dark purple tent was Billik, dressed impeccably in a new suit, with the sign reading the old words, "The Great Billik, Card-Reader and Seer."

"Mary . . ."

"For goodness sake, he's got a tent here at the amusement park," she said. "He *wants* people to come see him. He wouldn't be out here in the open if there was something wrong, would he?"

"All right," I said. "Let's go. I want to get a look at him up close and personal."

"No," she said forcefully.

"You *don't* want to see him?"

"No, I do . . . just, not, all together."

I looked at Billik, who stared straight ahead at the fair, as if he were alone in his home, looking out the window.

"Fine, Mary. But I'm going to see him first."

She made as if to protest, but then thought better of it. "Good," she said sweetly. "I hope he has some good news for you."

I strode up to the booth, but my heart was pounding. I wasn't sure why. Billik ignored me until I stood in front of his table and cleared my throat. He looked up and nodded at me to sit down, without saying a word. He began flipping some cards around.

"She bring some friends?" he asked.

"Who?"

Billik jerked his head in Mary's direction. "She bring you along?" His English wasn't completely right, but he spoke with hardly any accent. His skin burst out of his collar, but was clean and smooth, pale and shiny like a baby's. He barely seemed to look at the oversized cards that he was handling, as they made a slapping sound. A breeze started blowing and it began feeling more like May in Chicago.

"Tell her to stay away," he said. "She waste my time."

"I tried telling her to stay away. She thinks you have powers."

He stopped and looked up at me with the blackest eyes I have ever seen. "I *do* have powers. She has nothing for me to tell her."

"She thinks you do, or you will," I said.

"Stupid girl." He looked up at me and grinned. "You want fortune?"

"No, I—"

"Give me your hand." He grabbed toward my arm.

"*No.*"

"Who are your parents? Where do they work? You have nice house?"

I hurried away. Before I could even talk to her, Mary practically ran into the tent.

"What did he say?" asked Ginny, as we saw Mary eagerly sit down in the chair in front of Billik, who looked supremely uninterested.

"He says that Mary's bothering him. He seems like a complete farce. He's *mean.* You go up there and you'll see."

"No, I'm not. My parents would send me to a convent if they heard I was meeting with a mystic or a seer or whatever it is he calls himself."

Mary looked on with great interest at the cards that Billik was flipping around carelessly, and she eagerly held out her hand, which Billik pretended to study with poorly concealed boredom. He accepted the nickel she offered him like it was soiled linen.

I received some good news a few weeks later. My family was able to put some money together and I was going to go up to Milwaukee to attend Alverno, a women's college. Fall of '06, I packed my things, said goodbye to my family, and took the train to Wisconsin to begin classes. I wrote home frequently, and tried Mary several times, telling her about school and my classmates and the city, in hopes of getting her to speak with me again, but she gave me no answer.

I came home for Christmas, excited to see my family. All the aunts and uncles and cousins met at our house, and Ginny and I took a walk around the neighborhood to see if anyone else was out celebrating. All the houses looked lit up and warm, but as we came to the Vzral house, it was dark, with a wretched little black wreath on the door.

"What happened?" I asked.

"That poor family," whispered Ginny, who was becoming like her mother, more pious and maternal, as she grew older. "Tillie died the day before you came home," she said, referring to one of the younger sisters.

"Oh! That's so sad. First their father, then Tillie . . ."

"Actually," said Ginny, "Susie passed away right after you left for Milwaukee. They've lost two sisters."

"Why didn't you tell me?" I said.

"I didn't find out about it until much later," she said. "You know that family better than I do. I forgot, I suppose."

"What happened?"

"They say stomach trouble. For all of them. I hope it's not contagious."

We came home just as Mary had stopped by to say hello to my parents. She looked gaunt, much older than when I had last seen her. She seemed happy, though, and was cordial to me.

"How is your father, Mary?"

"Oh, he's fine, on death's door as he always is. But I've been working, and it's good to get out of the house."

"That's good news," I said. "Where are you working?"

"Some housekeeping here and there," she said lightly, trailing off. "Some bookkeeping too."

"Where?"

"Neighbors," she said, and abruptly changed the subject.

I hadn't seen Edward, my neighborhood boy, for a while and it was good to spend time with him again, away from my family and my classmates. I enjoyed school but being around so many other girls was tiring. The night before I left to go back, he asked if I would marry him. I said I'd think about it but of course I knew that I would.

Back in Milwaukee, Mary deigned to write to me again. I found out that she was working for Billik. She really, truly seemed happy, though, and told me stories of their fine house, his dusty cases of fortune-telling equipment that she wasn't allowed to touch, and the large sums of money that she kept track of, but knew nothing about.

"Is he paying you well, at least?" I wrote back.

"My payment comes in watching him work," she wrote me. "And his knowledge. He says that he's starting to see some good luck for me in the future. And love! I hope it's true."

"What's his wife like?" I responded, and she ignored this question in her next letter. She did congratulate me when I told her I was going to marry Edward.

I came back to Chicago for good that summer in 1907. We were hoping to marry in the winter, so we went to the parish to discuss the date with the Father and were surprised to see a coffin inside.

"Rose Vzral," he said, sighing and looking sad. "Only fourteen years old. If I believed in such things, I would think that family had a curse on it." I wanted to ask him if he believed in curses later when Rose's sister Ella died that fall. Stomach problems as well.

A month before the wedding, I had lunch with Ginny

and Mary. A few years previous I would have expected Mary to be drawn and bitter at any wedding news, spinster-to-be that she was, but she actually seemed haughty, although perhaps she kept tossing her head to show off the new earrings she was wearing.

"Those are beautiful, Mary," Ginny obliged.

"Aren't they?" she breathed. "They were a gift from my employer."

"Billik?" I said. "He makes that much money off fortune-telling?"

"The man has a gift," she said. "He helps people, and they reward him in return."

"Really? How so?"

"You remember how Martin Vzral was going to suffer from a competitor . . ."

"Yes, but he's dead now."

"That's beside the point. That family has made its own problems. The mother is a fool. She's holding onto that house of theirs. She would be better off to sell it to Herman. She can't rattle around in there like the crazy old bat she is. It's too bad, what happened to her family, but for goodness' sake."

"You're trying to drive the Vzrals out of their home?" said Ginny. "What does Billik have to do with it?"

"I just keep records of finances," Mary said. "The Vzrals owe everything they have to Herman. If it wasn't for him, they'd all be dead, or worse."

"Or worse, such as what?"

Mary just raised her eyebrows mysteriously and said she had to go. "I'm keeping house for him while he travels."

Although it rarely starts snowing in earnest until January or February here, God granted us a beautiful coating of snow for the wedding. The ceremony was lovely and we were giddy with the prospect of the future. Before we returned to my house for dinner and gifts and music, we had to pay Father Vincent his honorarium. As we were meeting with him and about to invite him over to the house, one of the Sisters rushed in and whispered in his ear. He frowned.

"What is it, Father?" asked Edward.

He crossed himself. "Poor Mrs. Vzral," he said.

Though I said a small prayer for her and the family, I soon forgot about it, until Mary, who seemed rather stoic throughout the wedding and the party, excused herself early, saying that she had to meet with her employer, who had come back to town.

"Mary, it's my wedding day," I said.

"I don't want to upset him," she said unapologetically, and slid out.

A few weeks later, Edward and I moved to St. Louis so he could set up his law firm with his friends from school. I tried staying at home for some time but got bored quickly, so Edward let me come work for the firm as a typewriter.

I received some good news from Ginny. She'd been rescued from contemplation of the convent when her shy admirer George from down the block finally proposed to her.

"No more excitement for me," she joked in her letter. "Except right now. The whole neighborhood is buzzing. Everyone is suspicious of Mary's friend."

"I'm not surprised that everyone is suspicious of him," I wrote back. "He's a very strange person. What does everyone suspect him of?"

I received a telegram from Ginny before I even sent my letter.

"*VZRALS MURDERED,*" was all it said.

She filled me in via letters. Based on some neighborhood

suspicion, Mrs. Vzral had been dug up and poison was found in her stomach, and how we did not guess that to begin with, I'm ashamed to even speculate. Billik was picked up a few days later.

Ginny sent me clippings from the newspapers. The city seemed more enthralled than horrified. Reporters kept comparing Billik to a previous murderer, Holmes, who was executed while we were still children.

I felt relieved that the strange man was behind bars, but I felt sorry for my cousin, that this man who she so admired, who didn't even seem to reciprocate, was now so disgraced.

"It's not true," she wrote to me.

I stopped paying attention to neighborhood gossip for a while after that, until in June '08, when I received a telegram from my mother saying that my uncle, Mary's father, had finally passed away. It was difficult to feel sorrowful, as nobody had ever really known him other than as an invalid that Mary was forced to tend to her whole life. I wondered if she felt relief or complete despondency.

I came home for the funeral. Ginny was starting to get big with her first baby and it was good to see her. Mary seemed rather unemotional at the funeral. Afterwards, I embraced her and said, "What are you going to do now?"

"I'm free," she whispered.

I smiled. "So what are you going to do with your new-found freedom? Go to school? Move? Get married?"

"I'm selling the house," she said, "But I'm moving to a smaller apartment in the city."

"I don't blame you," I said. "You've been in that house all your life. It's a shame that your father didn't leave you more to get a little house for yourself."

"No," she said. "I *did* get the money. Herman told me to

do it. He told me that that house is cursed, and that I should move."

"Isn't he in jail?"

"We write letters," she said. "It's time, Helen. It's a terrible thing that he's in prison but now that my father's dead, he's told me that his spirit isn't in the way anymore. He can see my future!"

I couldn't do anything.

I went back to St. Louis and did not return to Chicago for almost a year, as Edward and I found out that I was expecting my first. I hadn't heard from Mary since I wrote to tell her. She wrote me, requesting a donation for a fund she was organizing to release Billik from prison. I wrote a rather forceful decline.

She did respond though when I sent her the announcement of our son early in 1909. She congratulated us, sent a rattle, and slipped it into her letter that Billik was granted life in prison, not the death penalty. I sent her a thank you note but didn't comment on the latter. I was sick of hearing about him. After that, our letters were terse, when they existed at all.

In June of the new decade, I got the bad news that my mother was quite ill, so we took the children (now two of them) and went back down to Chicago to see her one last time. I managed to speak with her right before she slipped away. We stayed for the funeral.

It was good to be with Ginny, and I saw Mary for the first time in a couple of years. She looked even older and her clothes seemed threadbare, which was surprising. I'd heard that the sum her father had left behind for her was unexpectedly generous, and she was never a spendthrift. We embraced but did not speak beyond the formalities. She excused herself after the services.

"You're not coming back to our house?" I asked.

"No," she said quietly, but with an excited look in her eyes. "Her— . . . Billik? You remember him? He's been released from prison."

"Good news," I said.

"I promised him I'd go meet him. I'm so sorry to leave," she said, not seeming sorry at all.

I spent the rest of the day in a fury. Getting back home to St. Louis, I wrote to Ginny, "I've had it with Mary. She couldn't even be there as family after Mother died." I spent the next several days going about my business, but I could not stop thinking about how angry I was with my cousin, how she'd grown too selfish and foolish for even her own family.

"I'm sure she's sorry," Ginny wrote back. "I'll tell her you say hello and maybe she'll say something nice in return. I'm off to go visit her now, actually. It'll be the first time I see this apartment of hers. She says that she's not feeling well."

I looked up from my letter and stared at the wall for a few moments and then picked up the pen. I changed my mind, put it down, and rushed to the telephone, although I had a feeling I knew what I'd hear when I reached Ginny.

"Her stomach's been bothering her," Ginny said. "Possibly a cold or something she ate."

MAXIMILLIAN

BY ALEXAI GALAVIZ-BUDZISZEWSKI

18th & Allport

I have three memories of my cousin Maximillian. Two of them involve his fists.

My cousin was a short man. But like everyone else on the Mexican side of my family, he was built like a brick two-flat, heavy and hard, a cannonball, the way my grandmother on my mother's side was a cannonball, the way my uncle Blas was a cannonball. They were all skull, impossible to hug, but warm blooded, steaming, like just standing next to them could get you through a winter's day. My mother was like this. I miss her terribly.

But Max, my cousin, *Maximillian*, was young, sixteen or so when my memories of him first begin. His sister Irene celebrated her cotillion in the basement of St. Procopius Church on 18th Street and Allport. I don't know much about the planning. I was eight years old. But I know my sister Juana stood up in it. She was a *Dama,* and my cousin on my father's side, Little David, was her *Chambalan.* They went off doing their own thing, dancing, waltzing, the way they'd been practicing for weeks, my sister constantly fitting and refitting her dress, me calling her Miss Piggy because she was chubby and more *queda* than the rest of us darkies.

That night I sat with my mother and ate cake and people watched. My father, done with his shift at the basement door, hunched at a side table sharing a bottle of Presidente with his friend Moe. My cousin Chefa danced with my uncle Bernardo and my aunt Lola danced with her only son, my cousin, Maximillian. It was all beautiful, all quite nice. Then Stoney showed up.

I'm not sure my uncle Blas would've allowed any boyfriend of Irene's to attend the cotillion, but Stoney didn't have a chance. He had issues, most noticeably the tattoo on his neck that said *Almighty Ambrose.*

No one had been at the door at that moment. So Stoney and his four partners simply burst into the basement. They were obviously high. My father and Moe walked up to them. There was wrestling, chair throwing, screaming, and two gun-shots, pops that sang off the basement's polished cement floor, the massive concrete support columns. Then the police came and made arrests—three paddy wagons worth. But the moment I remember most, right before my mother pulled me under the table, was catching sight of my cousin Max, on his knees, his fist jackhammering straight down into Stoney's limp head over and over. I couldn't see Maximillian's face; his head was bowed. But I could see his thick shoulders, his biceps bulging within his dress shirt. Behind him my aunt Lola was pulling at my cousin Irene, my uncle Bernardo was reaching for Max, and my father had one of the gangbangers up by his collar. All of them were staring down at Max. All of them had looks of horror.

Maximillian ruptured something. His arm and fist were in a cast for months. I don't know what got worked out, but Irene kept seeing Stoney. Eventually they married.

Stoney never had a cross word for Max, not that I ever heard.

Memory number two happens a few years later, when I was

eleven. By that time Maximillian had turned eighteen, graduated from Juarez High School, and joined the army. We threw a going-away party for him in the yard behind his father's house.

I'd lived in this house for nearly a whole year, holidays included, back when my parents were split up over my father's cheating. They gave me my own bed, the bunk over Maximillian's. Like other houses were haunted, my uncle Blas's house was marooned. The Kennedy Expressway rumbled within yards of the back door. Out the front door the South Branch of the Chicago River turned. There were neighbors to either side, but still my uncle's house was lost. Living there made life desperate.

The party happened a year or two after I had moved back in with my parents, and though I'd seen Maximillian nearly every weekend since I'd left his house, at the party he seemed aged. He'd grown a thin mustache. He had on shorts and a Diego T. His muscles looked thicker than usual. His skin was dark, worn even.

Maximillian was never a big talker. But as the afternoon progressed and he continued to draw from the keg, he spoke more freely, eventually calling out my name like I was a friend of his from the street. "Jes-se!" he would say. "I love you, bro." And then he'd start laughing.

Late into the party, the adults were drunk and I remember Maximillian putting his head under the tapper and chugging beer right from the keg. He smiled and laughed as he gulped. He came up choking, spitting suds, and stumbled around the gravel yard trying to catch his footing, like he was momentarily blind, lost in his spinning head. We were laughing. My mother had her arm around my shoulder. My father had his arm around my uncle. When Maximillian fell on his ass we doubled over in laughter. We were roaring. And at that moment we seemed really together, my father, my mother, my aunt and uncle, my cousins, Irene and Chefa, Stoney, my sister, even my cousin's dog, Princess. For a moment we were a real family. Behind us traffic droned on the Kennedy Expressway.

Just out the front door, the South Branch flowed.

My last memory of Maximillian happens a couple of years later. I was thirteen. Maximillian was in his twenties. He'd come home on leave from Germany because his mother, my aunt Lola, had died.

As sick as my aunt Lola had been, her death was mostly unexpected. In just a few weeks her cancer had gone from manageable to terminal. The last time I saw her was two days before she died. She was back in St. Luke's Hospital and when I said hi to her she could not respond but to look in my eyes. Her look scared me. It was the kind of look that needed a voice to explain itself.

My aunt Lola was a kind woman. The months I lived with her she always had a steaming bowl of *frijoles* waiting for me when I came home from school, two or three thick tortillas waiting to be dipped and sucked like summertime *paletas*. My aunt's most remarkable feature was her bridge, which she'd pull from her mouth and set on the armrest of her La-Z-Boy as she sat and watched TV. When she dozed off I'd try to put the bridge in my own mouth. As my months of living there wore on I used to steal her bridge and move it to some other location, in her bedroom or on the kitchen table, then wait for her to wake and be forced to speak, her pink gums showing through her fingers as she asked if anyone knew where her bridge was.

They held her wake at Zefran's Funeral Home on Damen

and 22nd Street. Masses of people came, including cousins I didn't know I had. Though I loved my aunt, especially the *frijoles* she used to leave me, at the wake I felt no need to cry. Mourners placed flowers on her chest, blessings delivered to her open casket. At one point a boy standing next to me, a boy that had been introduced to me as my cousin, began to cry. He turned and gave me a hug. I wasn't sure what to do. So I patted his back. "I know," I said to him. "She was a good woman." The kid raised his head and looked at me like I was at the wrong wake. Then he turned and walked away.

After the viewing we packed into cars and lined up for the funeral. The procession was too long for our family. My uncle and his daughters rode behind the hearse with my father in his black windowless work van. A few cars back, Maximillian and I rode alone in his Chevy Celebrity.

We were silent as we drove down Pershing Road. Maximillian had placed our orange FUNERAL sticker on the top passenger side of the windshield and for me it was like a sunscreen even though the day was overcast. The blinkers of the Celebrity matched our speed, the tick-over lagging as we braked, then racing when we sped to catch the car in front.

At Oak Park Avenue we slowed for a red light. Our blinkers were on. Our orange sticker displayed. We followed the car in front of us into the intersection. Suddenly a red pickup took off from the crosswalk. The pickup broke through the procession just in front of us, then continued south down Oak Park. It was a short pause, but long enough for me to consider what an asshole the pickup driver was for cutting off the procession. We were on our way to a funeral. I had that much in my head when Max threw the Celebrity into such a sharp left hand turn my temple knocked against the passenger side window.

We chased the truck for three blocks, the Celebrity's blinkers clacking so loud they seemed about to explode right through the dash. Finally the driver of the pickup pulled to the curb.

Through the rear window of the cab I could see the man jerking around. He looked out of his mind, yelling to himself. As we pulled up behind him, his shoulder heaved and he threw the truck into park. His taillights flashed to full red. He kicked open his door.

We'd stopped in front of a bank parking lot. It was the middle of the day but the lot was empty. Black screens covered the plate glass windows as if the bank was actually closed for good. Trees lined the street. I felt a million miles from home.

The truck driver slammed his door shut as Maximillian was stepping out of the Celebrity. The truck driver yelled something. He was a big man, white, potbellied. He wore a flannel shirt. His neck seemed like one big chin and his jeans looked too tight at the waist. Each one of his steps had a little bounce to it as if he had learned to walk on his toes.

The man continued yelling as Max moved forward. Maximillian didn't say a word. He simply continued to close, his feet looking small, his shoulders broad, his tight waist neat with his tucked-in dress shirt. His tie had blown up around his shoulder.

As my cousin got within arm's reach, the truck driver raised his hand and pointed to my cousin's face. His mouth was still going. He was looking down at my cousin, a heavy mean look, eyebrows pointed in, teeth showing as he screamed. It looked like he thought Max was going to second-guess, that he was going to stop and start yelling back. Max simply kept on moving, and just as the man was ending a word, drawing his mouth shut, my cousin lit into him with a flush right hand that sent the man staggering backwards. Even in the car, over the now practically dead heartbeat of the blinkers, I heard something snap. The man fell to a seated position and Maximillian bent over him and hit him three more times, solid, deep-looking punches, to the left side of the man's face. The man fell sideways and was out cold. His short arm flopped over his thick side and landed palm-up on the street.

Maximillian turned and started walking back to the car. His face was red now, swollen. He was crying. He looked like he wanted to yell, to scream, but couldn't get anything out. The Celebrity's blinkers had stopped. The car had died. I wished we were back in the procession. I wished someone had followed us, my father, or my uncle, or Stoney. I looked in my passenger side mirror. There was nothing.

ALL HAPPY FAMILIES

BY ANDREW ERVIN

Canal & Jackson

I am riding backwards on the Ann Rutledge, otherwise known as the Amtrak 304 originating out of Kansas City. I boarded in Normal, Illinois from where we departed precisely at 5:03 as scheduled. Pleasant enough ride I guess if you discount the possibility of any number of law enforcement professionals waiting for me at Union Station. They could also climb onboard at any of the five stops along the way. Shit. Local statutes require the engineer to blow the train horn more or less continuously and some college-age hottie a couple seats up is hollering into her cell phone. It frequently amazes me how few people possess even the slightest inclination toward common decency. I am writing you this letter in a composition book made by the Top Flight Co. of Chattanooga, Tennessee. It has a stitched binding, not glued, and a heavy stock cardboard cover with a black-and-white marble pattern. 100 Sheets Wide Rule. Of course this is a nonsmoking train, which I am forced to admit is beginning to cause me some small degree of consternation. Over two more hours until I get back to Chicago. Reds are in town tonight. Zambrano's first pitch at 7:05. He's currently 15-8, and his 2.64 earned run average makes him our most effective starter this year. Better even than Maddux or Prior or Wood. Without any unforeseen delays a twenty-minute cab ride from the station will have me kicked back with an Old

Style by the start of the fourth. It is reasonable to expect the Cubs will already be losing by a significant margin. It is my belief that the long-term effect of noise pollution is something we are not yet able to comprehend. Approaching Pontiac now. The night we met you stabbed me with a sharpened No. 2 pencil. It happened halfway through the first meeting of our Russian lit seminar and I had to excuse myself to go to the men's room to inspect the damage. You were crying when I returned. We had never said more than one or two words to each other but I agreed to let you buy me a beer after class. Less than a month later you moved in. I never learned if the stabbing was accidental. Despite the huge production the press is going to make out of this thing it wasn't such a huge deal. You hear about these small heists, five grand here, seven grand there, but that's bullshit. I bagged eighteen thou and change once at a particular lending institution down in Champaign, but in the newspaper article the branch manager admitted just two. That kind of shit used to bother me; I know better now. His picture was in the paper looking all tough. Same dude that damn near pissed his pants. But it's in his best interest to lowball the figure so as to not send the public into a panic and to discourage future would-be perpetrators like me. Those university towns are the best. Big transient population, all the kids dress the same. Normal was the obvious choice. I showed up a few hours early just to walk around a bit, get some coffee and the lay of the land. At the campus bookstore I bought a red, adjustable baseball cap ($14.99) and a red windbreaker ($34.99), both of which were emblazoned with the university's pissed-off looking cardinal logo, along with this notebook (99¢) and a Sanford Uniball Grip pen ($1.29), which doesn't write very smoothly at all. My hope of course is that the FBI has bigger things on their minds right now than a hit in some bunghole town. This was my third job and I think it's my last. Shit. Let's just say I had no reason to expect things to get fucked up this bad. I wish she'd shut the hell up. Going into a weekend series with Prior and Wood on the hill we should be able to expect a sweep, but we lost two out of three to the Mets of all goddamn teams and are now just a half game ahead of San Francisco for the wild card. We are pretty much fucked. Christ a cigarette would be right on time. Dwight. No one on the platform thankfully. Not enough time to jump out. One long glorious puff, that's all I want. Ann Mays Rutledge worked in her father's tavern in New Salem, Illinois, where Abraham Lincoln stayed for some time. According to several accounts he fell madly in love with Ann but she was already engaged to a local landowner, John MacNamar, formerly of upstate New York, who left New Salem on business never to return. Illinois State University is home to Waterson Tower, which at twenty-eight stories ranks as the tallest university dormitory in the world. Vestibule on the ground floor has a white emergency phone. I tell 911 that my room is packed with explosives and if I get another bad grade on a psychology test I'm going to set it off. Hang up, smoke a cigarette. Then it's fire trucks, ambulances, the yellow tape. The bank's a block away, back toward the station. Baker's the worst goddamn manager in the game. We had the best young staff in the league. Kerry Wood gets his elbow taken apart and put back together like it's fuckin Legos. Last season he threw an average of 109.9 pitches per game and went 141 on one occasion. Just this season he threw 131 on April 17. Most of the tellers are outside trying to figure out what all the noise is about. They're wearing billowy, cream-colored blouses and multiple cheap gold necklaces. Only a couple kids in the place, depositing what appears to be an excessively large bundle of bills. It used to be that you could tell just from the look of someone if he was packing. Now everybody's got guns. The fucking college kids got guns now. I walk up all smiles and lift the front of my new windbreaker to show her the handle of the .22 slid into my jeans. Her name plaque says DONNA. Something's genuinely fucked up about the state of the world when we got college kids who feel the need to carry firearms. Joliet, knock on wood. Killing me this year, I swear. You'd think Baker would get his head out of his ass. Tommy John surgery, that's what they call it. In 1974, Doctor Frank Jobe of Los Angeles, California treated Tommy John's torn ulnar collateral ligament by extracting an accessory tendon from the pitcher's right, non-throwing arm and then weaving it around his left elbow using holes drilled into the bones. Fifteen minutes to game time. Shit. Almost in Chicago. Union Station was designed by the venerable firm of Graham, Anderson, Probst and White. Construction started in 1913 and lasted through the war. It's funny how things happen. On April 29, 1986, Roger Clemens set the all-time Major League record by striking out twenty batters in a single game. The same night, a chain reaction in the Chernobyl nuclear power plant led to an explosion that killed thirty people on the spot, caused the evacuation of 135,000 people within a twenty-mile radius of the plant, and sent a toxic cloud floating across a huge swath of Central Europe. On May 6, 1998, a paying attendance of 15,758 at Wrigley Field watched as Kerry Wood tied Roger Clemens's record. The same night, you returned home early from class to find one of my undergraduates naked under our bed, then left for Union Station never to return. Summit. No way I expected any trouble in Normal. I go in knowing it's going to be my last job so I want to make sure to score big. I've just had enough, you know? The stress is really something. I wish that bitch would shut the fuck up already. Jesus. Donna does the right thing. She grabs all the money out of her drawer and puts it into three of those heavy-duty zipper bank sacks. Looks like ten to fifteen even if the wads *are* filled with singles as I suspect. Couple twenties on the outside of each stack. It's smart. But who knows? Not like I can dump out my backpack on the next seat and count it out. Not till I get home. I drop the sacks inside my shirt. No one can see them with this big jacket on. But here's where I get stupid. Instead of walking calmly out and getting lost in the crowd outside, I pull my gun on the two college kids. That was a shitload of money they were depositing and I wanted some. Smaller of the two reaches into his armpit. He looks like he's getting ready to flap his arm to make fart sounds, but instead he draws out this gun way bigger than my little pea shooter. The sound is amazing. Something shatters behind me and this time I'm the one about to piss his pants. Shit. Never ran so fast. Heavy sacks of money bounce against my stomach. I push past the ladies smoking outside, toward the crowd. Throw the baseball cap under a parked car. Christ I hate the fucking Cardinals. Roger Clemens now pitches for the Astros, the team Wood struck out twenty of. Train's not for another hour, so I have to lay low and the best place to do that is among the mass of evacuated college kids. They're treating it like a holiday. You wouldn't believe the way these girls dress nowadays. I think I scored enough to keep me going till some other career path reveals itself. Maybe I'll try to enroll in grad school again. Union Station has a very unusual setup. The double stub-end tracks allow northbound and southbound trains to arrive at the same spot even if they're from different railroads. Something to think about. I boxed up your stuff and a month later your father and sister came by one night to throw it all in the back of a pickup truck. There remains the remote possibility there'll be a couple cops waiting for me on the platform. Unlikely but you never know. Those are the risks. Ann Rutledge finally agreed to marry Abe Lincoln, still a law student at the time, but she died at age twenty-two of typhoid fever. Some accounts say that her death caused the great emancipator-to-be to lapse into a permanent state of melancholia, one that affected the remainder of his illustrious life and career. This fucking curse. 131. I just don't get it. What the hell was Baker thinking? We could still face the Astros in a one-game playoff. Clemens versus Wood to determine which team makes the playoffs. Shit. We are totally fucked. Your flair for the dramatic was something I truly adored about you. Of course I never expected you to pull an Anna Karenina. Must have been right here somewhere. With trains coming and going both directions these tracks make Union Station, and I guess all of Chicago, a unique kind of crossroads. Doesn't happen anywhere else in the country. Another reason I admire this city. Sweet home. Shit.

MONKEY HEAD

BY M.K. MEYERS

Grand & Western

O n the hottest summer night Perryman had experienced in Chicago or maybe anywhere, he sat on the front stoop and watched boys assemble on bikes at dusk in front of the convenience store. *Assemble* may have been too orderly a word. With the introduction of just one more boy, movement would ensue. When that occurred, the boys began their nightly circling of the block. Leisurely pedaling their tiny bikes designed for much smaller children, they could have been a circus act in the making, one in which jackals, without the guidance of a trainer, attempted the complicated task of filling time.

With each pass, the boys gained the collective confidence of a mob, which provoked them to widen their circle to adjacent blocks until they ran into another group of boys, also out exploring the limits of circumference fate had provided. When the groups met, they might skirmish, a little bantering and shoving, but surely, Perryman thought, they'd all get back on their bikes because it was too hot even to fight.

A hot cap of air that would not lift had descended upon Perryman's block. Everyone who couldn't get out of town was compelled to live under it. The entire neighborhood had moved outside. Standing or seated in metal folding chairs, in clusters or alone, the old, the very old, and women accompanied by their young arranged themselves and their provisions, coolers of drinks and food at their sides, as if preparing to lay siege to their own homes.

The men stationed themselves alone, one hip supporting them in a metaphor of what the men imagined themselves to be, what Perryman had once imagined himself to be, a pillar upon which their families stood upright and off the ground. Alone from each other and their families, at distances that looked prescribed, these men smoked cigarette after cigarette, like sentinels. In the intermittent dark spaces between streetlights, they resembled solitary fireflies. Around them the neighborhood might have been lifted whole from an earlier part of America's short life, when people without TV or radio to separate them were reported to have mingled more. With time not yet fractured into tiny bits, they were said to have been more amiable and languid, and generally, although they didn't live as long, were said to have had a better time.

Around 10:00 that night a tribe of boys from another neighborhood passed down the block on bikes and slowed. Dressed alike in white T-shirts and tan short pants, they'd dyed their sneakers to look cut from the hide of a leopard or giraffe. With a quick thrust, one of the boys stuck a rubber monkey head, broken and roughly abused, on top of the decorative hood ornament lifted from a Mercedes that Bobby Pando, the block's drug dealer, had bolted to the nose of his Ford panel truck.

Everyone on the block knew Bobby Pando's love for his Ford panel truck extended beyond the Mercedes hood ornament. For its side Bobby commissioned a mural of a deer, or an animal with horns, standing atop a hump of green. Perryman had developed a nodding acquaintance with Bobby, one predicated on the understanding that Bobby Pando did not live on Perryman's block; Perryman lived on his. Often Bobby Pando strolled the block with his mate Stevie B. or the fellow called Mr. Panfish, and whenever he saw Perryman, he waved and called out, "Lou," which was not Perryman's name.

"Yo, Lou, what's new with you?"

"Nothing, Bobby, nothing's new."

"Lou, if nothing's new, that's something."

Once, gesturing him closer, Bobby cupped his hands to whisper directly into Perryman's ear.

"Lou," he said, "from now on, and I've talked this over with the guys," he thumbed air in the direction of Mr. Panfish and Stevie B., "you have nothing to fear on this block from anyone my age."

Perryman circled the day on his calendar, marking it: *Limited Good News*.

All that was left of the monkey head to let the world know it had been a monkey's head was one ear, a patch of raggedy black fur running across the crown of its head, and two near-enucleated button-shaped oogly eyes. There was its ear-to-ear toothy grin, but that could have belonged to any species, a small bear, say, or raccoon. It was remarkably little evidence to go on, but someone called out, just after the kids left, "Look at the monkey," and when no one disagreed, like the proving of many things, that first naming became what was thereafter called truth.

Coming back from whatever crime had recently engaged him, Bobby didn't see the monkey head immediately, but when he did, being drunk and happy and carrying an aluminum bat, he took a swing at it. He missed badly, smashing in one of his truck's headlamps and a chunk of its ornamental grill. All talk on the block ceased. Bobby had taken a big enough cut to fall down, and he did. The solitary men returned weight to both legs and approached the truck from all sides. Perryman moved with them.

A drunk's mood is a delicate thing, and Bobby's, as he righted himself from his fall, was no longer cheerful. Darkening, he turned to face the grinning monkey head. Always overeager at the plate—and elsewhere, too, some of the girls on the block muttered—Bobby swung again, this time harder, again falling and again landing his swing on the Ford's ornamental grill, more of it now in the street around him than on the Ford.

With difficulty, he picked himself up, and the foreign tribe of boys, back from some skirmish, set their bikes down and cautiously, as Bobby still had the bat, joined the loose circle of men around him.

When Bobby Pando looked from boy to man to boy to man, Perryman looked with him and saw faces made even more passive and blank by the intensity of their curiosity about what might happen next. Bobby turned from them to what was left of the rubber monkey's head, and looking into that face, pondering those oogly eyes and that ear-to-ear grin, appeared to be attempting to stick a finger in and take the temperature of the depths of some unfathomable confusion, perhaps his life.

There was just so much time a drunk needed to reflect on confusion, and Bobby, lunging sideways, took another cut, a good one, not at the monkey, but at the inner ring of boys. They easily danced back, swelling with a collective laugh, then settling, their mood now darkened, as they focused on the threat that was Bobby Pando.

But the gyro in Bobby's head had gone all topsy. It spun him and he went down hard, bat skittering free with a diminishing sound, a *clank, clank, clank* of aluminum on asphalt that drew the outer circle of men closer together. If they wished they could have reached out and grasped each other's hands.

Perryman checked his watch. It was close to 10:30, and Bobby, flat on the street, groped through shards of his ornamental grill and glass from his headlamp for the bat. Right then is when Perryman heard, and men standing around him later confirmed, a kind of hissing sound. The sound came from Bobby Pando. Some men said later, when they tried to explain, that it sounded almost like a song. "It undulated," one fellow offered, "sort of like a song."

Bobby tried to right himself. He was just beginning to assemble the complicated series of activities that would eventually, if accomplished in the correct sequence, enable him to stand, when a meaty kid, larger than the rest, evidently starting from down the block because by the time he reached Bobby he was traveling that fast, drove his bike over Bobby Pando. It was quick. A thump-thump as the bike passed over Bobby's back. And the song? Then everyone heard it. To Perryman, it sounded uncomplicated as death might turn out to be, just a quickly diminishing gush as something sang itself free from Bobby Pando's chest.

Panfish and Stevie B. assisted Bobby into his van, and Panfish slid into the driver's seat to squeal away, not with anger or urgency, but insolence. They peeled off, the monkey's head still in place, its one near-intact oogly eye facing forward.

When it was quiet again, or a city block's equivalent of quiet, the women, first one, then all, gathered their children, folded chairs, and closed coolers. They moved slowly because it was far too hot to move otherwise, but they moved, retreated inside or to screened front porches, and Perryman did, too, a shadowy shape joining other shadowy shapes looking out.

ZERO ZERO DAY

BY KEVIN GUILFOILE

Grand & Racine

The kitchen was small and square and further encroached upon by splintered cabinets and ancient appliances, the latter kept in working order by a combination of the tenant's unusual skills and his hard-to-find tools. The walls of the musty apartment cracked and peeled, but mechanical objects, clocks, lamps, televisions, and especially radios, had been restored like museum pieces among the ruins. Anything not electrical, like walls, bathroom tile, and ceiling paint, remained in a state of ongoing neglect.

—*Twenty-two-thirteen.*

—*Twenty-two-thirteen go ahead.*

—*Yeah, squad, do you have me logged on?*

—*Negative.* [Pause] *Try again now.*

—*Am I logged on now?*

—*Ten-four. I'm sending that job again.*

—*Ten-ninety-nine.*

This radio, Kimball Dent's original creation, had been cobbled together from sets abandoned in dumpsters around the city or in his shop downstairs by aborted customers who realized it was cheaper to buy new and better ones than pay to have them fixed. For Kimball, hunched over a late-night bowl of oatmeal in his kitchen, every banal word squawking through the receiver tonight between shrill fits of static was like a cut fastball thrown for a strike in the middle of a perfect game.

—*Keeler and* [unintelligible] *with a* [unintelligible].

—*Seventeen-thirty-five, I can't understand a word he's saying, his radio's garbled.*

—[Unintelligible] *Milwaukee and Keeler, stalled car blocking traffic.*

—*Ten-four.*

—*Gonna be a red Honda* [unintelligible]. *Need to order a tow.*

His heart beating at an accelerated rate, Kimball seized the scanner with both hands and repositioned it on the table for better reception. He didn't want to miss a single thrilling exchange.

—*Can I get an RD for a zero-four-six-zero?*

—*Your RD is Henry-King-four-zero-four-six-four-three, Henry-King-four-zero-four-six-four-three on event number zero-eight-six-two-five. Zero-eight-six-two-five.*

—*Ten-four. Thanks.*

The old analog clock on his stove read 10:55. If it continued like this for another sixty-five minutes, until midnight, he would be a witness to Chicago history.

—*I still can't log on. Hold me down going in for a new PDT.*

—*One-three-three-five, please call me in the sergeant's office.*

The Holy Grail of the police scanner hobbyist.

—*Can I get a female for a search?*

A Zero-Zero Day.

—*Twenty-one-ten.*

—*Twenty-one-ten, go ahead.*

—*Anyone know of a Dominick's near Paulina and Ogden with a Western Union* [unintelligible] *currency exchange?*

Last year there had been over 600 homicides and more than 3,000 "aggravated batteries by firearm" within the city limits. The last time Chicago had a Zero-Zero Day, a twenty-four-hour period, midnight to midnight, with no murders and no shootings, was 1999, and as far as Kimball knew there were no witnesses then. No ears listening in on the scanner with an appreciation of the event as it occurred. No one anticipating the countdown to midnight the way he and dozens like him were doing just now.

—*Yeah, uh, we were following a youth on a bike that fits the description of a suspect* [unintelligible]. *We have him on the hood.*

—*Twenty-one-ten, is that a negative on the Dominick's?*

In the middle of the Formica-topped table, on the other side of Kimball's oatmeal but still at arm's length, was an approximation of a laptop Kimball had Frankensteined from computers so obsolete that cash-strapped schools wouldn't even accept them as donations. Scanning enthusiasts from across the country were instant messaging with Chicago hobbyists demanding the latest news on the lack of news, and the conversation scrolled up the screen with the speed of a stock ticker. Curiously, cops and dispatchers weren't even acknowledging the feat over their radios. Maybe they were afraid of jinxing it. Maybe the different shifts and the different districts had no way of comparing notes in real time. Maybe they wouldn't have any idea what had happened until the CPD command staff had their briefing in the morning. It was funny to think the scanning community shared real-time intelligence better than the Chicago PD. That notion made Kimball chuckle. He spat wet cinnamon and oatmeal onto a small auburn oval of mustache and goatee, then rubbed his face with a moistened washcloth he kept on hand for mealtime grooming.

*—I just on-viewed a traffic accident at 95th and Pulaski.
Hold me down over here and dispatch EMS for me,
please, squad.*

—[Unintelligible] medic [unintelligible] contact the station.

*—Ten-four. Let me know if you need any more help over
there.*

His phone rang, a lovely clapper-and-drum trill. He
allowed those awful digital tones neither in his home nor in
his shop, where the synthetic tweeting might go on for minutes, unnoticed and unanswered under the din of labor, static,
and police dispatcher conversation.

"Hullo?"

"Dent!" It was Jen Colino. In the background, her own
scanner, an expensive Radio Shack Pro-96, belched in har-
mony with the homemade one in Kimball's kitchen.
"Amazing, huh? Amazing! Do you think it will hold up?"

"Dunno," Kimball said, now wondering if the cops
weren't right to observe a superstitious moratorium on dis-
cussion of the Zero-Zero in progress. "We'll know in an hour."

"Wanna come over for the finish? I'll open a bottle of
champagne at midnight. Like New Year's."

Kimball sighed. He didn't have a girlfriend, hadn't for a
long time, and Jen Colino was the only woman availing herself to him currently. They had plenty in common. She was a
scannerhead. She was sweet and kind of pretty, maybe a little fleshy around the face and under the arms, but no more
than he was. Jen was plenty attractive *enough*, was his point.
But if they became a couple she would be over every night.
She would make chicken and they'd track the scanner
together but she would want to talk. *Constantly.* Over the
dispatchers. Over the cops. Over the paramedics. Although
nearly every one of his friends was, like Jen, a member of the

All Chicago Scanner Club, Kimball believed his hobby was a solitary pursuit, and he wasn't ready to give up his bachelor benefits for a warm body on the couch just yet. "No, I don't think so," he said to Jen now. "I don't want to miss anything."

All his life Kimball had chosen paths he could walk by himself. Maybe his parents imprinted that on him when they made him an only child. When he was a boy he loved jigsaw puzzles, and from there it was a small step to taking apart radios and fitting the pieces back together. He liked keeping his own schedule. Answering to no one but his customers, who were in and out of his shop as quickly as it took them to set a television on his counter and get an estimate. The people he felt closest to, the dispatchers he knew by name and the cops he recognized by beat tags, didn't even know he existed.

Kimball cupped his right hand at his temple and leaned against the kitchen window, peering down at a refrigerated truck idling at the four-way stop below. With his eyes he could follow Grand Avenue east all the way to downtown but Racine only as far south as the Metra tracks on the other side of Hubbard. The Italian joint across the street was playing host to its Monday night lasagna regulars and a fleet of Caddies and Lincolns were squeezed into the angled parking spaces in the tiny lot. Along with the bakery and butcher and the storefront men's club down the street, Salerno's was one of the last landmarks of the old neighborhood. There was still an Italian for every yuppie on this thin sliver between the expressway and the meatpacking district, but you couldn't really call it an Italian neighborhood anymore, not like the Polish and Korean blocks up Northwest where hardly anyone spoke English and you had to check with your waiter twice before you put a spoonful of anything in your mouth. There were still a handful of aging or wannabe wiseguys about. A few of them passed the hot days in lawn chairs on the sidewalk in front of the bakery, telling tales of the great Italian migration of the '50s, from Cabrini Green up Grand all the way to Harlem. But in the condo sales brochures and restaurant listings, this neighborhood was River West now, a name as stripped of ethnicity as the realtors could manage.

"I could come over there," Jen offered.

"That's okay," Kimball said. "I mean, I'm kind of tired. I'm going to bed right after midnight." He added, "Or sooner, if somebody gets capped."

"Oh. Okay." The disappointed silence was interrupted briefly by a unit responding to an alarm at a Clybourn clothing boutique and then continued for thirty seconds or more, as Kimball lingered with one ear pressed against the phone receiver and the other listening for the dispatcher.

Then, the buzzer rang downstairs.

"Someone's at the door, Jen. I gotta go."

"Who would be coming over at this hour?"

Her words were armed with jealousy and Kimball wanted to defuse them. "Could be a customer," he said.

"You shouldn't answer. You'll miss the Zero-Zero."

"I'll call you tomorrow."

"Okay. Call me."

Kimball hung up the phone and walked to the intercom, smudged with greasy fingerprints, next to the apartment door. With some frequency, folks from the neighborhood brought their televisions to Kimball's apartment after-hours. It most often happened on nights of Bulls playoff games. A desperate basketball fan might arrive at his doorstep, TV set cradled in his arms like a sick baby. Kimball tolerated such visits and even encouraged them. His services might not be needed much anymore in the era of disposable electronics, but they valued his skills when appliance stores were closed for the night.

He pressed the button and talked at the beige box in the wall. "Yeah?"

"Kimball?" a voice replied. "Lemme in."

"Who is this?"

"Gerry!"

"Gerry." Kimball repeated.

"It's me. Genuine. My TV in your shop. You gotta let me in."

Genuine Gerry was a neighborhood character of indefinite Central Asian origin. Possibly Kyrgyzstan. Turkmenistan. Tajikistan. One of those. It would be a stretch to call him a neighborhood *resident*, as he didn't exactly have an address. To get by, Gerry relied on good weather and the generosity of others, and in Chicago the latter was just marginally more reliable than the former.

Story was he had been a Comiskey Park beer vendor. His nickname was from the Miller Genuine Drafts he once poured from his tray. Allegedly he'd been fired over an aggressive response to a drunken fan's insult. Since the spring, he parked cars at a new jazz club around the corner on Ogden, spending the hours from 7 p.m. to 3 a.m. in an aluminum and glass box the size of two old-fashioned phone booths welded together. His most prized of few possessions was a tiny, eight-inch black-and-white TV, but during the day it wasn't safe in the parking lot booth. By long-standing agreement, when he left his shift, Genuine would hide the television on Kimball's second-story back porch. In the morning, Kimball would retrieve the TV and take it into his shop for safekeeping until 6 o'clock on the nose, right at closing, when Genuine would stop by and retrieve it for the night. Twice Kimball had made minor repairs, once to the antenna and once to the loose knob, without charging Genuine or even mentioning what he had done.

"Yeah, okay," Kimball said. "I'll be right down."

Kimball slipped back into the kitchen to get a quick bead on news coming over the scanner. Nothing going on, just a trespassing call from the University of Chicago library. Gerry leaned on the buzzer three times in annoying succession and Kimball grabbed his keys, spun out the door, and sprinted down the steps.

Genuine was hopping on the sidewalk, arms rigid at his sides, his long, curly black hair, *Ace Frehley hair, you know, from KISS,* Jen had called it, bouncing around his head. Kimball had seen him high before, although he was never certain what combination of herbs, inhalants, liquors, powders, or pills got Gerry off.

"Let's make this quick, Gerry," Kimball said. "I'm kind of busy."

"Oh yeah, oh yeah," Genuine said. "You have a lady up there? Jennifer?"

"No, man." Kimball said. "Just . . . stuff. It's late."

"I know. I know. This is the case."

Kimball pegged Gerry at about his own age, forty, and wherever he was from originally his accent didn't sound foreign, exactly. His English was occasionally quirky but always understandable, even in his present state, and his dialect sounded more like a nasally amalgam of Chicagoese and urban slang than it did Middle-Eastern or Russian. His body rigid, Gerry continued to hop like he was underdressed for the cold. But the night air couldn't have been much below seventy.

Kimball pushed aside the padlocked iron cage that stretched across the door to his shop and unlocked two dead-bolts and then waved Genuine Gerry inside. Gerry rubbed his hands together and blew on them. "It's right here," Kimball said, walking quickly back to his workbench. He lifted the set by the handle and held it out, but Gerry was looking away, his eyes scanning the broken merchandise.

The indoor fluorescent lights were off, but plastic knobs and chrome trim twinkled in streetlight leaking between the iron bars on the window. Hundreds of small appliances lined every wall in the narrow shop. Some were awaiting repair. The ones that had been wiped clean and polished and dusted with compressed air sat near the front of the shop in antici-pation of their owners. Many were shells, partially hollow, which Kimball had cannibalized for parts.

Gerry counted the shelves with his finger, *one, two, three, four, five, six,* all the way up to the ceiling. "You got any of those flat screens in here? Whatyacallem? Plasma TVs?"

"Not today," Kimball said, still holding the television in his outstretched arm. "Sometimes, though. Most of them are under warranty. Repaired by the manufacturer. Occasionally I get one of, uh, dubious origin that needs to be fixed."

"Dubious?"

"Well, I don't know for sure, of course, but when a plasma comes in here I usually suspect it's been stolen."

"Uh-huh. And whaddya do?"

"I fix it. It's none of my business where it came from."

Gerry began walking the perimeter of the dark shop, examining each television, radio, toaster oven, and computer. He didn't look ready to leave. Kimball leaned impatiently on his left hip. Of course, if he didn't hate confrontation so much he would have told Gerry months ago to find a new place to stash his crappy little TV. The secret to a solitary existence is to never make waves. Entanglements are just like they sound, ways in which you and other people are hopelessly entwined. Kimball reached up on a shelf and turned one of several in a row of police scanners to low volume.

—*Go ahead.*

—*We're at the CITGO at* [unintelligible]. *We have an individual refusing to leave. It's going to be a black male* [unintelligible].

"Most of the stuff I get nowadays is old," Kimball explained. "Stuff with sentimental value, or obsoletes the Compaqs and the Sonys and the RCAs no longer make. Big console sets. Lots of record players. Tape machines. That kind of thing."

Gerry turned to face him. "I need money."

"What?"

"Hundred-fifty dollars. I don't give him, he cracks me up."

"Who?"

"The man. The man in the green car."

Kimball had no idea what Gerry was talking about, but he assumed the man in the green car was a drug dealer. What else could he be? On the other hand, what dealer would give a guy like Genuine a line of credit?

"I'm sorry, Gerry. I don't have any money." He was still holding the television, waiting for Genuine to take it.

"Maybe I take something from here," Gerry said. "Something worth hundred-fifty."

"No. No. No." Kimball walked toward Gerry and tried to force him, again, to take back his own set. "These things belong to my customers." Gerry was still studying the merchandise. "Come on," Kimball said. "You have to get back to work. Back to the club."

"This is why it's a good idea, Kimmy," Gerry said. "These things, they don't belong to you. I take them, you tell the owner it was stolen. *Oops*."

"No. Come on. Leave." He put his hand lightly on Gerry's arm and tried to guide him toward the door.

Genuine Gerry spun away from Kimball and when he regained his balance, his right hand was holding a pistol, pointed away, toward the wall.

"What the hell, Gerry?"

"You let me take something. I take something or I shoot it, your choice. You ever fix television full of bullets?"

—*Can I get a description? Suspect will try to blend in here.*

—*White T-shirt. Long black jean shorts. Short afro.*

"Genuine, come on. Put the gun away."

Gerry was leaning over a set of twin turntables Kimball had already repaired and tagged for pickup. "What are these?"

"Turntables," Kimball said. "Record players. You know, for a DJ." He made a noise in the back of his throat like a scratching record.

"I should take."

"No. No, you can't, Gerry."

Genuine took one step back, turned his head away, shut his eyes tight, and fired a bullet into the machine.

"Gerry! Shit!"

"I told you. You let me take or I destroy. Either way you lose."

"No. No. No. Look, settle down." Kimball studied the situation nervously. Gerry seemed terrified of his own pistol and he held it away from his body the way you would a snake or a lit match. "Gerry, *you* have things you can sell." Kimball held up the set. "You have a television. Obviously, you have a gun."

Genuine shook his head. "Television is crap. Gun is not mine." He waved at an old Waring blender on the counter. "What is this worth?"

"Not a hundred and fifty bucks."

With a sharp, stabbing motion, Gerry shot the blender twice at short range. The bullet pierced the glass pitcher and ricocheted off the concrete floor with a *ping*. Kimball ducked and covered his head, although if the bullet had been coming for him his evasive action would have been far too late. This had to stop.

He took a step forward. Gerry, his back turned, was looking for his next mechanical victim. Kimball put an arm around his shoulder. Gerry twitched but didn't move away. Kimball reached slowly for the gun. Genuine began to weep. He surrendered the pistol and put his hands to his eyes. "Please," Genuine sobbed. "Ple-ee-ease just give me money."

"Gerry, no."

Genuine turned to Kimball. His eyes appeared full of hatred. *Because he had seen Gerry crying? Because Kimball had taken the gun?* Between tears Genuine yelled, "You goddamn wop! You fecking dago!"

Kimball blinked at him. Wop? Dago? These were slurs from another era. Right street, wrong decade. And Kimball was a mutt bred from many ethnicities, Scotch-Irish, German, even a family rumor that would have made him one-sixteenth Sioux Indian and, if proven true, eligible for a low-interest business loan. But he wasn't Italian at all. Genuine Gerry didn't know the first thing about him and for some reason that made Kimball angry.

"Relax, Gerry."

"Give me the money!" Gerry had squared himself with Kimball and was waving his taut arms beside his head. Now that he no longer had the unfamiliar pistol in his hand, he seemed less scared and more agitated. Quietly, Kimball recognized the irony in Gerry's demands, which had become more confident and assertive now that Kimball had the gun. He also recognized the upside-down logic of his own fear, which had likewise and just as oddly become more intense.

"You're not gong to shoot me," Genuine said spitefully. "I know you. You're not going to shoot me." After one failed attempt, he lifted himself up on a gray, painted workbench and sat there, feet dangling. His tone was mocking. "Come on, Kimmy. Just a few bucks. A loan. It is nothing. Hundred bucks and I leave. No money, maybe I stay."

Tears gone as suddenly as they came, he now smiled an unfriendly smile. A menacing smile. The unhinged smile of a dangerous buzz. Something about it made Kimball hot under his skin. This was an outrage. He had the gun now, after all, and Gerry was still threatening him. *And threatening him with what exactly?* This is why he preferred machines to people. Machines perform exactly as you expect them to. There's nothing ironic about a machine. When a machine acts erratically, you find the broken link in the chain and when you fix it, the machine does just as it's supposed to. If you wave a gun in a person's face you never know what's going to happen. If you wave a gun in a person's face and you're still more scared of him than he is of you, how do you fix that?

Kimball pointed the gun at the ceiling, just to remind Gerry it was there. "You don't know me," Kimball said. "How do you know me?"

"What? For years I know you. You keep my TV safe. In your shop. We are friends."

Kimball still wondered how their relationship had become inverted. He had the gun in his hand, but he still didn't have control. Genuine continued to threaten him. Continued to blather on. Meanwhile, the Zero-Zero progressed into its final minutes and he was missing it.

Genuine Gerry? *Ungrateful* Gerry, they should call him. Here he was, robbing the one fellow in the neighborhood who had been kindest to him. Kimball had never been afraid to answer his door, hadn't become cynical about helping his neighbors, and for that he gets an addict blasting away in his shop, keeping him away from the scanner, insulting him at all hours, the waning hours of the most important day in Kimball's otherwise uneventful life.

"I fixed your TV," Kimball said.

"What?"

"Twice. It was broken. I fixed it." Kimball poked the gun at the new antenna and knob, which were clearly poached from another make and model.

"I did not know," said Genuine, but the news seemed to please him. "This what I mean. You are nice guy. I know you. Now, you give me money. I leave you alone."

—*He's in custody. We have him in custody behind the Office Depot. He's got blue jeans and a green shirt. First name of Jimmy.*

—*Ten-four.*

Cops and robbers, Kimball thought. On the street, the gun represents authority and power, but only when possessed by the willing. In a gangbanger's hands, or a cop's, a gun has influence because bangers and cops are expected to use it. A cop is supposed to exercise restraint, of course, but a suspect will give himself up because he knows the policeman is empowered by the law to shoot him. Genuine Gerry surrendered his gun because he realized Kimball was not. If there are two people, neither of whom is willing to use the gun, then the gun is as impotent as cooked spaghetti. And so is the man holding it. A cop doesn't have power in a roomful of cops. A cop has power over suspects. Over civilians. For you to have power, someone else must be weaker than you. And a man alone is by definition powerless.

"You don't know me," Kimball said, and then he did something unexpected, which was, of course, the only point of it.

He fired the gun.

Genuine Gerry yelped and fell forward onto the floor, his legs up in the air like a baby's. He was swearing. "You shot me! You shot me! You shot me!"

Kimball watched the blood ooze from under Genuine's hands, which were pressed tight, one on top of the other, against his thigh. Kimball knew from the scanner that if the bullet hit the right spot in the leg it could be a bad bleeder, and he watched evidence of that fact form an amoeba-shaped red pool across the painted concrete under Genuine Gerry's body.

"Call the police! Call the ambulance! You fecking dago!"

Kimball walked to the shelf and turned up the radio.

—[Unintelligible] *domestic. The neighbor just got home and said she heard a door slam inside the apartment. Ex-husband has physically abused her before.*

—*Ten-four.*

—*Let me know what you have when you get there.*

"Call the ambulance! I'm dying!"

Kimball looked at an old classroom clock on the wall. It was 11:45. "Fifteen minutes."

"What?"

"I can't call 911 for another fifteen minutes."

"Call them now! I am dying!" The skin on Genuine

Gerry's face had stretched itself tight across his skull. There was blood on his jeans and his hair. When he tried to close his bulging eyes, his eyelids didn't meet.

"Fifteen minutes, Gerry."

From the floor Genuine wailed in five-second bursts and cursed Kimball in Tajik or whatever. Kimball turned up the scanner's volume knob another quarter-inch and as he waited for the day to expire, he reminded himself to call Jen in the morning, as promised, after he had given his statement to the police. This had been a night of revelations.

He might even ask Jen to dinner.

ARCADIA

BY TODD DILLS

Chicago & Noble

I work the desk at the old folks' house, though I also live there. People come in, drug dealers, little high school gangbangers trying to score an initiation sale at the place. They figure a captive audience is all they need. I tell Benjamin, the 300-pound security guard, to toss them out on their knees. He's always happy to oblige. There are junkies in this place who haven't had a drop of their particular sauce in years, yet they never leave. They need the gatekeeper. They need me.

That's how I met Tristam, years ago; he turned out differently than many of the little entrepreneurs, though. After some college at the UIC—that's C Chicago-go, this shithole of a town—he flunked out, addicted to the city's second letter. He dropped by and was so skinny and haggard I didn't recognize him at first.

"Goddammit, boy, you look like shit," I said. "Plastic getting to you?"

We went on, as was our style in the days of old, about the plasticizing of the world around us. Plastic car rims, bumpers, plastic cigarette holders, plastic handles on doors to places like churches, plastic communion wafers (taking the symbolic one level higher) slated for reuse. Suck and spit, back into the offering plate. Then we struck a deal. Included in my diseased old man's daily dose was a single helping of the vanguard Ajexo painkiller. The combination of a Valium-like synthetic with just the slightest twinge of morphine-derivative punch, these pills were then mythic among the junkie set, regarded as a sort of withdrawal cure-all. I didn't take them, no way, since I was long off the hard shit and they'd have been the road back to death for me. Besides, pain I could live with.

In the spirit of God's good grace, I handed them over to the boy. He needed help.

But Tristam didn't keep his half of the deal: staying off the primary jolt. Time goes by and contracts lose their potency. Occasionally I'd start when on the bus on the way to a checkup, a prescription refill, and realize with the full weight of a catastrophe that the boy had gotten off at the park again to see the man who went by Valentino, recognizable by his perpetual attire: bright-red athletic jumpsuit, sneakers, and a fedora over his pristine afro. The pusher-pimp was known over the blocks for hard shit.

One particularly momentous day, I felt like a martyr, like I wanted to be Joan of Arc or some righteous-ass Palestinian or Iraqi. Tristam and I rode the bus east on Chicago truly without an idea of what would happen. What we wanted was routine, of course, however chaotic our lives might be; we could strive. It was all I could do to resist the urge to burn the whole fucking place down, myself with it. For me, the days start nervous.

I keyed my pilot to search the data bank for the right fit; I call it "pilot", but really it's custom, fabricated from the body of an old cell phone. It could get me into any city database long as I had the code. Old girl Jenna Simonsen of the Logan Square halfway house gave it to me in exchange for certain connections that only I can provide. At twenty-seven minutes past the hour, I ran a background check on myself, Mr. John Arcadia, to find I'd escaped from prison for the third time, but way back in 1987. More interestingly, I trashed the greenhouse of a neighbor in Waukegan, ended up in the hospital and with a charge of indecent exposure on top of other vandalism counts, a two-inch gash traveling the length of my buttocks. I got busted with marijuana two years later, and the cops put me in a boarding home with no hope of escape, which is to say without a goddamned chance, much less twelve jurors and a judge.

"There's my money," Tristam said.

The flunky pointed to the same park at the corner, by which we were presently passing; we stood each with one hand gripping overhead stabilizing poles like chimpanzees, myself keying the pilot in my other hand. The boy was getting bold. Valentino was there on the steps of the park's field house in plain view.

"You mean you're pointing him out to me now?" I said. "What about our deal?"

"Money," Tristam said.

"That mean he got money, or he gone take your money?" I said, knowing too well the answer. "Boy, I don't know why you just don't settle on your fix with me. Settle on safety."

"Who are you today?" he said, and before I could tell him about John Arcadia the greenhouse torcher, he gestured broadly back west, toward the church. "Meet you there," he said, and hopped from the bus, his skinny legs forever appearing like they ought to crumple under the weight of his body, however paltry. This time he stayed aloft, floating toward the pusher-pimp. And I may have been shaken, distracted, or angered by this, and maybe it prefigured things to come, but

I didn't get heated just yet over it. I imagine he knew well what he was doing, the fuck, cause I didn't miss a step, headed downtown for my checkup, preoccupied, scanning the pilot for further details.

In 1990, as it happened, I torched a service station, a blaze that singed the eyebrows of many a bystander when it got to the main gas tanks, and did time for it. In 1995 I got out and lit up the prison itself, which ain't here in the record, but I did do it. I'm liberal with history, you might say; the details are there to be eaten and spit back out however you like. They run television commercials about people like me, and usually there is some woman whose voice is overrun with that of a man, and she looks very silly sitting in her posh kitchen at a polished-titanium table talking about the booze and whores she's gonna buy on the vacation she's gonna take to Tijuana on her stolen credit card. I ain't in it for cash reasons, though. Money corrupts absolutely, to modify the old phrase. You might ask Tristam about that one. With me it's more in the blood, you know.

I found a seat finally and just when I got relaxed an old bum strode by and knocked my legs. He was passing out badly reproduced leaflets on which were printed the Lord's Prayer. The old son of a bitch stopped just by me and wailed on about the anointed cloths he was gonna give out to anyone with any bit of change whatsoever. He yelled through the bus, erupting brash and ugly in the center of this morning commute. Everyone ignored him but me. I could be him too, and was excited at the prospect for the moment, for I knew there would come a day when the pilot stumbled upon the fate of all gadgets of its kind, broke, and left me hanging with a story I couldn't play for keeps. I needed another option.

I asked the bum his name. He looked a little like me. He

stopped his sermon and turned my way, his eyes going wide.

"My name is your name, Jehovah," he said, which I promptly keyed into the pilot. "Jehovah," the old bum repeated.

The bus slammed to a hard stop, the vagrant swaying with the tide. Yeah, I could be this guy.

"Last name, social security," I said.

The bum's eyes shot wider still, and he broke into the prayer on his mangled photocopied leaflets, holding one up close to his farsighted eyes and shuttling out the rear door in the same motion, midsentence, at Larrabee. On his way out he dropped one of those "anointed cloths" he was talking about. It was bright-blue, a pretty picture against the ribbed black rubber of the floor. Before anyone else could get his or her hands on it, I jumped. It's a holy day, I figured. I remained standing in honor.

They were gutting the old Montgomery Ward building at the time, turning the commercial space into luxury condos. I looked out the bus windows from my spot and saw straight through the twenty-and-some floors of the monstrosity. Can't break a structure that solid, been standing much too long now, and the developers figured it to go the route of the rest of the neighborhood south of Chicago this far east since the retailer shut down, absolutely fucking filthy rich. It wouldn't necessarily work out: On the north side of the street of course sat the outer edge of Cabrini-Green, the miniscule streets dead-ending before Chicago Avenue in cul-de-sacs, the single-story brick boxes reminding me of projects in cities much smaller. Say Charlotte, Atlanta. Long time since I'd seen those places.

I could be Jehovah or any other body. Not like there was someone to tell me different. I got off the bus at State and trekked it two blocks south to the clinic for my checkup, then down to the old-school pharmacy on Superior to refill my many prescriptions. I left feeling truly like a savior in spite of the name on my health card. Arcadia I am not. I pulled the blue cloth from my pocket and brought it to my nose. It smelled like the bum, stale and musty, slightly sour with sweat and urban rot. But hidden deep in that stink was a sweet flower blossoming.

My prescriptions took up a ten-page stack of printouts from the doctor's computer. The pills came prepared in a plastic, everything plastic, slotted box, one small compartment to correspond to each day of the coming month. I don't know how I managed to keep up with them, Jehovah the meek, the persecuted, the resolute, the vigilant. I gazed up at the time on a digital display clock outside the Holy Name Cathedral, then at my plastic, everything plastic, watch and made my way to the next meeting, muscling to the back of the bus, pilot switched off in my little drug bag. Today, I would need it no more. My name was secure.

I was spot on time to the abandoned church, where I used to spend my nights and many days before the old folks' home took me, the state footing the bill. Tristam wasn't there. I took my day's meds sitting on the concrete steps before the boarded-up former door. I'd been waiting for the kid for nearly an hour when the nausea and pain kicked in, so I crept through the space between the half-kicked-through boards over the church's front door. I laid down in the dark of the vestibule in communion with the Saints, the wind and whine of the expressway now a fading memory, nothing present but the pain; I concentrated, pinpointed all my holy energy on a flash behind my eyelids and soon enough fell fast asleep.

When I woke the nausea was still present but the pain had subsided. "Tristam," I called out, expecting the kid to be conked out there somewhere near me in the dark. There was no answer, but I listened and could hear above the low outer din of his breath coming in long, slow gasps.

"Motherfucker," I said, crawling dazed toward the sound. Nothing. I punched what I took to be his leg, and a voice I didn't know boomed calmly through the cavernous dark.

"Who are you now?" it said. I got to my feet.

"Jehovah?"

Then a scrambling broke out and I was forced down onto my back, tackled. Tristam laughed through the darkness.

"Gotcha," he said.

"Goddammit, boy," I said. Tristam giggled and giggled on, and when finally I got a look at him, when he turned the flashlight on and I could see, I divined from the glare in his eyes and his slurry voice that he was fucked.

"I was just kidding, old man," he said. "Don't look so damn mad. You got the shit?"

"I'm holding," I said.

"Oh ho ho. Well, hand it over."

"I mean, you ain't getting anything until you hold to your side of things."

He sorta held there, held the flashlight pointed upward, held his body tensed in that brief attempt at comprehension of my words. And then when he fished through the muddled bank of connotations and meanings in his head, when he got what I was saying, I guess, he lunged at me, raising the flashlight high in the same motion as if to bring it down on my head. I caught his hand, and any fear the young man may have mustered in my head quickly turned to righteous rage. I wheeled out the only thing of particular strength I had anywhere near, the pilot, and in the gloom wheeled it around and caught Tristam on the side of his head. He fell hard to the ground, the flashlight rolling from his hand and coming to rest with its beam shining right in my face.

"You never wait for me to answer," I said. "What's my name, motherfucker? What is it?" He didn't answer. "You call me Jehovah, you hear? Jehovah."

I crawled over him and brought the pilot down on his head again and again and again. Tristam didn't move. I may have hit him ten times, twenty times, but I know I stopped, the pilot now an unrecognizable mass of cracked plastic, everything plastic, and other parts. I crawled from the vestibule and into the sanctuary, where the light penetrated the empty window spaces above, stripped as the place was of its old stained-glass windows, lighting on the old wooden altar, where I knelt and prayed for the first time in years, through it all the murmur in my head telling me that the fraud of the act was just that, a fraud, that I was praying to myself, that I alone would determine the route to salvation.

A week or so after I killed the boy I stepped up on the bus, strident in my conviction, noble as the street itself as I paid the bus driver, murmuring "God bless," and turned to face the crowded interior.

"I am Jehovah!" I hollered.

I opened my bag, bowed, and flung a handful of baby-blue towels into the crowd. I pulled a flyer up to my eyes and began to read, "*Our Father, who art in Heaven, hallowed be Thy name . . .*"

ALEX PINTO HEARS THE BELL

BY C.J. SULLIVAN

North & Troy

Alex Pinto shuffled down North Avenue. His head was bowed as he bumped into a young man coming out of Klecko's Hardware Store.

"Yo, pops, watch where the hell you walking. Damn, old man. You don't own these streets."

Pinto kept moving. He didn't hear the guy. If he had, there might have been a confrontation. Pinto felt that the young men of Humboldt Park were too disrespectful. They had no sense of the neighborhood. They lived here to either be killed on these streets in some stupid and senseless turf war or to finally get a decent job and move to the suburbs. The neighborhood of Humboldt Park would never be home to them like it was to Alex Pinto. This was a place they came to because there was nowhere else for them to go. Humboldt Park was not only home to Pinto, it was the only place on earth he wanted to be.

The young today would never understand that. This was the video-game generation. Everything came too easy to them, so when they had to dig down and fight for what should be theirs, they had nothing to draw on. No sense of self or family. It was all about them.

They needed to be taught a history lesson. Like how when Alex Pinto moved into this neighborhood in the 1960s he had to fight Irish, Polish, and Italian toughs just to get to the store to buy milk and bread. Back then the Latins were considered cockroaches by the tough-ass white working class. When the Latins and blacks grew in numbers the whites moved away. *White flight* they called it. Then the fires started. And the gangs came. And slowly the neighborhood began to die. Killed by neglect from the city's power brokers and the young men with guns, knives, and drugs, with no sense of community or pride. But Alex Pinto would never leave Humboldt Park. It was where his memories lived.

He never got to explain that to the young man because Pinto wasn't on the streets of 2005 Chicago. His mind was busy remembering a fight from thirty years before. He stopped on the corner as the fumes from the 72 bus blasted into his face. He thought he was inhaling the smoky air of the Chicago Coliseum. It was 1975 again. "Jungle Boogie" played on all the boom boxes on North Avenue. President Ford was on TV talking about his new federal program, W.I.N.—Whip Inflation Now. *Jaws* was the big hit at the movie theater on West Division. Everyone was talking about how the Arabs were becoming world players and had learned to dole out oil with a boycotting flare. Cars lined up on Cicero Avenue for an hour wait to get a full tank of gas.

1975 was a good year, at least for Pinto. All his hard work was finally paying off. All those runs in the early morning hours through Humboldt Park. All that time in Brick Gym. Jumping rope. Sparing. Working the heavy bag until his hands bled. He was finally catching a break. The *Trib* lauded him as a local fighter ready to battle for a championship belt in his hometown.

Pinto stepped off the curb and felt like his legs were once again twenty-five and full of taut muscle. He saw himself as a young Latin boxer about to make his mark on a city. Strolling down the sidewalk, he felt as if he was moving like a big wild cat. The people passing by saw a slow-walking gray-haired man with a face that had caught too many punches.

Pinto smiled as he remembered that after the 1975 fight—if he won—he was going to hit Felicity Disco and meet up with his backers and the best of the local ladies. He would have a championship belt and the city would be his. Pinto passed in front of Kim's Grocery as the Korean owner cursed at a Mexican shoplifter running away from the store. All Pinto heard was the referee telling him the fight was over. He'd lost on a technical knockout. He never made it to that disco.

Pinto had fought well that night. At the end of the fourteenth round he was ahead on all the scorers' cards. Pinto knew it. His corner knew. The rabid crowd knew. In three minutes their local boy would be crowned the new light heavyweight champion of the world. Alex Pinto, the five-to-one underdog, was about to upset the legend of Bob Foster. And there was a lot of local money riding on Pinto. Chicago was about to have a big payday.

But Bob Foster had other plans. He'd been champion for years. He was the best boxer the division had ever produced. He was smart, quick, and was always in a fight because he had a powerhouse right that gave him a puncher's chance. He sat on his stool staring at Pinto. Feeling his years. Angry that this kid had caught him unprepared. He thought this was going to be an easy fight. Figured Pinto was a rookie just happy to be in the ring with a legend. Foster saw a cocky young kid thinking the fight was his. He knew he had a short window to earn his redemption.

He came out in the fifteenth round and knew he had to knock Pinto out to keep his title. They met in the middle of the ring and touched their gloves. That would be the last time Pinto touched Foster. Foster hit him with a series of right jabs and left hooks that would have knocked out a lesser man. It was like Foster had set him up. Let him think he had it won. Pinto had boxed masterfully for fourteen rounds and now this. The crowd fell silent as Foster beat him senseless. It was like a force of nature had entered the ring. Pinto held onto the ropes as Foster punched him with sharp blows. The ref stepped in and ended the fight, perhaps saving Pinto's life.

On the corner of North Avenue and Troy Street, Pinto blinked up at sun and felt like he had just woken up. The August heat of the sidewalk was cooking the soles of his threadbare sneakers. As he looked at the Humboldt Park Library, he wondered how he'd got here from his Armitage Avenue boarding house.

He walked into the library and felt relief at the cool air pumping in from the vents. Pinto went to the microfilm desk, handed over his library card, and took out the August 1975 *Chicago Tribune*. He would spend this hot afternoon reading about the young man he once was.

After he went through August of 1975, and then March of 1972 when he won a Golden Glove amateur title, his eyes grew tired from the microfilm machine. Pinto decided to grab a magazine and sit in the lounge, where the regulars went. In the summer only the old were seen in the library. They were the ones who couldn't afford air-conditioning for those brutal August heatwaves. He grabbed an old *Newsweek* and nodded to a man he knew named Juan. Next to him was Olga. She always had a *Sports Illustrated* and read slow.

"Hey, champ, how you doin'?" Juan asked.

"Good, you ignorant Boricua. Don't you know you supposed to be quiet in a library?" Alex said.

"Used to be that way here. No more. This here is unciv-ilized times we living in. This is a horrible time to be alive. Especially if you're old," Olga said.

Alex nodded at her and sat down with a sigh. He read about an earthquake in Sri Lanka and his eyes grew heavy.

"Closing time. Come on, time to go."

Alex wiped some drool off his face and blinked at the security guard standing over him.

"What time is it?"

"Time to go."

Alex looked around the empty room and stood up on his shaky legs. He waved to the desk librarian and walked out to the rush hour of North Avenue. The air was a little cooler as he crossed the street and entered Humboldt Park.

When he hit the path he started to jog slowly. He'd do five miles today. He kept up his roadwork. He liked to think he stayed in fighting shape. Tomorrow he would work as a part-time janitor at Brick's Gym and after his shift he'd do some speed work and punch the heavy bag. He wouldn't be getting any more shots at a prizefight, but in this city it paid to stay in shape. Can't afford to get old and weak, he thought.

As Pinto jogged past the boat pavilion his body tensed as he saw a group of Spanish Cobras sitting on the benches. He knew all about these guys. Pinto had been a regular of the Latin Kings in the 1960s. Back then they stood for defending the Latins of the neighborhood against the whites and the the Chicago Police Department, the toughest white gang of all. Once he got into boxing and the Kings got into dealing drugs, he put the gang life down.

But these Spanish Cobras were a bad gang that caused a lot of trouble in the neighborhood. They mugged, robbed, and sold drugs to their own. He kept his head down and wanted to just move past them.

"Hey, homes. You. The boxer."

Pinto slowed and looked at the young man approaching him.

"Yeah?" Pinto said, jogging in place looking at the man.

"I hear back in the day you were some fighter. My pops tells me you were almost champ. Long time ago. That you, Alex Pinto?"

"Yeah, that's me."

"Damn. A pleasure to meet you. I'm Paco."

Pinto shook his hand and said, "Well, thanks, I got to go."

"Wait, homes. You want to earn some money?"

Pinto looked down on the ground. "How?"

"Doin' what you do best, homes. Boxing. We hold smokers out on Cicero. I'll pay you $200 you come out this Friday night. It's good. We tape it and sell tickets and take bets there. You will be a big draw. Big bets on you, papi. People remember you in the ring. You were a legend."

"Boxing? Really? Who am I fighting?"

Paco smiled at Pinto and said, "A guy about your age. You'll tear him up. Only thing is, you gotta bring your own gloves. You down?"

Pinto hesitated. That money was a week's pay for him. It would help. Get him some meat, fresh produce, and a decent bottle of wine. Maybe even a coat for the winter. But boxing? At fifty-five?

"I don't know. How come I never heard about this?" Pinto said as he moved his weight from foot to foot.

"Hey, it's our first smoker. Figured we start with the best and work our way down. Could be a regular gig for you."

Pinto looked at the benches. The other Spanish Cobras were smoking and yelling at a woman walking by. Paco kept his eyes locked on Pinto.

"So what do you say, homes? You down?"

"Give me the address. I'll be there."

"Cool, it starts at 8. Be there like 7:30. You're the first fight."

Paco handed Pinto a flyer and walked back to his friends. Pinto put the paper in his back pocket and continued his run. While he circled the lagoon he saw himself in the ring ducking a punch and laying his opponent out. That is how it will go Friday night. A guy my age stands no chance against me, he thought. I've kept myself in shape. I still have the tools.

Pinto finished his run and limped out of the park. He went to a small grocery store and bought a can of beans and a beer. That would be dinner. Under two dollars. He was keeping to his budget.

On Thursday Pinto woke up feeling good. He got out of bed and did a few jumping jacks. He shadowboxed as he reveled in the thought that he would fight once again tomorrow night. There should be some kind of senior league for old boxers, he thought. Tennis and golf had it. Why does age make you put down the things you love? Old men still had basketball and football leagues. Why not boxers?

Pinto spent the day at Brick's Gym on Mozart Avenue. He swept and mopped the floors. He tightened the ropes on the two rings. He held the heavy bag for a young lightweight. As he went about his chores he asked some of the young boxers if they'd heard of the smoker out on Cicero.

No one had, but they were young and had venues for their boxing skills. Pinto ate a bologna sandwich for lunch and read the flyer again.

THE JOKER SMOKER

SEE THEM FIGHT. SEE THEM BLEED.
BET ON THE BEST. BOO THE BUMS.

ONE BEER AND ONE CIGAR
WITH $15 ADMISSION. 8 P.M.
NO GUNS AND NO KNIVES.
SUPPORT YOUR COMMUNITY.

THE SPANISH COBRAS BOXING LEAGUE
1991 CICERO AVE. IN THE
OLD FLECK MATTRESS FACTORY

Pinto put the flyer away and went to the bathrooms to clean up that mess. As his day ended, Pinto put away his cleaning supplies and went to his locker to tape his hands and put on his boxing gloves.

He went to the speed bag and got a good rhythm going. The bag smacked the wood with a solid whack. Yeah, Pinto thought, I still got it. I can still make that bag sing. He went to a corner and bobbed and weaved while throwing multiple punches. That's how I'll take him out tomorrow, Pinto thought. I'll duck and come up and in. Body blows made young men want to quit. No way an older man can take the punishment I can still dish out.

When his workout was over he put his gloves in a bag and went into the office to see his boss, Mr. Rico, for his pay. Two hundred off the books. Enough to pay his rent and eat very lightly.

Pinto entered the office and saw a boxing poster

announcing a fight of his from March 17, 1974. That night he knocked out "Irish" Danny Walsh.

"Hey, Alex, you still working out. Good for you," Rico said from behind his desk.

"Yeah, well, you know I just want to stay in shape."

Rico laughed and patted his large belly. "Hey, guys our age are too old to fight. Me, I eat what I want and keep this here." He opened a drawer and pulled out a revolver. "This, Alex, is the fat man's equalizer. This will stop any young man. Dead in his tracks."

Pinto smiled as Rico put the gun back in a drawer and then slid his pay envelope across the desk. He thought about asking Rico if he'd heard of the smoker but then just put the envelope in his pocket. Rico was never a boxer. He never had that longing for his youth. To feel his body again and let his juices rip as he beat another man. And he knew Rico would tell him it was a bad idea. Pinto had enough dreams crushed in this life. He kept his own counsel.

"You okay, Alex, you need anything? You able to keep up your rent? You need anything, you come to me, okay, hermano?"

"I'm good, Mr. Rico. I'll see you Monday."

Friday night came and Alex felt those old butterflies in his stomach as he turned onto Cicero. He pushed open the door to the factory and saw a beat-up boxing ring with about 250 folding chairs around it. A few young men were setting up a table to sell beer and Paco smiled when he saw him.

"Hey, champ, you made it."

"Where do I get ready?"

"Right over there in the corner with the other fighters."

"There's no locker room?"

"Homes, this ain't the Coliseum. We do what we can. See that big ugly Polack over there. That's who you're fighting."

Pinto stared at the man. He had to be pushing sixty with a big gut and a face weathered from street living. He looked like a bum.

"Him?"

"Yeah, you'll tear him up."

"He looks like a homeless bum."

Paco got up close to Pinto. "Hey, the man needs money like you. Who you to judge anyone? You think you look any better? He used to be a boxer back in Poland. Almost made the Olympics in 1972."

Pinto moved back.

"So where do we change?" he said. "We use mouth guards? And how long is the fight?"

Paco laughed and said, "See, now you asking the real questions. You fight as you come. No boxing gear other than gloves. No headgear. You got a mouth guard, you use it. Your boy you fighting ain't got no teeth so I don't think he needs a mouth guard. The fight? Well, it is a little different. There are no rounds. We ring the bell and you go until one man can't fight anymore. No ref. No nothing. Just you and him in the ring. You on your own in there. Can you handle that?"

Pinto turned and said, "Yeah, I can handle that. But I want my money now."

Paco laughed, "My man, now you talking."

Paco gave Pinto two crisp hundred-dollar bills. Pinto put them in his front pocket and went to a bench to put on his gloves. There were seven older men with gloves on sitting on the benches. Their heads were down and they looked old and beaten. Pinto had to get away from them.

In the back of the factory floor he watched as a crowd of young men paid their money and took seats. Drinking beer and being noisy. The cigars were lit up and the smell of marijuana filled the air.

Pinto and his Polish opponent were called to the ring. Pinto stayed in his corner and jumped up and down, getting his legs loose. Paco got in the ring with a bullhorn and stared to yell.

"Welcome to our first smoker. In this our first fight we got Smokin' Alex Pinto going up against Punchin' Jan Pulaski. Both these men fought as pros. The line is even. Get your bets down. We jump off in two minutes."

Paco came over to Pinto and put his arm around him.

"Take him out, homes. Make us proud."

Pinto grabbed the rope and did a few squats. He watched one of the Spanish Cobras circle the ring with a video camera. The crowd was looking up at him, yelling that they had bet on him and he better win.

He leaned against the ropes and saw Jan Pulaski staring right through him. Pulaski didn't move. Just stared at him with a blank look.

The bell rang and Pinto slowly approached the center of the ring. Pulaski staggered out of his corner. Pinto thought he looked drunk. He threw a wild right that Pinto ducked and came into Pulaski's gut with a solid right. Pulaski belched and fell to the ropes.

"Kill him! Kill that old white bum!" a kid yelled from the crowd.

Pinto moved in carefully and threw a right to Pulaski's head. Then another right. And another. Pulaski took the punishment with no reaction. His mouth was bleeding but his body didn't move.

Pinto moved away and yelled though his mouth guard to Paco, "He ain't fighting."

Paco laughed and yelled, "Then make him."

Pinto stormed in and hit Pulaski with a left hook. Then a right cross. The Pole staggered and then fell to the canvas with a dead thud. He didn't move. The bell rang a few times and then Paco grabbed his hand and yelled to the crowd that Alex Pinto was the winner.

Pinto left the ring as he watched a few Spanish Cobras carry Pulaski out of the ring and sit him on a bench. Pulaski just sat there with his head down.

Paco slapped him on the back and said, "Hey, nice fight. You come next Friday, I'll give you $250."

"I'll think about it," Pinto said, then walked to the back of the factory and took off his gloves.

He left the factory quietly and walked down Cicero feeling dirty. Like he'd done something wrong. Sinful. Shameful. But as he kept walking he couldn't stop feeling good about being in the ring again and knocking a man out. Even if the man looked like an old drunk.

The next week Alex Pinto showed up on Cicero Avenue. He needed that $250. He told Paco he'd only fight if he were on first. He couldn't watch these other men flail around the ring.

That night he took out a forty-five-year-old black guy who looked like he needed to be on meds. The man threw punches like a wild man and Pinto was able to duck each one. The man was knocked out with a right to his liver.

He celebrated his second win with a ten-dollar bottle of red wine and a nice rare steak.

His third fight was against a Latin kid of about thirty. The kid looked like he hadn't had a decent meal in weeks, but he could fight. He caught Pinto with a smashing blow to the temple. Pinto had to dig down deep to fake the kid out. If he hadn't landed a right to the kid's throat that knocked him flat, he might have quit. The fight went fifteen straight minutes and Pinto ran out of gas.

The Wednesday before his fourth fight Alex Pinto was walking down North Avenue when a young kid stopped him.

"Hey, are you the boxer?"

Alex smiled at the kid. "You're too young to have ever seen me fight. Your dad told you about me?"

"Nah." The kid laughed. "I seen you on that new video. They selling it right over there. You the best of the Bum Fighters."

Alex froze and looked at the Latin man with a table set up with videos on it. He walked over to the table like he was in a dream. His legs grew heavy as he picked up a video and saw a photo on the cover of him knocking out Jan Pulaski, with the title: *The Best of Bum Boxing—See homeless bums beat each other till they bleed.*

"Fifteen dollars each, pops. Some of these homeless know how to fight. The shit is funny."

Pinto walked away, his face burning. He ran home to his room and screamed into a pillow with rage. Screamed and screamed until the night came and he fell into a dreamless sleep.

He didn't leave his room. He couldn't. There would be no more. It was over for Alex Pinto. He wanted death. This shame he felt. This creepy crawling feeling that he had lived his whole life so that cowards who never got into a boxing ring could point and laugh at him. He was a failure. Nothing but an old joke. A bum who boxed other worthless bums.

"Silence, cunning, and exile . . ."

That's how "Irish" Walsh had said he would live after Pinto knocked him out in 1974. Back then he laughed and thought the Irishman was just being dramatic. Now he knew how that felt. Well, at least the silence and the exile.

He sat on a stool and let his rage build. He thought about his whole life. It was all a waste. To end as the butt of a joke on a street-corner video box. A tag line. A broken old man. His face clenched as he stood up and punched the wall. That felt good. He did it again. Then again.

He found he lost track of time. Morning. Night. It all felt the same. He didn't eat. Sipped a little water. Had no desire or needs. They all faded away. He was in a void, an old man's purgatory. He knew he was hiding. Too shamed to be seen. The village idiot. The dopey old man who still talked about his youth like it would matter to anyone but himself. He would wake up and groan and just want to stay asleep. How would he ever face anyone at the gym?

As he circled his room in a daze, it came to him. He heard it. Clearly. Cunning would join him. It was like an angel's voice telling him what needed to be done. Then he knew. There would be only one way out.

He left his room on Friday at 7:30 p.m. He kept his head down and looked at no one. He moved quickly through the streets. He thought he heard a group of kids laughing at him on a street corner as he passed. He looked back and saw that a boy was telling a joke. But how did he know it was not a joke about Alex Pinto? It could be. He was the laughing stock of Humboldt Park. The stupid old man who boxed bums.

He went to Brick's Gym and avoided the few fighters left working out. He looked around and then pulled out a long, thin metal locksmith tool from his gym bag. He picked the lock to Mr. Rico's office. He knew Rico was gone for hours now and he didn't carry that gun on him. He closed the door and walked into the dark office and grabbed the revolver that was in the top drawer. He left the gym quietly.

When he got to the smoker, he went to a dark corner and put the gun inside his boxing glove. He moved closer to the crowd and sat on a milk crate and waited to be called into the ring. He kept his head down. Not from shame. That had left. No, he was hot. Red hot. He kept his head down. He didn't want anyone to see his smile.

This night he was going against a forty-five-year-old named Welch. But Welch would get off easy. He stood in his corner with his head down. As Paco got in the ring to announce the fight, Pinto threw off his boxing gloves and put the gun to Paco's head.

Pinto yelled, "All right, you bunch of parasites. You punks! You think I am some kind of joke? Everyone out of here. Now!"

No one in the crowd moved. They stared at Pinto and a few made moves to grab their chairs.

Pinto cocked the revolver. "Paco, I will put this bullet in your stupid head now if you don't tell them to leave. You heard that gun cock. Right? That means you got a second or two to live."

"You dead, homes."

Pinto pushed the gun into his temple. Paco shook and said in a whisper, "All right. All right! It was just a joke. Don't shoot."

"Then tell them to leave. Loud."

Paco called out, "All right! Listen up! Get out of here. Listen to this crazy old fuck. It's cool. Go home. I'll handle him. Get goin'."

The crowd started to move to the exit. A man pointed at him. Some grumbled. Alex yelled, "Call 911! Tell them the boxer, Alex Pinto, has a gun to this punk's head because Alex Pinto came to claim back his dignity which this *pato* tried to rob."

The gym emptied as Pinto pushed Paco away and aimed the gun at his chest.

"You think you can make a fool of me. Rob me of my good name. Make fun of me. Treat me like a bum. Strip me of my humanity. You think that is funny? Make fun of who I once was?"

Paco backed away in the ring with a weak smile and his hands up, "Hey, pops, what's your beef. I paid you for the fights. What's your problem?"

"My problem is I saw those videos you're selling. Bum Boxing. You played me for a fool. Made me a joke in my own neighborhood. Like my whole life was all a big joke to you. I ain't a bum."

Paco smiled and said, "Well, you ain't a boxer no more either, pops."

Pinto smiled back. Took a slow breath. Aimed the gun at Paco's kneecap and pulled the trigger.

Paco fell to the ground with a scream.

"Well, at least I was once a boxer. I once fought for a title. What have you ever done? Look at you. Your life is over before it began. And what did you do? Make fun of people. Sell drugs. Ruin others."

Paco kneeled on the canvas. He held his shattered knee and squirmed with pain. "Come on, papi. Don't kill me. I won't tell anyone."

Pinto stood over him. He gave him a small smile. "You want mercy, boy?"

"Yes."

"Why?"

"It was just a joke. I paid you. I'll get rid of them all. No more videos of you. All gone. It will be forgotten. No one will remember."

Pinto held the gun up and said, "Too late. When you were in diapers, I was out here on these streets trying to do what was right. Well, you know what? I'm tired of doin' what's right."

Pinto aimed the gun and shot Paco once in the head. Paco fell back, his torso leaning on the ropes. His eyes were still open. Pinto threw the gun on Paco's lap.

He stayed, dancing around the ring, throwing punches, seeing Bob Foster in front of him, surprised at the fury that came out of the gloves of a young Alex Pinto.

Pinto thought that he looked like a good contender against Foster. He heard the sirens down Cicero Avenue and he went to his corner to wait for the bell to ring for the next round.

PURE PRODUCTS

BY DANIEL BUCKMAN

Roscoe & Claremont

The rain streamed off the porch roof and the black sheets dissolved Chicago and they thought themselves behind a waterfall. Mike put his hand on Susan's cheek, her hair windblown against his knuckles. She held her breath and they bit each other's lips. After twelve years, it was what they did to make things feel new. And the rain kept coming, beating the leaves from the maples and the elms, turning the gutters into rivulets floating Starbucks pastry bags.

They went upstairs to lie down and the rain fell harder with the late darkness. He held his wife against him, her back warm and damp. She felt the rain through the screen, more than he did, and pushed into his chest until he moved. There had been long days of rain and they never knew the rain from the sky. If the sunlight came, it showed hard before the dusk, and made the streets steam. But there were two weeks before they would talk about the wet summer, a month before the rains ruined July with low, gray skies.

Mike Spence had told Susan he was going to be a cop over delivered Thai food. His academy class was starting in three months down on Monroe by Rico's, where they once drank vodka martinis, singing Dean Martin songs with a bartender friendly over past tips, and watching the fallouts from the police trainee runs spit and hold their sides. Who the hell could they chase, he'd laughed. No soldier would lower himself to be a cop. Now he was thirty-five, a veteran, and he hadn't won a thing. I wrote a book about me, he thought. Winners and losers. That was the risk.

"This is nothing," his wife said.

"I start in ninety days."

"I don't think it's what you want."

She sat up and drew the bedsheet around her breasts and pointed in his face. He looked out the window. A writer, he was thinking. Just because that idea moved him didn't mean it was moving. He felt crazy sometimes, even undone, like he'd been climbing hard but the ladder was up against the wrong wall. In the early darkness, her eyes searched his face.

"Why do you still get this way?" she said.

"I'm no one way anymore," he answered.

"You get these ideas," she said, "but life isn't a story. You were just talking about going to Iraq with Quakers. Last year, you were going to backpack through Cambodia. You always attach yourself to something that is not your own."

He looked at her and then at himself in the wall mirror. Her biceps were bruised from wrestling with autistic boys in her special education class. In grocery stores, people eyed her arms and stared at him while she scanned cat food and mangos through the self-checkout. A dyke is going to hit you someday, she'd laugh. Just leave you for dead.

"You're not a character," she said.

"You don't know," he said.

"I know you're not a character."

Mike knew his wife saw a bloated cop parked in the wagon outside a 7-Eleven while his partner got a coffee and eyed the Indian girl's breasts. Pooja, she'd be thinking. My husband's partner will be eyeing Pooja.

Later, in his shaded room, Mike read his work when Susan was quiet outside the door, listening. There were noises she made, noises she thought he didn't hear, the way she coughed from breathing slowly through her nose, the floor creak from her shifting weight. As a kind of game, he made his voice like slick rocks, doing Barry White, Al Green, Isaac Hayes. He tried making her laugh, breaking her cover, but she was silent. The abortion had been the price to keep his life, not hers. It was making her eyes hard. A cop, she'd said. After we did it for you to write. He forgot her coughing and read in the bulb light.

I saw these guys who looked like Todds in the loop after rush hour. I gave them last names.

Todd Miller. Todd Turner. Todd Stevens.

They were always squinting from the white heat still glinting off bus windows. Six-thirty was the earliest I ever watched one leave the First National Building, humping the sidewalk in the white heat of summer, swinging a briefcase up Dearborn Street, then long-stepping amongst the women with popcorn in the Picasso's shadow. Todd's father taught him how to stay low and know how much things cost. He kept a fraction in his head and headed to the El after ten hours at Sidley and Austin, jamming down the subway stairs slick from spilled popcorn. He moved like a golden retriever and loosened his tie. Humiliation for Todd was going from wild-caught Sockeye Salmon at Whole Foods to the flash-frozen farm-raised fish Costco lets you buy if you pay the fifty dollars a year. He had to ask Jennifer to eat that, look her in those swim-team blue eyes and say things were weird at work.

I wrote a book about having been a soldier for Todd. He needed to see drunken barracks fights on the weekends, know what he missed when Jacky Bozak and Ernie Chopper threw hands, strung out on crank and Michelob, and my best friend

Edward Dilger had Charge of Quarters after the senior NCOs went home to duplexes and house trailers. I didn't hold back for Todd. He'd read how Dilger beat his knuckles bloody on Bozak's plate face, himself a new corporal and six months to discharge, but couldn't make the wired Polack stop choking the hillbilly. Todd couldn't leave this earth, suddenly and beautifully with Jennifer in the collapse of a Whole Foods parking lot, and not experience Bozak's frozen skull take Dilger's punches. It was like watching a sledge head begin breaking up concrete. Chopper strained to keep his eyes open while his lips went dark.

I waited at Whole Foods meat counters after the novel came out and bought chicken while Todd picked free-range T-bones, his handcart heavy from organic artichoke hearts in cans. He wore fleece and suede slipper walking shoes and I knew he'd mess himself if Dilger even aimed his eyes at him and got cold. Edward Dilger taught himself to have still eyeballs by shooting coyotes with a .223 Ruger for the twenty-dollar bounty in Hall County, Texas. Todd never watched a guy like Dilger get dragged off by two MPs for having punched Bozak too long, until his eye hung sideways and he collapsed against Chopper's back and dripped blood on his shaved head.

Todd never paid twenty-two dollars to know about guys like my buddy. He did pay dearly for chicken breasts already rubbed with herbs. The army paid Dilger, and Sidley paid Todd. The guy couldn't see the problem.

I'd written about how Dilger was a good soldier, but when the MP sticked him by the stairs, four of his teeth bounced off the cinderblock wall like pellets. The CO took his stripes three days later for not calling the MPs first thing. Todd couldn't be human unless he saw Dilger in Key West two years after the army, Dilger making Manhattans at Sloppy Joes, and knew that he'd started shooting speed under his tongue. But Todd probably had some college friend whose parent committed suicide junior year, just after a year in England, and finding Dilger dead in his apartment bathroom didn't shock him. He loaned heavy for Northwestern Law School and didn't spare cash for other people's pain. If he died tomorrow in the collapse of the Whole Foods parking lot, he'd sleep forever in his Range Rover like the pharaohs in mountain tombs.

In May, after the abortion, Mike and Susan drove Interstate 80 from Chicago to the Rocky Mountains. They rented an old timbered cabin in the pines at the bottom of Estes Canyon. There was good shade from the trees and a fast stream coming down from the mountains and a narrow gravel road that dropped steeply from the highway and stopped in the jagged black stumps at the bank below the cabin. There were cottages up the highway, circled by birches, and if there were people, they did not see them. It was early in the season and very cold and rainy at night.

The stream came straight from the Continental Divide, where water became other water, all-powerful and cold, but the trout were gone from the shallows and they could not drink the water any more than they could from the Chicago River. If they'd not sent the deposit, he would have left over it. An alpine stream, the Internet ad read. Cold, clear snow runoff. He assumed he could dip his cupped hands and drink sloppily, letting the water numb his mouth, but the rental manager dropped off two cases of Evian for the week. Screw this place, Mike said. But Susan calmed him, the way she did after the happiness about his first novel faded like a new car smell. She made him look north where the woods and the canyon walls were all one thing, like a great idea, strangely jagged and soft, but always the same. They were here to let go. They were here to wash it all away and see if they could feel clean again. Relax, she told him. She lowered her voice to say it.

At night, they wrapped themselves in one blanket and sat watching the clouds blow down from the high range. The sky turned green and the lightning splayed like fingers. They tried to make love and it went badly so they held hands and talked about getting new cats and perhaps their own house in the cornfields south of Chicago. They talked like they believed the abortion was not the sad and humiliating thing it truly was. They were cautious with each other. They never talked about the bad dreams or the weak feeling that went to their knees. Sitting still under the blanket, they would make themselves laugh by naming the new cats after cartoon characters or friends they'd had. When the jokes went, they listened to the slackening rain, holding each other, both seeing him in the waiting room with *People* magazine while she lay dilated before the doctor. Then later, when the clouds blew through the canyon, they would decide the farmhouse they wanted must have white clapboards and a long front porch and stained glass in the eastern windows to color the sunrise. I'll build a fireplace from river rocks, he said. I'll cut the wood, good hackberry. She lay her head against his shoulder, her hair wet from the leaky awning. I'll sweep the porch and try not to wake the sleeping cats, she said.

All week they held hands and hiked trails of slate rock slick from the wet spring. They came upon elk herds sleeping in scrub meadows, ground squirrels running between holes like vaudeville comics, and one night watched a coyote nosing by the car. They stopped and studied waterfalls, shooting rapids, boulders dropped amongst birch trees like monoliths. She took pictures, holding the camera up and down to get in his height. We pick up from here, she said. One day after the next, he thought. Like walking.

They took Interstate 80 home through the stout hills of Nebraska, where cattle herds balded pastures and fat kids with sunburned legs waved from overpasses. The sunlight was low and even and white. Susan found new stations when the distance beat the signal. Outside Cheyenne, they heard Joy Division's "Love Will Tear Us Apart" on college radio, and listened through the static. He wished they could sing it together, let go the way dogs howl.

"I can't believe they're playing this song," she said.

"Go with it," he said.

"I didn't like it then."

She turned down the volume and he heard the wind over the sad, growly singer. Ian Curtis was a put-on, she said. She'd talked about dancing in the aisles at Talking Heads concerts back in college, really throwing her arms above her head, and for twelve years he tried imagining it.

Mike first saw people scrubbing their windshields with greenpads at a truck stop near Kimball. The insect guts darkened the glass like window tint, but his remained clean enough to see Susan's reflection without spots shadowed on her face. They must have hit an odd stretch of air, he thought. Smiling guys with RVs stood upon stepladders and worked their elbows, watching Susan walk for the rest room, her hand squeezing her purse strap. Look at the ass on her, their faces said.

"You can't get the bugs all the way off with a squeegee," a man in a cowboy hat told him. "Not out here. Go get you some green pads at the Wal-Mart in Brownson."

Mike nodded that he'd make do and the man shrugged his shoulders. He went looking for Susan because that morning she'd cried on a Texaco toilet seat outside Cheyenne, sobbing so hard her eyes were still swollen at noon. He'd stood outside the door, his shadow broken on a propane tank, asking her what she wanted from him. My eyes are all puffy, she'd said.

"Remember," the man called out, "it's the bugs' world in Nebraska and we just live in it."

Mike drove off and set the cruise at eighty-five and read the mileage sign for North Platte, Kearny, Omaha. Sure, Tex, he thought of the man. It's probably just like you say.

Ogalala was a hundred miles away when the bugs came out of the white sky like spilled coffee. They stitched the windshield. He looked hard through the smears and heard them hitting while Susan searched the radio for a stronger station. He couldn't see and the bug shadows spotted her cheeks. She scanned and listened for a half second, caring more about a clear signal than the music.

In Chicago, they went on dates again. Just the two of them. They were making steps, like they talked about in the mountains, and meeting at restaurant bars, the same places from ten years ago, an Italian place on Racine, or a Lebanese bistro far north on Clark. Then, they'd drunk martinis because people were doing it again, he Stoli, she Absolut, and laughed about inside jokes with friends they last knew had moved to Seattle. Lance was Heineken, then Bombay and tonic when he bloated. Elizabeth liked Cosmopolitans. It was the pretty glass, the faded red vodka. In those days, they were all just off work, the loop or the near north side, where women swung Coach bags and pigeon feathers fell in the puddles. They sang Nat King Cole songs with the jukebox and thought things were one big wave.

Tonight, Mike and Susan ordered their martinis and sat alone at Rico's. The bar was clean, but scratched. She played with her olive stick. Mike wanted to tell her there wasn't enough air in their apartment for two, and it was good they left the place to fill back up. Open windows, a hard wind, the curtains pushed to the ceiling. But she would only look at him, her eyes becoming wet. We were just in Colorado for two weeks, she'd say. Air isn't the problem. Now, they sat where they once drank grappa like they knew something special, and said nothing about him becoming a cop. She was sure he'd pull the plug, that it was already an old idea he had of himself. You wait, he thought. I can't lose in that world.

Mike watched the waiters watch the 6 o'clock news. There was a fire west on Harrison, around Cicero, an eight-flat lit up like a wedding party. Kids aped for the news camera.

"You think Lance and Elizabeth ever married?" he said.

"No. She left him for a doctor."

"How do you know?"

She pointed to the rest room through a doorway, by a pay phone. Two busboys looked at her where they folded silverware into cloth napkins.

"We used to talk in there. She was scared Lance's dreams were too tied up with him going out."

"He wanted to design computer games."

"She said he only ever had plans on barstools beside you."

"He knew what he wanted to do."

"I bet the doctor dumped her after she left Lance."

"Where's this coming from?"

"That girl was like a monkey with men," she said. "She always had her hand on a branch before she swung. One has had to break."

"You want to get a table?"

"You really thought Elizabeth was something."

"Maybe we should finish our drinks here."

"Whatever you want to do."

"She was our friend."

"*He* was *your* friend. Women make the best of being stuck together."

Mike kept quiet and drank, letting the cold vodka numb his gums before he swallowed.

Later, he left Susan lying awake and ran the city dark with an open smile. He caught the raindrops in his mouth and sprinted between the rat-proof garbage cans while the garages dissolved from the rain. He felt good, he'd drunk light, and the shoes were taking the shock while he hit puddles behind used car lots and donut shops with chained dumpsters. The clouds sopped up the city lights. He stretched his legs and he felt only the cold rain stinging his throat.

Back home, he stood in the bedroom doorway, sweat and rain wet. His wife lay in the TV light with the cat across her leg. When she'd first heard him, she started making sobbing noises, though now she was done with that. He knew she'd tried crying, but stopped after her ducts gave no water. On their third date she'd cried as badly, telling him about her college abortion over vodka tonics and T-bones beneath the Sinatra painting at Rosebud on Taylor Street.

"Six miles in forty-one minutes tonight," he said. His running shorts still stuck to his thighs.

Susan said nothing, her eyes sad and dry. He still found them beautiful, like chocolate syrup, the way he told his buddies after their first hook-up, but now, after twelve years, her brown eyes demanded an emotional admission he was afraid to stop paying because his buddies were all gone.

"Forty-one minutes," he said again. "I'll sleep through the

police academy. Remember at Rico's when we'd watch the fat trainee cops run down Racine?"

Susan was silent. Mike wanted to put his finger in her face, but he didn't. She looked at the cat while she stroked its cheekbone. He knew he couldn't touch his wife even if he put his hand on her mouth.

One day he'd remind her they were from different towns, but the same Illinois with brown rivers and cornfields running to the sky. He needed to get that straight again, remind Susan of her limitations.

"I know Harvard accepted you senior year of high school," he'd tell her. "You wrote an essay on Freud and dreams for a contest, then presented it to the Rotary Club in a long dress. You had slides of diagrams and spoke into a microphone. The bored, gray men sat in folding chairs with their legs crossed."

Susan would shake her head. Her eyes might blear while her finger pointed at his nose.

"You have no idea," she'd tell him. "There is no way you could know a thing."

"The day the envelope came," he'd say, "you saw the rain dance on pickup hoods parked amongst the clapboard houses. The gutters were high with muddy water from the flooded fields. You held the letter and watched the weather coming over the interstate, the paper flecking wet, knowing your mother would worry all night about the creek rising behind the house. You cried with closed eyes, alone beneath the willow tree, happy you could blame your wet face on the rain."

"I didn't see any of it. Not the way you say."

Mike told his wife nothing. He only watched her look away and rub the cat's ear between her thumb and forefinger.

He knew they liked fighting more than understanding, and because of it, they'd forced each other away. She was there for the cat, not him, and he could feel good about that if he let himself. Either way, he thought, he'd jog different alleys tomorrow night, dreaming he could run until the dawn broke over the two-flat roofs, the morning light coming fast, chalky, then the palest blue.

DEATH MOUTH

BY AMY SAYRE-ROBERTS

Roscoe & Broadway

Turn at Cornelia. Follow the scent of fresh bread and sidewalk heat, the stale belly breath of the city. It raises a slight glow on the upper lip, a contagion like an unseasonably warm September. It will lead you to Dahlia's. I like having espresso here at the end of the day. There's always someone to meet at Dahlia's; you never know what you'll discover. I met Matthew on a night like that, a humid, Ciabatta-scented evening. Geographically, it's easy for a straight boy faking his way around Wrigleyville to get "lost" and end up on Halstead or Broadway. He will say something like, "This is Boystown?" A beat. "I didn't realize." Sure.

I sat a few tables in from the door to observe the comings and goings unnoticed; like a praying mantis, I court stillness and wait for an innocent to walk into my grasp. Sebastian, my favorite waiter, sidled by with drinks for another table, "Cover girl, 12 o'clock high." Matt stood in the door, a young blond woman clutching his arm. The creative ones like to bring along a girl, someone to hold their hand. The boys want to check it out on the down low. They might as well be holding a Kewpie doll.

Let me just say, in terms of the market, Matt and his little doll were prime real estate located conveniently near the intersection of virginity and Vine. They wanted the same thing—someone to be gentle with them. He was looking for a door, and what can I say? I'm a gentleman. I held it wide open.

We made eye contact several times. I was RKO classic in a black cashmere turtleneck and chinos. Absolutely turned out. I get a color every four weeks, r4 with a touch of 3 to set my eyes. Armani Fatale. I wrote StephenLaFraise@hotmail.com on a hundred-dollar bill and waited for him to pay. I bumped into him at the counter and let the bill fall from my pocket. He picked it up and held it forth like a daisy.

"I think this is yours."

I looked at his eyes.

"No, I think it's yours. If you want it."

Reading the bill from his palm, his mouth puckered a red oval.

Ciao, bella. I turned on heel and walked away. Really, I only speak Italian in coffee shops and where otherwise appropriate. French is my native come-on language.

I handled him like silk. He emailed me three days after the hundred-dollar night. We played around—friends, not for long, but at first. It took about a month. I love slow seduction, the foreplay, the gradual building of an orgasm. He was such a baby, a kitten learning about claws.

Matt's foster parents were a loving Christian family who could not even comprehend the idea he might be gay. Denial. He became depressed. Denial. He considered killing himself. Denial. Blah. Blah. Blah. The first night we made love, he gave me a suicide note he wrote. A note he kept, anticipating opportunity.

"It helps me, you know, relieve the pressure just to keep it around, like I have an escape."

I used to buy that bathos bullshit. I thought I was everything to him. I told him he didn't need it anymore. He gave it to me. The ultimate submission, admitting I was his father, his lover, a conqueror on a stolen horse. I held onto it, like a relic to Matt's innocence. Proof apparent on the bride's bloody bedsheet.

Problem is, you can't count on virgin loyalty. At first it's all doe-eyed devotion, but then he got confident and curious. A month ago he broke up with me.

I was tri-folding the new logo Ts when my lost boy sashayed into the store and dropped bullshit all over me like it was a shower. He knew I hate distraction when I'm arranging displays.

"He's punk," he said. The second thing Matt told me about Eduardo, his new boy off the boat from São Paulo.

Matt has balls. We've only been apart one month and he's regaling me with tales of his new lover like the wounds are licked and clean. Curiosity again, why does no one learn from the cat?

I said, "What does that even mean?"

"I mean he's Sex Pistol, old-school punk. Jesus, he has a bi-hawk."

Trés chic. If there's anything better than a mohawk, it surely must be two. "You're joking. He sounds like a walking hygiene issue."

"You know, Stephen, this is exactly why we broke up. You are so judgmental. I mean, get an edge already. You are so limited in what you find interesting."

"What are you now, the minister of high culture? I've known Labrador Retrievers more discerning than you, Matthew."

He pulled a pout, the one I used to find irresistible. The pout that used to signal make-up sex. Now used for effect, could it have been less effective? But I'm not even sure to what end.

"So when's he coming in?"

"To the store?" Matt laughed out loud. "Eduardo would not be caught dead in here, he's totally anti—"

"Anti-what?"

"Exactly. Anti-everything that relates to consumerism. He makes his own clothes, with all these patches and stitching, you really can't imagine."

True statement: I really can't. I once orchestrated a series of Italian silk suits with fishing line and mobile footlights that became a pilgrimage, a Via Dolorosa to couture devotees. Working at a clothier does not equate to being a fabric waiter; Dress Accordingly is the hottest clothier in Boystown. I'm twenty-eight and still going strong, ageless really, born on the tide of my talent for tailoring. I can take you from gruel to cool in less time than it takes to steam milk. Show me the *derrière* I can't make smaller, the thighs I can't camouflage, the legs I can't lengthen. They don't exist. I feel like Warhol.

"Stephen, I so want you to meet him," Matt says. "I mean, come on, we've not been together for almost two months. We're friends. Aren't we?"

I sigh. One month, but who's counting?

"You really should know him, he has something. It's intangible."

"How strange, considering you do such a good job describing it."

The purpose of the pout was soon to be revealed. He couldn't actually think I would meet his Neanderthal lover. I don't play children's games, not even when I was a child. Matt Burton didn't know which way his dick was pointing until he met me. I made him in this community and here he is, a born-again fag sporting his red Italian tennis shoes and instructing me as to the finer points of his new lover. All that improvement and the best thing he could catch was a *Mad*

Max wannabe with Portuguese subtitles? Where did I go wrong? After all, I *had* shown him a way out.

It was a door we all sought at one time or another. I remember finding my own. Mr. Gautreux, my high school French teacher. It might have been the easiest coming out in history. Born in French Guiana, he was a sleek panther moving about in a man's body. Married with two children. For me, it was evolution, a shadow seeking skin. I had nothing to admit, merely to accept. We spoke a new language and parented a new race. Our own silent society, one eye watching for a signal and swollen lips needy to speak.

Matt's voice is a buzz in my ear.

"Stephen, are you listening to me?"

Yes, back to now. Was he always this petulant?

"I'm sorry, what were you saying?"

"Scars are becoming art, Stephen. Eduardo is so beyond the tattoo. I mean, some of his friends were talking the other day. They say the most heinous righteous things. Anyway, one guy, Martin, he's from London and wicked smart, he says, 'The gunshot wound is the new tattoo.'"

"Jesus, what kind of barbarians are you involved with?" I flubbed a fold and had to start over.

"Seriously, Stephen, I have not been able to get that idea off my mind."

"Well, get it off, that is fucking insane. Not to mention illegal, dangerous, and plain stupid. There is no bliss in your apparent ignorance."

"He's a Brit. They have a radical different perspective. Scars are art."

"Even worse. Is there a culture more consumed with their own grandeur and absolutely no evidence to prove them correct?"

"Stephen, please, there's a couple bands playing at the Underground. Eduardo sings lead in Johnny Come Lately? They are amazing. Will you come? You can meet him after."

I see the pout give way to wide-eyed "please me." I couldn't believe it. He actually wanted me to enter the lair of this bi-hawked creature. He wanted Mr. Macho to meet *moi*. He wanted his brute to set his oversized brow on me. Allowing his hip quotient to skyrocket by teasing his new lover with the old. Now I was a sexual resume? *Touché* and no thank you, *cheri*.

I didn't intend to take Matt up on meeting his *nouvel amor*. I completely forgot it for the entire week. Even that night, I don't think I subconsciously ordered the parsley penne instead of the garlic pesto for social reasons—I wasn't planning on getting closer than arm's length to anyone. Well. I went, but didn't wear my best. I had an image of sweaty young Goths pressing their black-clad bodies upon me by mistake or purpose; as arousing as that might be in some scenarios, it was turning my stomach and I had no desire to wear it home on my sleeves.

I stood at the stairs descending to the Underground Pub thinking, why do the rebellious always embrace filth?

I was doing my best to move toward Matt through the crowd without spilling my drink or touching anyone. The lights went down. Nothing to do but stand still and hope for a short set. The entire room grew silent as the thick darkness settled over us and our pupils expanded into black holes devouring light. Eduardo took the stage like a newborn deity. Strobes flashed and he stood bathed in purple footlights. He had surgeon's hands, long, tapering fingers that curved around the microphone. The guitar strapped to his back like a warrior's sword. Looking at his face, I remember Matt saying, "He's half-Brazilian. Exotic." For once, Matt had not overstated. Eduardo. Juxtaposed, I see Matt's simplicity like a cashmere cotton blend that you thought worked when you bought it off the rack, but didn't wear well after all. A knobby knit peeled off and discarded at my feet.

Eduardo leaned into the mic. "September is dead and the October bacchanalia is upon us. Feel this one in your blood."

I did. I felt an unused chamber surge and flash brilliant, a spectra behind my left eye. The blue-white burn of startling truth seared me. I longed to bite down.

I didn't move through the entire set. Matt introduced us when the next band went on. Eduardo wasn't like Matt had described. He'd been worshipped in a previous life. I knew right away, Matt had no idea what he'd discovered. Eduardo, idealistic and lordly at the same time—his words were a dizzy aphrodisiac tingling the arch of my foot and waking my belly-button to connect a new cord, to rebirth.

"Do you dream, Eduardo?" I said. His name cream-coated my tongue and I anticipated the swallow.

"*Sonhos*. I live by them."

I've found an equal, I thought. Nothing is going to separate me from him. "He's one of us," said a jeweled whisper.

I watched him stroke Matt's face, but when the boy leaned in with lips close to his ear, Eduardo's eyes found me. Unspoken agreement. We knew, as easily as one tiger recognizes another. It's not the first time a blood sacrifice was made in his honor. I'm sure the scent of such allegiance was as familiar to him as it was to me. We are not like other people, we're an unknown matter born of divine illumination and escaped velocity. Matt's presence is a sudden impurity on my new found love. Eduardo and I are capable of heights Matt cannot conceive. Like a fingerprint on fine crystal, everything filthy may be polished away.

* * *

Death is beautiful and it need not be difficult. After the first night with Eduardo, I dreamed the whole production in great bruised sky colors. For Matt, I thought, it should come softly, a fragile sigh in his sleep.

I'm a devil for details. Matt's departure from my life needed to be as tendered in hypocrisy as his entrance. I planned to wear a new pair of dark adobe leather pants that night. So it had to be clean. Clean and quiet. Easy enough, I thought, to get him drunk and go about the X method. Drugs and suffocation. Good night, sweet queen. I took my time shopping and found the perfect poison. HPNOTIQ liquor, product of France. It was Smurf-blue and bottled as to confuse the consumer whether it was bath gel or liquor. I bought two bottles.

We met at the Pepper Lounge. I used to blow the bartender and now he lets me bring in special bottles of choice. Matt proceeded to get drunk while we discussed everything from Johnny Depp to Mandarin collars; we never were at a loss for words with each other. Sleeping pills go down as easy as speed.

"Matthew, Eduardo's incredible."

"This is so different than I thought it would be."

"Really, I kind of always figured we'd be here, sooner or later."

Matt, the pathetic little peasant that he was, ate it all up. I thought for a second he was going to offer me a goodbye fuck in return for my tenderness. But then he started to feel the blue liquid settle in and I helped him to the bathroom. "Look, let's get you cleaned up. Want to come back to my place?"

"Oh yeah. Okay. I'm so sorry. I feel like shit. I just need a shower and some coffee."

"It's early yet, we have plenty of time."

"Stephen, I'm so happy."

"Me too, *mon ami*, me too."

He passed out on my bed. I lay down close, propped myself on an elbow, and studied his profile. "They all look like angels when they sleep." I pulled on my kitchen gloves and couldn't resist one last goodbye. I bit down hard on his bottom lip before slipping the plastic bag over his head, secured it around his neck, and poured a subtle Bordeaux. Never underestimate how the right wine enhances an experience. His slow breathing against the bag crackled like dry kindling. "Burn. Escape and burn, little soul. You are no longer inseparable from skin."

I cranked *Never Mind the Bollocks* up to ten and took a deep breath to find my center. You should never rush moments like these; they simply do not come knocking all that often. I put the gun in his hand and, cupping mine over his, pointed it at his left shoulder. The sleeping pills did their work, and he barely twitched when I pulled the trigger. The scar, a death mouth tattoo, was going to be gorgeous. Now we all have what we want. I'm so happy.

Later, people will tell the cops they saw me leave the bar with him. People will say they saw me leave the apartment without him, maybe. I don't care. I'd tell them too. It's just some fag with a fetish committing suicide. The city gives and the city takes away. The cops think we're a freak show anyway. No matter, the police don't care and his Christian foster parents sure as sin don't care. I got tickled thinking about that. And so we part. I left the note he gave me, the one he wrote, for just such an occasion, under his left hand. He was right to leave it without a date and his thoughtfulness made me smile.

I lay one finger on his wrist. The throb was mine.

"Eduardo is full-on." The phrase made me laugh and it echoed a howl in the quiet room.

"He's full-on."

It was the first thing Matt had said to me about Eduardo.

And the last thing I said to Matt.

Eduardo was just coming off stage when I walked back in the club. He watched without moving as I covered the last distance between us.

"Well."

"Like smothering a baby."

"You are a wicked, wicked boy, Stephen."

"I'm *your* wicked boy now. Any complaints?"

"Not from me. Come on, I want you to meet some people."

He took my hand and drew me across the room behind him. The crowd gave way, then closed quickly over the wake of the new king.

LIKE A ROCKET WITH A BEAT

BY JOE MENO

Lawrence & Broadway

High black cat is the worst kind of luck. It's the luck of knowing your ghostly number is up. It's the luck of the zero, the no one. It's the record that automatically plays whenever the radio comes on. Like Donna Lee with the trumpet blaring.

"Shirley stole this record too," Seamus cursed. "She took this one."

He'd borrowed a coupe and the night was warm so we were out driving. At the time, he was up to number nine. Mister Ten might go walking by anytime. "Pull over," he said suddenly. I slowed the automobile down, figuring it quick.

At the corner of Broadway and Lawrence, there was Cannonball Adams, the piano player, with a girl, standing unsuspecting. He was telling her the ideas he had about her—her legs and hair, the way she looked like a movie star in the lights of the evening. She was buying it because she wasn't his wife. The girl was on the corner listening to the music Cannonball was whispering and he began leaning in at her with his enormous hands, and it was then that Seamus opened the passenger side door.

In a flash, Seamus was at the corner and had already slugged the fellah in the back of the neck. Seamus gave him two chops to the head and a shot to the kidney and then one more to the crown, which laid him out pretty well. Seamus hadn't fought in the ring in years but he could still move like lightning. Then the heartbreak. Seamus raised his foot up.

"No, no, not my hands, not my hands," Cannonball pleaded, and he had hands unlike any other man, three times the size of most men's, they were the hands of a monster really. Seamus snarled and stomped down hard with his size-elevens on the sap's fingers, a step on the right, then the left, then back and forth, then again. The girl didn't like the idea. She swung her purse at the side of Seamus's head. It only made him madder. He turned and grabbed the purse from her hand, then turned again. He came shuffling back to the automobile but he was slow now and sad. He closed the automobile door and I took off quick like that.

It was quiet for a while. The ghost of a small black cat cut across the snow, from one corner into a dark alley, its shadow stretching thin and long. That cat, and me seeing it, was just about the worst thing that could happen at that moment. I swore to myself. We went on driving and I looked at Seamus, and what he placed between him and me on the front seat made my eyes ache, but badly. It was the girl's white purse: small, square-shaped, etc., etc. He had taken the girl's purse for some reason.

"How come?" I asked, and he looked down, embarrassed, then turned his head and started to open the purse, sad that the whole thing had ever happened maybe.

"He was number ten," he said.

"How come the purse then?"

"I don't know," he frowned, out of breath. "You want it?"

"No," I replied. "It's bad luck. I won't touch it."

"That settles it," he said, "I don't want to think about Shirley again," and even as he was talking, I was sure neither of us was having it. Cannonball Adams was number ten, the tenth fellah to have fooled around with Shirley. Somewhere out there, I was sure, was number eleven.

I glanced over at Seamus's big red face. He looked like he had lost the big fight. His left eye was twitching. He shrugged his thick shoulders then emptied the rest of the tiny purse in his lap. Inside there was a handkerchief and a makeup kit. A pair of fake eyelashes fell on out next. They landed right beside me, just like that, almost blinking. I didn't say a word. I just stared at them. They were thick and black and tired and lovely. He tipped the purse over and what came out next was like a song where the lady singing mentions your name, but directly, something like, *"I'm in love with a boy who makes my heart spin/I'm in love with a boy, a boy named Jim."*

It was a white business card that fell out, with a picture of a blue genie coming up from a lamp. I picked it up and saw that, on the other side of the card, it read:

THE BEARER OF THIS CARD IS HEREBY
GRANTED THREE WISHES

It was those moments, those strange moments where I caught the lines no one else seemed to be hearing, those strange moments like the one I was having, that made me want to go into a church again so badly.

"What's it say?" Seamus asked.

"It says I got three wishes."

"Three wishes? What for?"

"For finding it. Sure," I said, "three wishes? That's easy."

"Sure."

"For my first one: huh. Well. Well, I wish I could sleep more soundly."

"How's that?" Seamus asked.

"I'm up all night. I hear things. I get afraid. I get afraid ghosts are sitting in my parlor, you know. I'm counting sheep until daybreak."

"A grown man like you?" He smiled. "You oughta be ashamed."

"Sure I am. Ever since I was a kid, though. I get in bed and that's all I think about. Ghosts."

"You're gonna throw away a perfectly good wish on nonsense like that?" Seamus grunted. "Really. You oughta be ashamed. Why don't you use it on something you need? Something you always wanted, maybe."

I looked down at my sad Stacy Adams with the hole in the toe and said, "O-key, then, I take it back. For my first wish, a new pair of shoes."

"You're gonna waste 'em on a pair of shoes?" Seamus moaned. "That's terrible."

"That's what I need."

"That's terrible," he repeated.

"O-key, then you can have the next one."

"O-key," he said, and I should have seen it coming, down the block, right up the street. "O-key. I wish I knew where Shirley was right now." He whispered it and I nodded, without a word, letting that one pass as quickly as I could.

"O-key, for my last one . . ." I said. "Huh, I dunno. Maybe I'll keep it for a while."

"That's smart," he said, but even as he went on talking, I was already thinking. I held the card in my hand and thought of my Slingerland traps, the greatest drum set I had ever had, pearl finish with red sparkles, my kit which was now sitting in the front window of a pawn shop on Ashland, and the thought was this: "*I wish I don't end up a two-bit just like everybody.*"

2

It was our job to drive around. Seamus had been hired to collect certain things from certain people and he would give me a cut of his pay for me to drive, because although he could set a fellah twice his size down on his back, he couldn't keep his hands still on the wheel. It was a decent enough job but nothing I was too proud of. Seamus would borrow a car from his employer and then we'd drive around all night. It was always easier at night and the music they played on the radio was always a lot luckier.

In the soft gray silence of morning, after we drove around, searching for certain people on street corners, in bars, in the arms of girls they did not trust, I'd mope back to the apartment to try and sleep. It would be too quiet. At one time a lady with a pet canary had lived in the apartment beneath me and they sang along together, every morning, the lady being lonely, wishing for some man to do her duet with maybe. Then the little orange canary got out of its cage, crawled in a hole, and got caught in the wall. For a while, very, very late at night, the lady would sing and it would sing back from behind the plaster. But then it was quiet and not even "Body and Soul" would help locate where the bird had vanished. The lady moved out finally. There were still white sheets all over the furniture and it made me wonder if, like the rest of the town, she had given up on something.

I'd come home alone, lock the apartment door, and switch on the light. If I looked in the hallway mirror I might see a ghost. My uncle, who was a night watchman, taught me how to spot them. There was a ghost of a bootlegger who would appear in my bedroom late at night, dressed in a borrowed white sheet with two black holes for eyes. You could try and convince him he didn't belong there, but it was impossible. The only way to get rid of him was to switch on the radio and slowly turn the dial until there was a song he recognized and somehow it would remind him that he had died. It was a shame. Here I was, a grown man, superstitious and afraid of the dark, and being afraid of the dark is what got me into the kind of trouble I was always in.

3

Like the way it usually went, Seamus came by the next night and asked me to help him put the fix on Mr. Number Eleven. He was all busted up about it. He was stuttering and wringing his hands nervously. I locked the apartment door and took my glasses off because I was not about to go through breaking them again, and he said, "All you got to do is drive me, Jim," and so I put my glasses back on my face.

The elevator arrived and we stepped inside. The two old black cleaning ladies were already there. They had boxes and bags of garbage and old clothes and were whispering to each other. One of them was saying, "It's not like they didn't try to help him. He just went off on his own. He couldn't get it off his back, that stuff. He moved in with that white girl and he couldn't be good, and just like that she stabbed him to death. That girl, that girl's gonna reap what she sows. I told her. She needs the cure. The only thing gonna save her now is Jesus. But she's not interested. She won't hear it. She ain't never gonna be happy until she lets herself be saved. I know it. I've had my share of it. Hardening your heart like that. I don't know what you call it, but it sure ain't living. That boy's dead two days now, stabbed. My man's been gone for ten and it hurts like yesterday." The lady looked me over and smiled and said, "What size are you?" and I said, "Size?" and she said, "What are you? About a nine?" and out of one of the boxes came a pair of black shoes. They belonged to whoever had been stabbed, and even in the shaky light of the elevator I could tell that they would fit fine.

4

The fix was going to be put on a fink named Langley. He had a horse face and played the trumpet around town with Davey Trotter, the clarinetist and arranger. Apparently, Langley had also slept with Seamus's wife and now, including Cannonball Adams, the count was up to eleven. Most of them were musicians, stage actors, or semi-pro fighters, one was even a southern jockey. The wife had a hot spot for anyone whose name was in lights. It seemed to me that if Seamus found out about one more, just one more, it might end in someone's murder maybe.

When we got out of my building, I saw that it was snowing again. Also, there was an automobile sitting there waiting. This was a surprise because, like I said, Seamus did not own an automobile. For a second I wondered if it was stolen or borrowed, and then he said, "You drive, all right? I can't. My hands are too shaky."

"Whose automobile is this one?" I asked.

"I found it," he replied, and I nodded and he gave me the keys and I started it up. It was a late-model Chevy Coupe, maybe '55, '56, and it looked like it had been black once but now it was dull brown and green and a junkyard. It was an eyesore, only being a few years old, which must have meant something. Seamus got in the passenger side and lit up a square and his left eye started to twitch a little. I took it as bad luck immediately.

Seamus had a thick red scar over his left eye from the

time when he was eleven and got cut by his older brother in a fight over a purse the both of them had stolen. It was when he was still just a kid and stole ladies' purses, not for the money, he just went through them to look at their makeup and nylons and handkerchiefs and everything. That cut-up eye seemed like it belonged right on Seamus's face. He went through life squinting as hard as he could, smiling a quiet, cock-eyed smile to himself. Because of the cut and the row with his brother, though, he learned to fight. Truly, he was the squarest, most honest person I knew, him being a kind of two-bit hustler too, I guess.

He was younger than me, somewhere in his late twenties, a big Irish kind of pug. He had very short blond hair and a thick neck. He'd been a middleweight fighter for a while and hadn't made much of a name for himself. His wife had thought he was going to be famous, and spent all the dough like he already was. So he went out and did a stupid thing. He got arrested knocking over a liquor store with his bare hands, and because he didn't have any priors and hadn't been carrying a weapon, he made parole pretty quick. But the dame hadn't waited, in any sense of the word. She headed out to Hollywood to be discovered as an actress. She was gone before Seamus came home.

"How'd you hear about this fellah Langley?" I asked him.

"Clovis told me. He said Langley was bragging about it the other night. He said the guy said, 'You know that has-been pug that hangs around the Back Room? Well, his wife has a soft spot for horn players.' He said some other lousy things I don't want to repeat."

"Do we go by his place?" I asked him.

"No, Clovis says this fellah owes him some money. He's setting it up."

"So that's Clovis's angle," I said. "He still owes me a dou-ble sawbuck himself."

"They're going to be at the Back Room. That's where Clovis said to meet him."

I said o-key and turned the radio on. "Now's the Time" by the greatest, Miles Davis, blared to life. I snapped my fin-gers, taking it as a good sign. In a moment, the song was over and "Salt Peanuts" rolled on. Then, an old Duke Ellington tune, "Mood Indigo."

"The radio is good luck today," I said. "One good old good one after another." I glanced over at Seamus and he was somewhere else. He was staring straight ahead and tighten-ing his hands. He had the blank look of revenge on his face. It was there in the sad resignation of his small eyes. It looked like he had just found out his wife had left him again. It was still snowing as I took the next left and headed toward the other side of town, away from the bright lights.

5

The record playing was "Swanee River," another old one, when we came in. Clovis sat at a table alone in the back, drinking. He looked sharp, like always: wide-shouldered and black, his skin the color of some distant world, the soft face and round cheeks that gave away his good nature. He saw us and then nodded his head and we watched his eyes move to the left where Langley was slow-dancing with a tall female patron. Langley had his horse face buried in the dame's soft blond hair and seemed to be very occupied with it: like a blue jay of happiness, him with his eyes closed, getting dreamy, petting the girl's hair, sighing softly. For a moment, I felt sad having to interrupt him. It didn't seem right separating a fel-lah like that from the one thing that might make him happy.

But Clovis finished his drink and stood up very carefully, backing away from the table. And then, just like that, he winked.

"Is it you that's been saying those things about my wife, Langley?" Seamus shouted. "Is it you that's been saying she's got a soft spot for horn players?"

The blond girl got the idea and cleared out quick. Langley looked at Seamus, sized him up, then glanced over at Clovis and frowned. In a flash, he made a reach for a highball glass and tossed it toward our heads, then ducked for the side door.

Clovis sighed and shook his head. "A couple of amateurs, you two," he said.

"I'll get the automobile," I whispered, and headed around front.

I started the automobile up and Clovis climbed in the passenger seat beside me. "Don't say it. I know I owe you twenty, Jim," he said. "Next week."

"You've been saying that for three weeks," I mumbled, and threw the gear into drive. The coupe took off like a rocket. We spun around the corner, sliding in the snow. I turned down the alley and saw Langley doing his best to pull himself over a barbed-wire fence. He was about seven feet off the ground and all knees and elbows.

"There stands our man," Clovis said.

I always liked Clovis, not so much because he was some-one I felt I could trust, but because he was someone I admired for his reputation of being a ladies' man. He had one of those tiny elegant mustaches, a thin line just above his lips, and smooth-looking hair with just the right amount of relaxer. Also, most of the time he was holding some pills, black beauties, west coasters, bennies, some kind, and he always knew a few good-looking white girls who thought he was an amateur photographer. He'd take pictures of them. They were what I might call *forbidden pictures*. He had this portable Polaroid and a whole collection of close-ups of white girls undressing. He would show you them if you asked, and usually I was very interested. He might have been one of the best coronet players that ever lived, the way he played so slow and sad, if he sat still long enough to listen to himself, but that was a no go. He would sit in sessions around town but, for the most part, if a dame wasn't involved, he had no interest in being still that long.

"Now what?" I asked, and it was at that moment, Seamus came around the corner.

"Now you turn your head, Jimmy, because this is not gonna be pretty," Clovis said with a grin.

"Please, no!" Langley shouted, and it became apparent he was no longer climbing. He was stuck at the top, his pants leg snarled by a ring of barbed wire. Seamus saw this and moved down the alley, slower now, taking his time. He took off his hat and his coat and rolled up his shirt sleeves very carefully.

"Please, please, let me get down first!" Langley shouted. "To be fair about it."

Seamus went up and grabbed the fence in both his big hands and gave it a shake. It was like making a wish with a dime, easy. Just like that, Langley fell on his back right at Seamus's feet.

Then, "Please, wait, wait a minute . . . she . . . she didn't mean anything," Langley muttered, and in my mind I imagined a big red dictionary which opened to a page that read:

she didn't mean anything *she did not meen 'en-e-thin*\\
slang phrase 1: at this moment, exactly the wrong thing to say.

I put the automobile in park and turned the radio up, and this radio was sending me secret messages of good luck again because it was Gerry Mulligan's big sax trembling. I looked away as Seamus swung his hand back and *snap*! Langley, the poor fellah, couldn't have done a thing to avoid it coming. Seamus hit him a square one in mouth and I saw Langley fly forward, his hands dropping to his sides, and then I couldn't see what was happening because they were on the ground, in front of the automobile. Seamus was very quiet about it all and I saw him swing again. Some blood specked along the snow.

Langley was yelling, "She didn't mean anything! She didn't mean anything!" and each time he said it, Seamus lunged forward. "Please, my, my teeth," and Langley being a trumpet player must have registered with big Seamus finally. He stood up and took a step back and his foot went right into the sap's teeth.

"Yikes," Clovis mumbled, and Seamus was putting his coat and hat back on, frowning.

In a moment, Clovis climbed out then and dug the wallet from the back of poor Langley's pants. He robbed the poor sap and I hadn't thought he was going to do that. He got back in the coupe and threw Langley's wallet down in the front seat and took out the fellah's cash, then slipped me a twenty. I said, "No dice, Clovis," and handed it back, but quickly.

We were driving away and I was beginning to think I'd never ever be lucky again because I was just another two-bit among two-bits and there was nothing but scientific evidence of bad luck all around me. "High black cat," I said, keeping my fingers crossed to ward it off. "High black cat."

6

We went by the pawnshop on Ashland after that because I wanted to see my traps. They'd been sitting in the window a week before and now they weren't and I wondered who the heck had bought them and what madman was playing them right now. We were standing outside the Friendly Pawn— Clovis, Seamus, and me—and my traps, the greatest drums in the world, were gone.

7

We cruised downtown next. Clovis had two joints and we smoked one up at Harbor Point where Randolph rises above the rest of the city. Up there stand three or four high-class apartment buildings that stare out over the entire lakefront. I let the radio play and it was an old Count Basie side on then, "Dark Rapture," and I was getting stoned. Then Seamus sat up quick and said, "I'm going to go try and call my wife," and he hopped out of the automobile and was gone just like that. It was his trademark disappearing act. You might be at a nightclub or in a taxi, and he'd mumble something about calling his wife and then disappear, but there'd always be enough money in the spot where he had been sitting to cover his tab.

"He's got a screw loose, that one," I said.

"Too many uppercuts to the head," Clovis said. He searched around and lit the second joint. I laid back and I kept thinking about those Slingerland traps and who was playing them, and just then I realized it. Christ Jesus, I was late again.

We hit the Blue Note after that because I was supposed to sub for a trap player. When I showed up they said I had fouled up and the band had to call someone else and the baritone player said some comment like, "Jimmy Rabbit? I thought he was dead. Whiz-bang, baby, maybe you'd be better off if you did," and I said, "Fuck you, my man," and he said, "No, fuck you, my man," and because of that situation, I lost about thirty bucks.

At the last minute, the alto reed player, a kid named Bobby Lincoln, a white kid who was straight as an ace on the alto sax, said he'd rather have me playing than the fellah they had called in. The fellah they called in looked like his mother had just dropped him off, and the way he was sweating and shaking, his face white as a ghost and him being black to boot, was a bad sign for everybody. By then it was 10:00 and they were scheduled to start on the hour and so it was on. I got up behind this very slick set of white Pearls and let them all have it. The first song I played was for the baritone player and it was a slow Earl "Fatha" Hines tune and I held it all in, right on time, waiting for my chance, etc., etc. The second song came and I was on and it was for the organ man who had said what he had said to me, and it was "Now's the Time" by Charlie Parker and my drums were saying, *"You can fuck off, my man, you fucking wannabe, dig this show I'm laying down and I know it's good because it's making your ten-cent organ solo sound like a million bucks."*

Later, the band, a five-piece with an alto and a baritone, said they needed a steady drummer and asked if I was interested and I said sure. Then they gave me my cut, which was only five bucks, and I said, "Excuse me, what is this all about?" and they go on to tell me the drinks are not free, and like a fool, I said, "Then you can count me out," and heck, I had needed that job and I needed that money, but badly. Then Clovis came up and said we should split and I said sure and he said promptly and I said what's the hurry and he said,

"Cannonball Adams just walked in," and like Clovis said, there he was.

Cannonball was white, muscular, with soft brown hair that was deftly parted, even with both his hands broken. It was a cinch his wife had combed his hair for him. He marched directly up to Clovis and I at the bar. He was in a soft tweed coat, both his hands in oversized white casts, his lip split and one eye still red and puffy.

"Well, gentlemen, I just came here to tell you a certain associate of mine is looking for you," and I couldn't think who that might be, so I said, "So why is this fellah looking for me?"

"He is representing me," Cannonball grinned. He was knocking his casts against his pocket, trying to pull out a cigarette. I shook my head and obliged him.

"So, he's representing you?" I repeated as I lit the smoke for him. "So?"

"My associate says he can't make any money off me because I can't play the piano. I can't play the piano because you and your pug Irish friend broke my hands. I owed this associate a sum, so now my associate is looking for you two to collect what I owe."

"I bet," I said.

"My associate is to come by here right before midnight," Cannonball grinned, and the clock above the rows of glass and liquor shouted out *five to twelve* and I had to think, was I a real posy in bloom? Yes. And my luck was only getting worse; worse, joe, worse.

8

Like magic, it had become morning. We found Seamus near his apartment on the corner of Broadway and Wilson. From down the block, I could see he was standing out front in the snow, smoking, and his big, misshapen nose was mashed and bleeding. He was holding his ear, which was swollen as big as a stone, and for some reason, standing there in the snow, he was smiling.

"What happened to you now?" I asked. "Number Twelve?"

"Nope. I ran into Cannonball's associates. They took what they think I owed them."

"How much was that?"

"My wristwatch and my wedding ring."

"That was it?"

"Yep. They're strictly small-time. I think one of them is going to have to learn to breathe through his ears from now on, but they got what they wanted."

"Is that why you're smiling?"

"Nope. I got a telegram from Shirley. She's moving back to town, she says."

I shrugged my shoulders, not knowing what to think.

"I just sent her one back. I told her, in my book she's still o-key."

I nodded. I thought my good friend here might be truly crazy.

"I got something else," he said.

9

It was in the back of the trunk of some automobile down the street, a white Ford, another one he had borrowed or stolen. Cold and desperate, we all stood around behind it and watched as Seamus inserted the key and the rear panel sprang up.

It almost made me cry, what I saw. There, beside a spare

tire and a soft blue blanket, was a single red sparkle drum, just one, a floor tom, with its silvery legs and all.

I didn't know what to say.

"It was all I could afford," he whispered, "the one. I was gonna try and buy one at a time, but they sold the rest before I came back." I shook his hand and smiled, glad like usual, that he was my friend.

The city seemed to be very pleased with itself then, cool and silent and steady. We went to go get some coffee and eggs at a place on Wilson. As we were walking, I looked up and caught a snowflake on the corner of my eyelash, it just landed right there, and to me that was as good as any good luck wish. It was then I noticed that the snow was falling. It was really falling.

MARTY'S DRINK OR DIE CLUB

BY NEAL POLLACK

Clark & Foster

The guy at the end of the bar was dead. Carlos had seen dead guys before, so he knew. They usually didn't get many customers in Ginny's, especially not before 5:30, which was when Carlos had started his shift, slapping the mop around the pool table: A couple of bikers had gotten into it the night before, leaving the usual dried residue of blood, saliva, and Leinenkugel. Tonight, the guy slobbered in and took the stool by the window. He sat hunched, not out of some deformity, but just overall weakness, his hair long and gray and greasy under the Cubs hat, his eyes brown and wide and blank, staring at himself in the mirror, or maybe through the mirror, at something beyond.

"Get you something?" Carlos said.

No answer. Carlos set the mop by the pool table and walked through the hutch. The guy had flakes of dry snot on his mustache, which was as peppered and unkempt as his hair. He gave Carlos a little nod, though even that looked like a struggle, and raised his right hand familiarly. Carlos thought this was strange, since he'd never met the guy before. The hand shimmered turbulently.

"You want a drink, man?" Carlos said.

"Whuhhhhhh," the guy said. "Wiiiiiiiiiii."

Carlos spoke wino. He reached under the bar, pulled out a little tumbler, flipped a few ice cubes into it, and added a double shot of well whiskey. When a guy was this far in the bag, brands didn't matter.

"Run a tab?"

"Ahhhhhhh," said the guy.

"All right," Carlos said. "That's two seventy-five."

The guy folded his arms on the bar and put his head down into them, without taking a sip of his whiskey. His jacket slid halfway off his shoulders. Screw it, Carlos thought, I'm not gonna shake this dude down. He can pay me when he wakes up.

A half hour later, the guy's arms slid off the bar. He hovered there on the stool for a second, arms flopping, before momentum pitched him forward. He bonked the bar; he tipped sideways and then he fell, his head hitting the bottom rail before he stopped, facedown, fully sprawled, on the floor. There wasn't any blood, but Carlos still didn't want to touch him. Carlos called the apartment upstairs.

"Ginny," he said. "You'd better get down here now."

Then he noticed the business card. It had fluttered across the room, settling under the jukebox. Though he knew enough to stay away from the body, this he decided to touch. He walked across the room and picked up the card. It said,

MARTY'S DRINK OR DIE CLUB
PHILOSOPHERS, STATESMEN, MEN OF CHICAGO
Johnny Quinn, Treasurer

Below that was an address, and Johnny Quinn's signature, in a shaky hand, and then underneath that, in red lettering, all caps:

MEMBERSHIP EXPIRED

The red letters smelled strong, like they'd recently been applied with a Sharpie. Carlos was no better detective than he was a bartender, but he guessed that this dead guy was Johnny Quinn. And he definitely knew Marty's.

In those days when the city gave real estate breaks to connected developers like stocking stuffers, there were two types of neighborhood bars: those that understood and cared about the changing landscape, and those that didn't. Ginny's fell in the latter category, one of the few leftovers from the 1960s hillbilly takeover of Uptown that had sent everyone else fleeing except for the most committed members of Students for a Democratic Society. Ginny had basically given up around 1987, when her sister died, and now she was one code violation from the end, which would happen soon enough. By this time next year, a mid-scale seafood restaurant would be serving up nineteen-dollar swordfish steaks in this spot, and Ginny would be sleeping on her son's foldaway sofa in Schaumburg.

Marty's was the other kind of bar.

When he'd been alive, Marty Halversen operated his place with a sense of whimsy. If any other working Chicago bar had once been a speakeasy, the newspaper reporters and Wild Chicago producers hadn't discovered it yet. Marty had liked to boast that his liquor license was the third issued by the city after the end of Prohibition. He'd put the license over the bar, in the same frame with a picture he'd taken of Capone drinking in his basement. By the time Marty left, those days of potluck Sundays, sponsored basketball teams, and neighborhood golf outings were fading, but the new owner, a neighborhood kid named Scott Silverstein, spoke just the right mix of regular-guy sympathy and monied schmooze to keep it going. He loved giving tours, showing cameramen and tourists Capone's secret cashier's booth, the trap door to the basement, and the old still that he'd preserved so well.

At night, the place filled with actors and bankers and lawyers, anyone willing to dress down a little and appreciate original fixtures and tin ceilings but also willing to spend five bucks on a *weiss* beer. The regular crowd still gathered to drink with Scott and raise a glass to Marty's memory and the glories of what once had been. The old patrons still had their corner of the bar. Scott could put in all the kitschy lighting he wanted. They owned the bar's soul.

The regular crowd was in session when Carlos walked into Marty's. He saw three guys conspiring around the bar toward the back, deep in conversation with a bartender leaning against a brightly painted wooden mermaid. Shot and beer glasses had accumulated. One of the guys looked to be in his mid-sixties, with a long, confident face, like a neighborhood Kirk Douglas. The other guys, including the bartender, were around forty. Carlos went over to them. One of the younger guys, pudgy, short-haired, and excitable, was in the middle of a monologue.

". . . A movie just isn't a movie unless there's a talking ape in it," he was saying.

"When was the last great monkey movie, anyway?" said the other young guy, who had his blond hair tied back in a ponytail.

"Any of you work here?" Carlos asked.

"My name is Schultz," said the pudgy guy. "I know nothing! Nothing!"

They broke up laughing. Carlos had no idea why. He pulled the card out of his pocket.

"I found this on the floor at Ginny's," he said. "You know this dude?"

The older guy, in his last year or two of distinguished handsomeness, took the card from Carlos. A severe look crawled across his face. He let out a puff of air.

"Ah," he said. "Little Johnny Quinn. To sleep, perchance to dream."

"The cops took his body away awhile ago," said Carlos.

"Was yours the last face upon which he gazed?" the man inquired.

"I was behind the bar, and he just fell down," Carlos said.

"A sadder day we haven't seen in these environs for some years," the man said.

"What does this mean," Carlos said, "*Membership Expired*"?

Eyebrows raised at the bar.

"The game is afoot!" said the guy with the ponytail.

"Who is Keyser Soze?" said the monkey man.

"Monsieur Poirot," said the older guy, "my name is Francis Carmody. We've been waiting for you!" He spoke to the rest of his fellowship. "Gentlemen," he said, "this man has a suspicious nature. I suggest we repair to our hideout a little bit later to alleviate his concerns with libation!"

The guys all raised their beers. As one, they said, nearly whispered: "Aye! Aye! Aye and aye! We drink, we drink, we drink, or else we die!"

What the fuck, Carlos thought.

Francis Carmody lived in a split-level bungalow a few streets west of Clark, on a block that still housed many people who'd been consciously alive in the 1960s. He'd owned the place for more than forty years, and had the accumulated basement of newspapers, magazines, and lyric opera programs to show for his tenure. An ill-placed match could have burned down the neighborhood. A decade previous, the paper volume had reached critical mass, but rather than recycle—a habit which Mayor Daley, an unlikely environmentalist, encouraged in all Chicagoans—Francis did something wholly out of character: He built an addition onto his house. It was the only improvement he made in all his decades of living there.

Francis needed the addition because he collected films, and not DVDs, either. Francis didn't believe in digital images. One could possibly make the argument that celluloid was equally dishonest, but if one made that argument, Francis would shut down the spigot and you'd find yourself drinking alone.

At about 9:30 p.m. on that Wednesday, Carlos found himself walking through the back door of Francis Carmody's 350-square-foot home theater. Carlos had been lured there with the promise of free booze. The last movie he'd seen was *The Chronicles of Riddick,* and then only because his date had a thing for Vin Diesel and Carlos hoped that little tingle might carry over into afterwards. So Francis's collection of framed posters from Jean Harlow and Errol Flynn movies didn't mean anything to him. Carlos didn't remember Jessica Lange as King Kong's girlfriend, much less Fay Wray. And when Francis announced that the evening would feature, after selected trailers and shorts, a double feature of *The Informer* and *The Lady from Shanghai,* to Carlos he might as well have been announcing lessons in medieval Catalan.

"These films were beloved by Johnny Quinn, blessed be his memory," Francis said.

A bottle of high-end vodka had appeared. Carlos didn't see where it came from, but these guys had been buying him drinks for hours, and he was already close to hammered.

Francis Carmody poured little tumblers for them all. "We quaff sublimely for Johnny," he said. "For he drank too wisely, and never from the well."

"Indeed," said the guy with the ponytail.

They took their seats on comfortable couches that smelled of two generations of cat, facing a screen that looked like it'd been rescued from a high school janitor's closet. Francis stood behind them at a projector. Behind him was a wall of film canisters. He pulled one down and pressed a button on the wall to his left.

"Laura," he said, "we're ready for the boiled meats."

On cue, a hunched woman in an unattractive housedress appeared, bearing a tray of flabby hot dogs, hydrogenated buns, and the appropriate condiments.

"My wife, Laura," Francis said to Carlos. "The bulwark of my soul."

She put the hot dogs on a table in front of the couches and shuffled out of the room without a word.

"A fine lady," Francis said.

They watched a Carmen Miranda short, then one starring Esther Williams, followed by a Chuck Jones cartoon that made fun of Hitler. Francis poured the vodka between each reel. Francis showed *The Lady from Shanghai*, but the movie stopped after an hour, without an ending.

"Art is at its purest when unfinished," Francis said. "I believe Johnny Quinn would agree."

"Hear hear," said the guy who liked monkey movies.

Finally, Carlos, who'd floated along on an existential sea all evening, oblivious from drink, said something.

"What are you talking about?" he said.

"Ah, the natural inquisitiveness of youth has surfaced at

last," Francis said. "Boys, shall we lift the veil of ignorance from his eyes?"

Francis stood in front of the screen, lecturing without a pointer.

"The only thing more intoxicating than the free flow of drink," he said, "is the free flow of ideas. On the rare occasions that the two combine, it's possible to know the face of God. Once, philosopher-kings who worked for a living, men who knew their way equally around a factory floor and a lecture hall, ruled Chicago. Their era was short but glorious. The city could barely build enough taverns to hold them all. They loved their learning and their drink, and the platonic joys of sophisticated male friendship. I was one of those men.

"So was Marty Halversen, the finest man I ever had the privilege of knowing, a scion of the Navy and a veteran of the slaughterhouse, and the holder of a degree in English literature from DePaul. He was a man truly worthy of the title *tavern keeper*, a great poet, a lover of women, and a friend to the neighborhood. I revered him more than my own father. Much more.

"Marty believed above all things, as do I, in the enlightenment of the human soul. To that end, we chose the finest thinkers of all the fine thinkers we knew, and we formed Marty's Drink or Die Club. We were young then, so the club's idea seemed fanciful. There would come a time, we joked, when our doctors would tell us that we had to stop drinking or else we would die. But not to drink is, in essence, to die anyway. Therefore we made a pledge, forged at the bottom of a glass: If one of us received the Hippocratic word, then the rest of us were bound by fraternal duty to make it come true."

At that, Francis held a glass as if for a toast, and everyone in the room drank on cue. He continued: "For twenty-five years, the club met happily. We formed a protective shell of ideas and camaraderie around ourselves, our intellects serving as a shield and a balm against the bitter shocks of the wider world. Then one day Marty came in the bar with his face ashen yet resigned.

"'Gentlemen,' he said to us, 'I have heard the bad news. According to my doctor, my liver is Dunkirk. He's told me that I've downed my last. He even brought in a specialist, who confirmed the toxicity of my X-ray. It's all gone to shit.'

"Oh, we thought, the shame! Our leader, the owner of our resting place, had been stopped from drinking by diagnosis. But what he said next sealed our fates in the afterlife: 'I expect you to honor our pact,' he said, 'and to honor it this afternoon.'

"We laughed. Death to us, though we certainly found ourselves aging, was still a metaphor. But not to Marty, who had us in years and in gallons consumed. He produced four vials from his pocket and placed them on the bar.

"'Three of these contain tap water,' he said. 'The other is pure tetraethyl pyrophosphate. Colorless, odorless, and generally fatal. You will each take one vial and empty its contents into my last glass of Bushmill's, which I will now pour.'

"He did so, a double.

"'Within an hour,' he continued, 'I'll be dead, and you'll all be culpable. Yet none of you will be. It's not murder if you have the consent of the murdered. Or maybe it is. Regardless, we need to assume we won't get caught. But once this pact is sealed in embalming fluid, you must all promise to follow me when your own day comes.'

"We promised what Marty asked, though not without

some subtle tears, because we understood that a strange combination of whimsy and duty had now bound us all to the same end. But before that happened, we agreed that the club shouldn't die with us. For every light extinguished, another would flicker on. Our shining white city of the mind would burn for generations. Marty downed his final whiskey, patted us each on the back in return for the favor of merciful death, and walked slowly toward the door. He turned and waved, silhouetted in the arch by the late-afternoon sun, and went home to his bed. Ronald was there at the bar . . ."

The guy with the ponytail said, "Yes, I was."

"Stopping in for a shot after band practice. We knew him to be a young man of the neighborhood, resolute in character and ethical in judgment. He had discovered our club, as sometimes secrets slide off drunken tongues, particularly when trusted bar regulars are talking. He agreed that day to take Marty's place. And two years later, when Mickey Lasker got the news from his doctor, Will, our monkey-film expert, took the night off from spinning records at Medusa's and became one of us. He, too, had learned of the club late one night, by accident, and he, too, is a forgotten genius of the North Side. Scott Silverstein joined the fold soon after upon the unfortunate demise of Leonard Loveless, former drama critic for the lamented *Chicago Daily News*. The papers all said that Leonard passed of natural causes. But we knew that he had drunk and died.

"Now we say goodbye to Johnny Quinn, a man of independent judgment who never crossed a picket line. Barely ten hours ago, we stood at Marty's and one of us slipped him the drops that caused him to breathe his last. And like those before him, he drifted off with grace."

Francis Carmody opened a cabinet and a record player

slid out on a tray. He pulled a 45 out of a sleeve. That, Carlos decided later, is when things *really* got weird.

The room had grown excessively warm. It smelt sour and gassy. Francis put a record on the player and hustled to the front of the room, where the other members of Marty's Drink or Die Club were standing. They'd linked arms, and they gestured for Carlos to join them. The song started, so they didn't notice too much when he didn't. They sang along with the record:

> *I've been a wild rover for many a year*
> *And I spent all my money on whiskey and beer,*
> *And now I'm returning with gold in great store*
> *And I never will play the wild rover no more.*
>
> *And it's no, nay, never,*
> *No nay never no more,*
> *Will I play the wild rover*
> *No never no more.*

The song made no sense to Carlos, but as the men sang, it was obvious that it moved them deeply. When they reached each chorus, he could barely make out the words over their blubbering. This made Carlos very uncomfortable. Men in his family didn't show emotion like this, not even in private after midnight. The song, mercifully, came to its final verse.

> *I'll go home to my parents, confess what I've done,*
> *And I'll ask them to pardon their prodigal son.*
> *And if they forgive me as oft-times before,*
> *Sure I never will play the wild rover no more.*

And it's no, nay, never,
No nay never no more,
Will I play the wild rover
No never no more.

They unlocked arms and Francis just kept talking.

"Boys," he said, "Johnny Quinn is forgiven all his sins, if he ever committed any. I only hope that you will have the same mercy on me. For I can't imagine my tenure on this soil will last much longer. I can feel myself fading even now."

"Blow it out your hole, Ahab," said the ponytailed guy.

"I grow old, I grow old," said Francis. "I shall wear the bottoms of my trousers rolled. With your indulgence, I'm going to play one more record. As you all know, I was once a featured performer at the Hanging Moon on North Avenue, back in the time when songs had lyrics you could understand. The great Moses Asch himself, of Folkways Records, recognized my talents, and I made this recording. When you hear it, I want you to remember the words, and remember me by them."

"Do we have to?" said the monkey man.

"You do," said Francis. "I'd like to think it was Marty's inspiration for our club."

He put the record on. Carlos heard tinny banjo music and a voice that sounded nearly forty years younger. But it was definitely Francis. The song went:

Play that banjo long and loud
And raise your glasses high,
Sing about the life I loved
And how I chose to die,

Praise me like the king I was
And not the rook or pawn,
Embrace your sin and drink your gin
And remember that I'm gone.

Even over the music, Francis talked. "It's a particularly melancholy moment for me," he said. "So many friends lost. So many millions of words. So much profundity. And now I alone remain of that first generation as the final distillation of a way of life. When will it end? One doesn't know. But one does know that young Carlos here has borne witness to our ritual."

"Indeed!" said the monkey man.

"As such, in our tradition, we should nominate him to take Johnny's place."

No way, Carlos thought. This wasn't even something he *wanted* to understand.

"But," said Francis Carmody, "Carlos has shown us nothing to indicate that he possesses the intellectual integrity to fulfill the bylaws of Marty's Drink or Die Club. Agreed?"

"Agreed!" said the other members.

"Therefore," Francis said, "as is our tradition, we offer young Carlos a choice: Maintain silence about what he knows, or die."

Carlos slowly backed away from them, toward the door.

Francis held up his glass. He indicated to the others that they should stand. "Do you accept our terms, young man?"

"I gotta go," Carlos said.

He ran for the door and flung it open, and as he escaped, he heard Francis Carmody say, "Do not betray us, Carlos! We'll find you!"

* * *

It was early November. The night felt crisp and cutting. Carlos's head should have been a fog, but as he ran out of Francis Carmody's backyard and down the side streets toward Clark, he felt nothing but clarity. Maybe he'd go back to Truman College after all, get that two-year degree and then see what was possible. But he'd never go back to Marty's again.

The digital bank clock said 1:15. Just then, the Number 22 came, as if sent by the bus fairy. Carlos got on and slid his card through the reader. His Uncle German's place was just fifteen blocks up in Rogers Park; he'd get there by closing time no matter how slow the bus ran. German always had a pot of *menudo* going this time of night. Carlos could already feel it, warm and fresh and greasy, in his stomach.

He couldn't wait to get sober.

BOBBY KAGAN
KNOWS EVERYTHING

BY ADAM LANGER

Albion & Whipple

One morning in the summer of 1978, Mom's Jim said he couldn't take it anymore and moved out on her for the third and last time, with the intention of finding his first wife. Shelah went away for the summer to Camp Chi, where I had contracted something like dysentery two years earlier and my mother wouldn't let me go back. So I was stuck with Grandpa and his nurse Hallie at the house on Whipple Street, where Mom said we would stay until she'd saved enough money from her job at Crawford's Department Store so that we could have our own place again.

My mother had grown up on Whipple with her sister and her folks. Now, Grandpa still slept in his bedroom, I slept in my Aunt Evelyn's old room, Hallie slept in Mom's old room, and Mom slept downstairs on the couch. The place hadn't been fixed up in years; the paint on the canopy was peeling, the basement moldy, the linoleum floor warped and cracked. There was an overgrown garden full of weeds and a garage packed with boxes, tires, rusted hoes, broken rakes, and Grandpa's white Lincoln Continental. No one had driven the car in a decade. The garage was locked, and Grandpa had long since lost the key.

The first I heard of the robberies came from Mr. Klein, a

retired contractor who lived with his wife Fran directly across the street from Grandpa's in a little red-brick house with chartreuse shutters and a lawn jockey out front. It had started at the Bells's house on Richmond. The thieves hadn't gotten much, Mr. Klein said, just a Mixmaster and a color television. They'd fared better at Mrs. Kutler's on Richmond, scoring not only the TV and radio, but also all her heirloom jewelry. What impressed Mr. Klein most was how professional the burglars were; there was never any sign of a break-in and they always seemed to know exactly what they were looking for. Even though they hadn't gotten anything from the Singers's house on Francisco, somehow they had known that Mr. Singer kept his cash under the bedroom carpet. But nothing like that would happen on Whipple Street, Mr. Klein assured me. All summer long, he would be sitting on his porch, watching.

Inside the house on Whipple Street, when Mom still wasn't home from work, and Hallie read Agatha Christie mysteries while my grandfather slept, I'd wonder when the burglars would hit our house. It was full of antiques and my late grandmother's jewels. It seemed as if it would only be a matter of time. Who would put up a fight? My grandfather needed help getting in and out of the bathroom. Hallie was sixty-three. My only hope was that the burglars would wait until Mom and I moved into our own place again. I had never liked Mom's Jim much. When he was out late drinking at Alibi's, I'd imagine that he was in my bedroom staring down at me. But whenever I turned on the nightlight, no one would be there. Now I wished he would come back.

Mr. Klein's tales of burglaries didn't impress Jason Rubinstein. He and his uncle, Bobby Kagan, had just moved to Albion

Street from Albany Park, where, to hear Jason tell it, the streets were becoming overrun with Korean gangs; every night he fell asleep to the sounds of gunfire.

Jason and I met at Beginners Woodshop at the JCC. Though he and I were in the same grade, he was a year and a half older, more than six inches taller, and probably fifty pounds heavier than me. He claimed to have fingered Robyn Rosen in the nocturnal mammal house at Lincoln Park Zoo and to have lit off firecrackers during the Elton John show at the Chicago Stadium. If you jammed your thumbs into some-one's temples, he said, their heart would stop.

When the JCC canceled Woodshop due to overall lack of interest, Jason and I took the opportunity to start walking our bikes alongside the Chicago River drainage canal on the rubble-strewn site of the old Kiddieland amusement park. Jason showed me what a used condom looked like. He also pointed out an empty Ziploc bag, which he said had probably contained marijuana. Sometimes we'd bike past the Lincoln Avenue motels.

"That's where the hookers take their johns," Jason said.

I nodded, needing but not asking for further explanation.

Jason said he'd learned everything he knew from his uncle, Bobby Kagan. Bobby was slim, with a full head of black curls. He walked with his shoulders hunched forward, his hands dangling down in front of him. He wore bracelets, neck-laces, and pastel shirts opened at least three buttons. Before he started speaking, something he always did quickly and breath-lessly, he'd swipe an index finger across his nostrils, blink his eyes, and swallow hard. He said he worked for the White Sox, but I figured he was lying. One time, he said he was in charge of concessions. Another time he was a scout. Once he said he'd done color commentary for the Sox farm team, the Iowa Oaks.

Still, he managed to get good seats for Jason and me. And not only for Sox games. During the first half of that summer, we saw the Sox three times at Comiskey Park and sat on the third base side during Bat Day. We also got to sit behind the visitors' dugout for Cubs games at Wrigley Field. Bobby Kagan always drove us to and from the games in his red Cadillac DeVille with whitewall tires. He'd buy our Cokes and hot dogs with one of the hundred-dollar bills that he peeled off a roll he kept in his right front pocket. But he'd leave before batting practice and wouldn't return until the ninth inning, when he'd say he'd met an old friend or had some business to take care of. Whenever I spoke, he'd cut me off. I sensed that he never listened to what I was saying.

One night, though, in Bobby's car, after the White Sox had taken a twi-night doubleheader from the Twins, I said that I was glad we were coming home late because Mr. Klein had told me that the burglars had never struck after 10:00. And for the first time that I could recall, Bobby seemed genuinely interested. What robberies, he wanted to know, what had they taken, who had told me all this, who was this Mr. Klein, what did he do for a living, and which house was his?

I told him what I knew about the robberies. The most recent one had taken place at a retired policeman's house on Tripp. They had taken his collections of clocks and belt buckles, as well as his framed Colt .45s. Bobby Kagan seemed impressed with my attention to detail.

"You oughta be a cop," he kept saying.

On this drive from 35th and Shields all the way north to West Rogers Park, I felt more comfortable than I had ever been with Bobby Kagan, and the most comfortable I would ever feel. Before the drive, I don't recall him ever looking me in the eye. Not long afterward, he started dating my mother.

During the second week of July, the night of my thirteenth birthday party—we had played .500 and had a picnic in Warren Park—Jason and I slept in sleeping bags on the floor of Shelah's room. The following morning, when we came downstairs, Bobby was in the kitchen with my mother. He opened the refrigerator and pulled out a carton of half-and-half. Two days later, mom handed me a five-dollar bill and told me to buy dinner for myself from Brown's Chicken because "Bob" was taking her to the Sox game. I started to protest.

"What?" she said. "You think you're the only one in this house allowed to have fun?"

Jason and I were sharing the five-piece chicken dinner in Chippewa Park when we saw two squad cars speeding west on Touhy. Their blue lights were going, but their sirens were off, which meant, Jason said, that they were trying to break up a crime in progress. Before finishing our drumsticks, we were back on our bikes, following the cops to Maplewood Avenue, where four squad cars had double-parked in front of a bungalow. A white-haired lady in a housedress and slippers was standing on her lawn, while police officers walked toward her with flashlights in their right hands, left hands poised over their holsters. As Jason and I leaned against our bikes and watched, one of the cops asked what we were looking at. Jason just stared straight back at the cop.

"I ain't looking at nothin'," he said.

When we got to Mr. Klein's house, Klein inexplicably already knew more than we did; he said he'd heard the news over his police radio. The victim was Mrs. Ruttu. They'd gotten her TV and her hi-fi. The most "brazen" aspect of the crime was that the burglars had taken everything while Mrs. Ruttu slept in her front room, and Klein now had theories about the culprits.

"Probably Arabs or Mexicans," he said. "Someone new to the neighborhood."

I listened intently, but Jason kept sniggering as if he doubted either the facts or Mr. Klein's sanity. Whenever Jason laughed, Mr. Klein would stop for a moment, stare sternly at Jason, then continue. But when Mr. Klein said it was a wonder poor Mrs. Ruttu hadn't died of a heart attack and Jason laughed again, Mr. Klein stood up and said he'd tell me the rest of the story when my friend had gone home.

"Fran," he shouted to his wife, as he opened his screen door, "I'm comin' in!" And then he slammed the door.

I told Jason it didn't seem right to laugh about a woman nearly having a heart attack, but he told me he wasn't laughing at that. He was just laughing at the idea of somebody sleeping while someone else carted off a TV. Burglaries didn't happen like that. Half of the time when thefts were reported and there was no sign of forced entry, it meant that the victim knew the robber and had planned the crime, hoping to collect insurance. That's what Bobby had told him, anyway.

"How does he know so much about it?" I asked.

"Bobby knows everything," he said.

In early August, armed with information provided by Mr. Klein, Jason and I sat down at a back table of the Nortown Library with a Xeroxed map of West Rogers Park, and plotted the robberies, searching for an overall pattern in the dates and times when they had happened, but found nothing. The robberies had taken place during mornings and evenings, in houses and apartments, on Tuesdays, on Thursdays, on weekends. They'd happened on Farwell, on Fairfield, on Granville, Bell, and Washtenaw. Not on Whipple Street, though, Mr. Klein was always quick to point out.

We read the accounts in the *Nortown Leader* newspaper,

in the police blotter and particularly in the front-page story of the Metro section that ran the week of August 3 ("Police Still at a Loss"). With my father's old army binoculars, a Polaroid camera, and a portable tape recorder, we'd case out houses and apartment buildings on blocks that hadn't been hit yet. But after Mr. Isaac Mermelstein approached us wearing an Israeli army jacket and a yellow hardhat and told us to get off his sidewalk, after Mrs. Weinberg called the cops on us, after my mother honked her horn and told us to stop loitering in alleys like a "couple of hoodlums," we went back to the drainage canal and the Lincoln Village Theater, where we would sneak into movies we had already seen, then go to Jason's apartment and listen to his Led Zeppelin and Yes tapes.

On the night that Jason tried to get me stoned, we were sitting in his front room, and he was already pretty high from the half a joint he'd smoked. Mom and Bobby were at Park West at a Boz Scaggs concert, and Jason and I were watching *Saturday Night Live* with the volume turned down and "Roundabout" playing loud. The actors' lips were moving perfectly in synch with the music, Jason said, handing me a lit joint. I told him I wasn't interested, but he gave it to me anyway. It dropped on my shirt, burning a hole by the left shoulder, at which point I panicked, ran to the bathroom, and dumped about a quart of water on myself to make sure the fire was out. When I got back to the front room, Jason was laughing.

"Go get yourself another shirt from the dresser, dork," he said.

I'm sure he meant his dresser and not Uncle Bobby's, but both rooms were dark and I couldn't figure out which was which. I rummaged through Bobby Kagan's dresser. While grabbing for an undershirt, I saw a wad of cash, all hundred-dollar bills.

As I lay in bed that night, listening to my grandfather breathing, I considered everything I knew about Bobby Kagan, how he had thousands of dollars in cash, how he lied about his job, how he seemed so interested in what I knew about the robberies, how he always disappeared for hours during ballgames. I thought of what Mr. Klein had said: Someone new to the neighborhood was committing the robberies. Bobby Kagan and Jason had only lived on Albion since May.

I had already made vague plans to try to follow Bobby, but when my mother got home at 2:00 in the morning and I told her of my suspicions, she couldn't stop laughing.

The next day, Mom was working and Hallie was taking my grandfather to the hospital for a checkup. I'd planned to spend the day tailing Bobby Kagan. But when Jason called to ask me what I would be doing, I couldn't tell him the truth, so we spent the day biking through Caldwell Woods, where invariably every summer the bodies of two or three teenage runaways would be dumped, and then went to Superdawg and ate cheese fries.

When I got home, there were two squad cars in front of my grandfather's house. Mr. Klein was standing on his porch, squinting, until his wife came out and said, "You watched enough, Joe. Later you'll watch more."

Hallie was talking to two cops on the stoop as my grandfather looked at the ground. I let my bike fall on the front lawn and made my way up the stairs.

My mother was sitting at the kitchen table, talking to two male police officers. She was smoking, but when she saw me, she suddenly stood up, put out her cigarette, and grabbed my hands. "I have to tell him what happened," she told the officers.

She told me not to get upset, that we had been robbed. Then she led me upstairs where all the bedrooms were in complete disarray. Dresser drawers were turned upside down, file cabinets lay on the floor, the carpet in my grandfather's room was slit open, everywhere were clothes and books and towels. My grandfather's bedroom didn't smell like urine as it usually did. The thief had thrown everything to the floor, and the room was pungent with mouthwash and aftershave.

My mother put her hands on my shoulders, looked me straight in the eye with an uncharacteristically concerned look. "Are you okay, honey?" she asked.

I nodded. Actually, I felt fine. I'd spent so much time dreading the robbery that when it occurred, my most profound sentiment was relief. I felt comforted by all the police in the house, remembered what it was like to live in an apartment with Shelah and her friends coming in and going out, with mom and Jim laughing and dancing and listening to the radio, instead of just silence and my grandfather's breaths.

When it was clear I was neither afraid nor upset, my mother changed her tone. "Don't start telling the cops your theories," she said, "If they ask you what happened, tell them the truth, and the truth is you don't know."

I was about to remind my mother that Jason Rubinstein was the only one to whom I had mentioned that my grandfather would be at the hospital all day. Who else other than Bobby would he have told? But I recognized my mother's tone. It was the same one she had used when I went with her to the auto insurance appraiser and she'd said, "Remember, don't tell them what you think happened because you don't know what happened," the same one she had when she and Jim had driven up to take me home from Camp Chi and she'd said, "If anyone asks, tell them Jim's your uncle." So when Officer Maki asked what I knew about the robbery, I said that I'd been at Caldwell Woods all day with Jason Rubinstein.

Once the police officers were gone, the house felt emptier than ever. I couldn't wait to get to sleep, then wake up the next morning, visit Jason and Bobby Kagan's apartment, and see if I could find anything new like Grandpa's cufflinks or any of his paperweights. I lay in bed listening to my mother talking to Bobby on the phone, telling him what had been stolen, then saying that tomorrow night would be great, and yes, she would meet him downtown.

The next morning, I noticed Mr. Klein across the street. He wasn't watching the neighborhood, he was doing the *Sun Times* crossword. When I asked if he knew that our house had been hit, he said that he'd been sitting outside all yesterday. He'd seen my mother drive to work with her Crawford's bags, had seen the ambulance pick up Hallie and my grandfather, had seen the ambulance return later that afternoon, then my mother coming home, and then the squad cars. He didn't know how he could have missed it.

I asked Mr. Klein if he'd seen a red Cadillac DeVille.

"Not even that," he said.

"It's enough, Joe," I heard his wife Fran say.

During the night, I concocted a plan that would allow me to search through the apartment on Albion Street without arousing Jason's suspicions. I would suggest a game of hide-and-seek. I feared that Jason might find the idea babyish, yet I couldn't think of another way to be alone in Bobby's room. But when I reached the apartment, Bobby Kagan was there.

He was wearing a white headband, white tube socks with red stripes on them, no shirt. Now that he was dating my mother, he had invented nicknames for me.

"Benny," he said, "Benito, what's happening?"

There were more than a dozen questions I wanted to ask Bobby Kagan. Why hadn't he been able to pick up my mother the previous night? Where had he been between 5:00 and 7:00? Where did all that money in his dresser come from? But he was the one asking questions before I could pose any of my own. Was I hungry for pancakes? Did I want to see the ballgame tonight? The Sox were playing the Angels. Though he had some business to take care of, he could drop me and Jason off and give us money for a taxi home.

"How do you get such good seats?" I asked.

"I work for the Sox, Benski," he said.

"What do you do?" I asked.

"Public relations, Benovich. I thought I told you that already."

Midway through the game that night, with the Sox down 7-0, I sensed that Jason had grown bored with me. He disappeared for the fifth inning and when he returned and I asked where he'd been, he said he was talking to some girls. I thought he was lying, but during the seventh-inning stretch he left again, then came back to ask if I wanted to join him and the girls in the upper deck. I asked why he couldn't bring them back to our seats; we had the better view.

"Because no one's in the upper deck," he said. "And if no one's in the upper deck, no one can bust you for spitting on people in the boxes."

In the front row of the empty right-field upper deck of Comiskey Park, Judy Petak and Brenda Lawton, two gum-chewing girls with Le Sportsac bags slung over their shoulders, had ditched their parents and were crouched down in front of the green seats. Then, suddenly, they would spring up, spit as far as they could, and duck back down. I don't know if the girls heard Jason when he introduced me, but my name made no impression.

I excused myself to go to the bathroom, and when I returned, Jason was making out with Judy Petak, and Brenda Lawton was spitting her half-chewed gum down. I had the twenty-dollar bill that Bobby Kagan had given us and I figured I could find a taxi in front of Comiskey and Jason wouldn't mind at all if I disappeared. But once I'd made it out the main gates and had searched vainly for a cab, wondering if I would survive a bus or train ride through the city at night, I heard Jason calling after me.

"What the fuck's your problem, man?" he said.

I told him that I hadn't expected him to follow me. He was welcome to stay.

"How am I supposed to do that when you have all the money?" he said.

We took the El back north; Jason had grabbed the twenty-dollar bill from me and said that he wouldn't spend that money on something as stupid as a cab ride. I said that it was probably dangerous to be riding the El so late, but he just laughed.

"If anyone wants to mug me, I'll just give them you as collateral," he said.

We sat next to each other on the train, but we didn't talk much. Every so often, Jason would just say how "goddamn stupid" I was, while I spent most of the ride staring out the windows, hoping no one would pull a knife on me then get pissed because I didn't have money. But when we got to Argyle Street, I grew exasperated with Jason telling me how goddamn stupid I was.

"Maybe I'm stupid," I said, "but at least I'm not so stupid that I don't even know what my uncle does for a living."

"What the fuck are you talking about?" Jason asked and snorted. "I knew you were dumb. Are you crazy now, too?"

"If I'm so dumb, what does he do?" I asked. "Sometimes he's a scout, sometimes he's in public relations, which is it? Do you know?"

"Yeah," he said, "he just doesn't like me to talk about it."

"Why?" I asked.

"Because it's illegal."

I couldn't believe how matter-of-fact he was. I asked him why he wasn't more upset about it. What would happen when Bobby got caught, what would happen to Jason? Where would he live? What would happen if someone caught Bobby in the act and shot him dead?

Jason Rubinstein regarded me with a seemingly indelible sneer. When I was through, he exhaled with a sharp, sardonic laugh. "You're pretty hopeless," he said. "Bobby doesn't rob people."

"Then what do you call what he does?" I asked.

"He's a ticket scalper, you freak."

As the El curved along the tracks, streaking toward Loyola, I stammered, but couldn't get out another word. We were supposed to get off at Morse, then take the Lunt bus home, but Jason got out early. When I tried to follow him, he froze me with a stare.

"Fuck you, asshole," he said.

In the past, no matter where I'd been, I'd always feel dejected when I saw the house on Whipple, could feel my world constricting around me until I could barely breathe. I'd smell the urine and the disinfectant, hear the breaths and the voices. This night, I didn't mind so much.

As I walked in, Hallie was seated at the kitchen table. In her right hand she clutched a paperback Agatha Christie book: *Elephants Can Remember.* But her hand was trembling and her eyes weren't moving over the page.

"She's in the garage," Hallie said when she saw me.

I walked through the den, onto the porch, out the back door, and through the yard, navigating a path of dead tomato plants, weeds, and wildflowers. There was a dim light in the garage. Bobby Kagan's Cadillac was parked in the alley. Cupping my hands over the garage window, I could see Bobby in an open leather vest, blue jeans, and boots. With one hand, he was roughly grabbing my mother's hand, leading her around, while with the other hand, he ripped open boxes and reached into Crawford's shopping bags, every so often pulling something out—a necklace, a handful of cufflinks, a roll of hundred-dollar bills—and gesturing with it in front of my mother's face before shoving it into his pockets. Her cheeks were red and her eyes were huge. I couldn't tell if she was angry or afraid. I ran into the house, then back outside with my Pat Kelly baseball bat, not paying attention when Hallie told me to stop.

I quietly slipped out the back gate and into the alley and walked a few paces north. I stepped into the light spilling out of the garage, walked around the red Cadillac toward the garage door, which was open three-quarters of the way. Bobby Kagan stood with his back to me, his hand still gripping my mother's arm hard as she leaned against the hood of my grandfather's dusty old Lincoln. There were streaks of gray soot on her pale-blue dress. Boxes and bags were scattered around the Lincoln. I could see the TV from my grandfather's living room, I could see the necklaces, the rings, the paperweights, the bracelets. My palms were slippery as I gripped the bat in my hands and my mother's eyes shifted from Bobby onto me.

"Get away!" my mother shouted at me. "Just get away."

She squirmed out of Bobby Kagan's hold and then pulled down the garage door. I dropped my bat and ran down the alley.

All night, I just sat on the front stoop with a rubber ball, bouncing it up and down, waiting for a police car to drive by with its flashers on and its siren off. At dawn, I heard Bobby Kagan's Cadillac rumble away down the alley, then the sound of the back door to the house open and shut. In the morning, I was still there as my mother walked down the steps. She was dressed for work and there were two Crawford's bags in her hand.

"I know," I told her, "I didn't see a thing."

I kept waiting for Mr. Klein to appear on his porch. I wondered what he'd seen and what he knew. But his shades were down, and Mr. Klein didn't come out all day.

THE OLDEST RIVALRY

BY JIM ARNDORFER

I-94, Lake Forest Oasis

The Illinois border burned orange under the falling sun. The rays singed the scrub and trees along the freeway and tempered the big rigs turning on Highway 41. The whitewashed barn demanding, in tall painted letters, that motorists "*Vote Republican*" was completely engulfed. A joke popped into my head.

I looked in the rearview mirror. Andy was orange, too, except for a yellowish spot on his chest. That was the light from the television he wasn't watching as he looked out the window. The way he had been since we left Green Bay. He'd been silent, except for when he slurped his soda or crunched on some chips. Neck curving against the headrest, he struck the image of adolescent ennui.

"Hey, looks like God's a Bears fan, too, huh?" I said.

His face crinkled, as if he were searching for something interesting in the plowed fields. He locked his eyes on mine in the mirror. He waited.

"The sun, it's making everything orange. You know, the Bears' color. Look around."

He looked back out the window, supremely unamused. Not that I could blame him. It's a long way from Green Bay to Chicago, even longer when the Bears smack the Packers around. I knew it was going to be bad when Gary Berry was laid out for five minutes on the opening kickoff. And it was.

Favre's first pass picked off. Marcus Robinson looking like Randy Moss. Cade McNown—Cade McNown!—looking like Dan Fouts. That boneheaded onside kick. We had listened to the blow-by-humiliating-blow recap on AM 620 until I heard Coach Sherman credit his team for almost coming back.

"You don't brag about almost coming back against the Bears! At home!" I turned off the radio. "Sorry." Andy hadn't said anything.

Less than fifteen hours from walking into the office. I could already see the wannabe-hip systems guy grinning at me through his wispy Fu Manchu. "Too bad about your Packers," he'd say, to which I would respond: "Yeah, I guess it wasn't our day."

All this from a putz who couldn't name the Bears' starting O-line.

Andy wouldn't get off as easy, I knew. He was only seven when we moved to Wilmette from Milwaukee five years ago, but he still bled green and gold, as they say on AM 620. That was my one accomplishment as a parent, I told my neighbor John Doolin. He laughed, but I hadn't been completely joking. I worked at it. I bought a dish so we could watch games together. I'd tape the game if I got stuck with clients in the corporate box at Soldier, and we'd watch it later. I'd call him from my hotel room when I was on the road and he'd give me the highlights. Andy'd put up with a lot of crap on the playground over the years for staying faithful. Last year had been the worst, after Walter Payton's ghost blocked the Packers' last-second field goal attempt and delivered the Bears a victory at Lambeau.

Andy still confided in me back then, so he told me what the kids said. "Cheesehead" became "Cheesedick." "Packers suck and Favre swallows." "Favre's a bigger pussy than you are."

That one hurt Andy the most. And they knew it. Skinny and small as he was, Andy wanted to play football. He didn't because we wouldn't let him. It killed him. "I want to!" His eyes would be red and wet. I always gave the same answer: "You're not big enough." "You played and you were shorter than I am." Swallowing my first response, "This one ain't my call," I'd point out my glorious career as a junior high receiver ended after racking up zero receptions and two concussions in two games. I thought Andy had good speed for a corner, but it wasn't a fight worth having.

"Well, we're back in Illinois now. Better get ready for all the shit we're going to have to take, huh?"

I looked in the mirror again. He wasn't going to humor me, even with my just-us-boys vulgarity. And I couldn't blame him. The shit he had to take went beyond abuse about the Packers. He'd get it for not having a credit card. Or for not having a cell phone. Or for having sneakers that cost only two figures. All these appurtenances apparently were standard issue for sixth graders at his school. He'd go to Natalie on this stuff and she'd come to me. I wouldn't have it. Natalie would point out we weren't in Milwaukee anymore. I'd walk into another room. She'd follow me. This apparently was a fight worth having.

I budged once. I told Natalie he could have cell phone when he was in seventh grade. That was a mistake. "Why wait if you already agree in principle?" And she wondered why I left the room when we argued.

The fields gave way to trees. I looked at the clock and gauged how far along the DVD must be.

"Fourth down?"

He looked at the TV. He'd begged us to get the TV with DVD-player option when we bought our paramilitary suburban vehicle. And after that he'd begged me to transfer my Packers videotape library to DVD so he could watch games on road trips. An hour outside Lambeau I put this one on as a surprise. I thought it'd be just the thing to get him out of his funk.

"Yeah."

November 5, 1989. Packers vs. Bears at Lambeau. The Packers were down by six at the Bears' 14 with forty-one seconds left. The Packers lined up in a four-receiver set and Majkowski went under the center. I was watching the game in a bar with friends from work. No one was breathing.

"Man, that was a good game."

"I don't know. It wasn't as good as the one Grandpa took us to."

That would have been December 18, 1994. The last game at Milwaukee County Stadium. No, not many games were better than that one. Not that the Packers played well; they should have put the Falcons away early. Despite all this "greatest fans in the world" hype about Packer backers, boos came lustily from the stands. And I could feel the chilly fear around me when the Packers lined up at their 33 with 1:58 left and them down 17-14. But people went nuts when Favre hit a stumbling Chmura for a twenty-five-yard pass; the crescendo of footstomping and screams hit a peak as the Packers called for a time out at the Falcons 9 with twenty-one seconds left. And when Favre dove into the end zone with fourteen seconds left, it was as if the Holy Spirit had come down. The people around me started shrieking in tongues and weeping and kissing each other. They would never be able to watch the Packers play in cramped, rickety

County again, but it was all right. They were close to the promised land.

No doubt Andy remembered the County finale for Grandpa. Grandpa explained the plays to him. Grandpa explained the penalties to him. Grandpa explained that he'd probably never see a better quarterback than the guy wearing No. 4, so watch him close. When Andy needed to go to the bathroom, he asked Grandpa. He knew Grandpa would cut a wider path through the howling crowd than his scrawny dad. Grandpa still had the body of the linebacker who'd played for Washington High School during the '50s and of the Harnischfeger worker who had shaped giant mining shovels with his hubcap-sized hands. Andy was too young to notice how Grandpa's walk was a shuffle instead of a stride. He couldn't see the way Grandpa squeezed his eyes shut every few steps. And he probably didn't realize Grandpa's hand on his shoulder wasn't guiding him; it was resting on him.

I'd hoped seeing the Packers beat the Bears would make Andy happy. I'd hoped spending all this time together would make him talk to me. I'd hoped, and I realized this as I saw the sign for the toll booth, to hammer life into the shape of an uplifting movie. Instead, Brett Favre screws up and Mike Sherman talks about making a good comeback.

I wanted him to see the Packers win because I couldn't think of anything to say that would make him happy. That would make him realize he wasn't a wimp. Because my own dad had been able to do that. The morning after my second concussion—blindsided by a freckled safety with the ball bobbling in my palms—I woke up to see dad at the end of my bed. He'd just pulled a shift and was still wearing his coveralls. I could smell his armpits and the Pabst he'd knocked back after work. "Hi," I said.

"You're not big enough," he said. "But you are tough, and you know, you can be tough in other ways. The way you study—so hard?—that's being tough. Not everyone can do that. Reading long books, that's tough too. That's stuff I can't do that you can do. And if you do that, you're going to be able to do some things I can't."

So I hit the books harder than Ray Nitschke. Dad'd find me sitting at the kitchen table at 2:00 in the morning and pat my head. When he saw my report cards he'd hit me so hard on the shoulder I'd bruise; we'd smile at each other while I tried to rub away the pain and not squirt a tear. I wanted to be tough. I kept at it through high school and as I pursued my business degree at Marquette University. That's where I met Natalie, who got me with the blond patch in her dark-brown hair and her ability to talk for hours about something called "branding." She needed less sleep than I did. A consulting business hired me after graduation and she went to work for a cheese company. Not long after that we went for our MBAs at Kellogg. She went to one of the world's biggest packaged-goods companies, I went to a well-known consulting firm with offices in every major city around the globe. She now spent her every waking hour trying to give personalities to frozen foods; I was the reason my boss issued a no-poaching order to the partners. Nat was looking on the Web for homes in Winnetka.

I can say without being at all reductionist or overly schematic that my dad's words that dismal morning set me on the path I took. But I couldn't say those words to Andy. My dad was a guy who carried beer barrels under his arm at block parties. I was a guy who got knocked out the only two times he ever suited up.

Andy's head bounced when we hit the toll both speed

bump. As I fished some change out of my pocket, I saw an empty toll gate. I hit the gas.

In the mirror, Andy was still looking out the window. He had missed the best part—Majikowski throwing what looked like a touchdown pass and the place going crazy. Then the flag; Majikowski was over the line of scrimmage when he threw it. This time the fans howled. As if to soothe their rage, the top ref went to his tape player to review the play. For nearly five minutes.

"Is Parkinson done looking at the tape?" I knew the answer.

"Yes."

I slowed down to drop the coins in the change basket. The gate lifted. I looked at the clock, counted to five, and started by imitating the ref: "Upon further review . . ." And then I repeated the roar that had filled the bar before Parkinson could explain himself: "THE BEARS STILL SUCK!" I could see the look on Bears kicker Kevin Butler's face. Ditka's face so red I'd hoped the heart attack would hit him then. After four years of losing to the Bears, the Packers pulled one out. After watching the 1985 Bears go to the Super Bowl, the Packers had humbled them. It was all the sweeter because of the way the Bears showed their loser mentality: In later team guides, an asterisk hung over the score. "*Instant replay game*." The game they could never admit they lost.

"Can we stop at Wendy's?"

"Sure."

The lot was a third full. I spotted marks of road-tripping Bears fans. A weathered flag mounted on a window of a mini-van. A dozen bumper stickers seemingly holding together the disintegrating rear bumper of an Aspire. A Bears helmet in the back window of an Audi. I grabbed my hat from the passenger seat.

"All right, let's put our gear on. Got to hold our heads high, win or lose, right? Otherwise, we might as well be Bears fans."

I turned to Andy. He stared back at me. He made a face and put his hat on.

Listening to Andy order three double burgers with bacon, I wondered if he didn't have a growth spurt ahead of him. He asked for barbecue sauce for his fries. Nat never let him eat like this even though he was bony. But after the loss and knowing what tomorrow would bring, I wasn't going to stop him. Maybe Nat wouldn't have either.

We passed a family with two boys younger than Andy as we looked for a place to sit. All of them were wearing growling Bears sweaters. The older boy smirked at us. The minivan, I figured. I didn't look around for the drivers of the Audi or the Aspire. We took a table by the window.

"They should be able to take the Lions and the Niners," I announced. Andy was halfway through his second burger. It was the first thing I said to interrupt our watching headlights pass beneath us. "But after the bye, man, it gets tough. Miami. The Vikes. The Bucs. Ugh. If they don't start looking better, they're not going to make the play-offs."

"Yeah, but do we want to limp into the postseason anyway? I mean, why not just get the draft pick?"

"But you can't play like that. The guys won't play like that. They have to look good if they want to get the big money, you know?" I took a drink from my soda. "And the coaches would get run out of town if they did that. You know that. The fans own them; they wouldn't like that."

"The McCaskeys don't seem to mind losing."

"As they say: 'McCaskey has no Ditka.'" I tapped my cup against his as he swallowed the last of his burger. He didn't reciprocate. "Just as long as they beat the Bears at Soldier, huh?"

"Could we go?"

My face muscles tightened; I felt my lips draw taut. That was a popular ticket for the firm. They always tried to get a big client in there for that one, and they always wanted a show of force. Andy looked away.

"Maybe . . ."

"I gotta go to the bathroom."

"Okay. I'll clean up."

I didn't enjoy going to the box. I hated it. The chit-chat and bullshit bonhomie with clients or prospects over beers and wings—we were all such regular guys in our luxury suite—while talking business. How to get ready for Y2K. How to open a plant in Mexico. How to find reliable partners in China. Usually the game was background music. Only a few of them could even follow it. Any time one of them said something, it was just rehashed Chris Berman or Dan Pompei.

"What we need are more Grabowskis," said one west suburban metal bender busy plotting to move a couple of lines to a maquiladora, invoking the word Ditka used to describe blue-collar guys he wanted on his teams.

"You probably got a guy named Grabowski who'll need a new job soon," I had replied. It was a joke. That's what I told my boss the next morning. I was told to consider myself lucky we had kept the business. He left it at that.

I prodded the wrappers and stray French fries onto the tray. I spotted a napkin crumpled under Andy's chair and reached for it. My shoulder hit the tray, sending my cup tumbling over my back. It hit the floor and sprayed ice across the floor. I swore and started to pick up the cubes. Mama Bear was watching me with a thin smile as I set the last shard on the tray.

I dropped everything in the trash and headed toward the bathroom, wondering what was taking Andy so long. The nut and candy stand by the bathroom was closed. I heard someone yelling. I started to run. I heard words now:

"Favre sucks. Why don't you get a real team?"

My hands were on the door.

The bathroom reeked of stale whiskey. The fluorescent fixtures cast a nicotine-yellow glow. I looked past the bank of stalls and saw Andy. He was pressed up against the wall near the sink. His eyes were wide and wet. His fingers were spread against the tiles. The only parts of him moving were his carotids, throbbing.

The man standing between us had half a head and fifty pounds on me. A Bears helmet patch was stitched on the back of his army jacket. Wiry black curls sprung from under his knit Bears cap. From the way he rocked in his heavy boots, I was sure he was the source of the whiskey odor. Then he started slurring.

"What, are you going to start crying now, you little pussy?" He stuck his gloved hand at Andy. "That faggot Favre likes to cry."

And then the man's body tensed as if to take a step toward Andy. And maybe he did, I can't be sure. I don't remember it clearly. I remember what happened next as a fragmented sequence of impressions.

My hands against the man's back. His headlong fall toward the stall door. The door opening as his face hit it. The sharp, hard crack. The heavy *whumpf* on the floor. The door bouncing back and forth several times before settling shut. The man's boots sticking out from underneath it. Then the smell: sharp, sweet, and sour at once. Like something rotting.

Andy was shivering. I realized we had to get out before someone else walked in. "Andy," I said. He didn't look up from the floor. I said his name again; no answer. Then I saw he was looking at something.

The liquid was black in the yellow light. The first trickle streamed along the grout line on its way to the sink. But it was chased by a faster current moving across the tiles.

"Get over here, Andy."

He looked at me, looked at the floor, and looked at his shoes.

"Andy, get over here right now. We have to get out of here."

His eyes repeated their motion. Then he broke for the stall. I hopped over the widening puddle and cut him off. I hugged him and lifted him off the floor. Just as I stretched my leg over the puddle, he kicked the stall door open. I caught a glimpse of the stain the man's head made on the toilet. I don't know how much Andy saw.

I set him down at the exit door. "Walk," I said. "Walk, just fucking walk."

Mama Bear's hand was locked on the forearm of her crying daughter. The lines were getting deeper at Wendy's. A kid was playing the mechanical crane game near the doors, trying to maneuver the claw toward a stuffed rabbit in the corner. No one said a word to us, no one looked at us. No one shouted, "Stop!" We were just two sorry-ass Packers fans scurrying on our way home.

Driving, I figured the scenario. A hidden camera in the bathroom must have caught me pushing the guy. Cameras in the parking lot probably followed our escape. At least the film would show I didn't mean to kill the guy. They wouldn't try to get me for murder. Manslaughter, maybe, but even then I'd probably get some slack; the guy could have hit Andy for all I knew. But there would be a trial. And even if I won, I would lose my job. No reputable consulting firm could employ someone who killed a stranger in a rest stop bathroom. They'd treat me well—no doubt partly out of fear I'd go postal. At a minimum we'd have to leave Wilmette; Nat might very well move out.

The next toll came up. Did the workers have my plates and description? I imagined my foot pressing on the gas pedal—the grill could take out the toll gate, I had no doubt. But then I realized: They wouldn't stop a killer without backup. No police cherrytops were spinning up ahead and a state employee wasn't going to try to be a hero. I slowed down and in my pocket my fingertips effortlessly set on a dime, a nickel, and a quarter. The toll booth worker was wearing headphones and smoking.

"Go Packers!" I shouted before I rolled up the window.

I got off at Tower Road and followed it through leafy Winnetka. I stayed five miles below the speed limit. But even as I kept my eye on the speedometer, my hands didn't feel the steering wheel; every tiny bone still rang from the man's shoulder blade. The balls of my feet were still pressing against the wet tile floor. My calf muscles ached from stretching for maximum push. I couldn't see Andy in the darkness but I knew the fear I'd seen when I opened the door still filled him. The men's room was staying with us.

A BMW brighted me and sped by in the other lane. He honked once he passed by. I waved, sincerely. Having somebody behind me would have made me nervous.

I went south on Green Bay Road along the Metra tracks. The stores in downtown Winnetka were dark and the auto repair shops looked abandoned. I flipped off the ridiculous cursive Kenilworth sign, a joke Andy and I shared. But once again, he didn't take the bait. I went east on Lake and a few blocks later turned onto our brick-paved road. I always said the best part of our suburban battlewagon was that you couldn't feel the ruts.

We sat in the car for a while after I pulled into the garage. I was waiting for Andy to say something until I realized he was doing the same. I was the father, so I went first.

"Well, I've got some work to do before I turn in. You?"

"Social studies homework."

"Okay. Well, we'll get them the next game, right?"

"Right."

Listening to his footsteps overhead, I went to the liquor cabinet and poured a Scotch. Then I went to my office. Two Macanudos lay in the top drawer. They were to have been lit up by us if the Packers had won. Looking at them now, I couldn't believe I had conceived such a horrible idea. It was so horrible I couldn't help but laugh. When I calmed down, I unwrapped one and sliced off the end with my Packers cutter. I lit it. After a couple puffs I went to the front room. I wanted to see the police as they came for me up our bumpy narrow street. Or maybe they would *walk* over; the Ridge station was only a few blocks away.

I stared into the lit windows of the Georgians and bungalows across the street for a peek of my neighbors. No luck. Scaffolding loomed in John Doolin's backyard. He'd blown out the back to add a home theater. During the summer it had been copper gutters. He was a broker.

"It should really help the value when we try to sell," he

said at a block party over the summer. "People expect that kind of viewing experience today. It's getting to be like central air."

"When are you moving?"

"Oh, no, we don't have any plans now. But when the time comes."

"Right, when the time comes."

"And I'll say now, I couldn't have picked a better time to liquidate some stocks to raise the money." He paused and looked both ways. "I unloaded in February."

"Did you tell your clients you were doing that?"

He'd laughed, twisting a fallen leaf under the toe of his loafer. "One or two."

When Andy and I set off to watch the Packers lose, John's son Steven, who was in the same grade as Andy, had been playing catch with his little sister. Both were wearing Cade McNown jerseys. It made me laugh. How was I to know? But now as I stared at the dark, empty lawn, I recalled a day years back: Steven running in circles and kicking up leaves in a Favre jersey. And in the seasons after the Super Bowl, he wasn't the only kid on the block sporting No. 4.

And that's when it struck me: For as much as I hated the kids who were going to torture my boy the next day, it wasn't entirely their fault. If their parents, most of them nominally Bears fans, even some of the ones from out of town, couldn't teach them to hate the Packers, you had to wonder what exactly were they being taught. I tried to imagine a kid in my Milwaukee neighborhood of duplexes and bungalows wearing McMahon's jersey. I couldn't. So no wonder they walked around Old Orchard gabbing about nothing on their cell phones and buying movie tickets with plastic. If they weren't being taught something as basic as *you don't wear a Packers jersey*, what were they being taught? The question answered itself.

After I finished the cigar I went to the kitchen and took out the Scotch bottle again. Then I went to the den and turned on the TV. I kept the volume low so I could hear the police tires slither over the bricks.

The news at 5:30 a.m. mentioned a body found in the Lake Forest rest stop; police were investigating. When I heard Andy's feet coming down the stairs I hid the bottle under the blanket and feigned sleep. After he left, I called in sick. By 8:00, it appeared the man had slipped but police were investigating. At 10:30 the police gave a name to the body: John Radkovich, a thirty-two-year-old landscaper from Lincolnwood. He'd watched the game at a friend's in Lindenhurst. "Yeah, he'd been drinking, but not so much," his droopy-eyed host said, unconvincingly. On the 5 o'clock news, Radkovich was divorced with one son. They showed a picture of him and his ex. She had slapped him with a restraining order when he was caught creeping in the bushes around her house after hearing she was engaged. She didn't appear on camera, but was kind enough off-camera to tell the shivering reporter that John had fought a "long-running battle with the bottle." As it turns out, he had been the driver of the Aspire.

The death of John Radkovich registered sixty seconds on the 10 o'clock news; the segment included a safety expert noting how many fatal accidents occur in bathrooms, so people should be vigilant. There was no mention of a crime being caught on camera, of a car being spotted fleeing the scene.

The police didn't come that day or the next. Or ever.

I didn't have any problem getting out of luxury box duty. It was simple actually. All I had to say was, "My son wants to go to the game with me Sunday night."

"Do you want to bring him in the box?"

"No, I think he'll want to sit outside."

"I can get 50-yard-line seats for the two of you. Would that be all right?"

Was it ever. The Pack whipped the Bears 28-6. Drive after grinding drive capped by Tyrone Williams returning a pick for a touchdown. Shane Matthews was no McNown. Andy was as excited as I'd seen him in months; he was smiling, jumping, and high-fiving a couple Packers fans sitting two rows behind. The Bears fans around us were tolerant and one even told Andy that Favre was the best quarterback he'd ever seen.

I wondered what they'd think if someone had told them not three months ago I killed one of their fellow Bears fans. Would they have believed it? This guy who takes his son out on a Sunday night to see a game? Who called for beers for the woman whose call wasn't heard by the vendor? They would have expected some mark probably: excessive stubble or a twitchy eye or a haunted expression. Some physical manifestation of guilt. But not a trace of that. And not because I was hiding it. I didn't feel it. I'd slept soundly since the first few days, when I realized I wasn't going to get caught. It didn't hang over my thoughts either. And, to be honest, Nat and I had been having our best sex in years. Nothing like a crisis averted to reawaken the animal passions. I was still enough of a Catholic to wonder if I should be guilty: I killed a man, after all. But it had been an accident. And while he'd left behind a son, who's to say his ex's new husband wouldn't be a better man? What kind of father can a man be, really, if he's berating a small boy in a public rest room?

For years I'd been putting food on the table by skillfully finding ways to take jobs away from hardworking guys, men just as good as my father, real Grabowskis, and send them to another country. Every time I did that, I knew in some way I was killing those guys. Sometimes, indirectly, not just metaphorically. Analysts at Doolin's firm repeatedly called for corporate America to cut jobs, to "contain" costs, to be a little more nimble. Bill Chait two doors down was a lawyer who fought workers' comp cases. House after well-maintained house in Wilmette was paid for by taking a little bit from the Grabowskis. Of course I could live with accidentally snuffing a landscaper from Lincolnwood. So could any number of my neighbors. We'd all had plenty of practice.

ABOUT THE CONTRIBUTORS:

Miriam Berkley

JEFFERY RENARD ALLEN is an Associate Professor of English at Queens College of the City University of New York and an instructor in the graduate writing program at New School University. He is the author of two books, *Harbors and Spirits,* a collection of poems, and the novel *Rails Under My Back,* which won the *Chicago Tribune's* Heartland Prize for Fiction.

Paula Wheeler

JIM ARNDORFER was born and raised in Milwaukee. He now lives on the far North Side of Chicago—in broadcast range of the Packers Radio Network—with his wife and son. He has attended four Packers-Bears games and the teams have split. He is a reporter for *Advertising Age* and a contributor to *The Baffler.*

Nathan Mandell

DANIEL BUCKMAN is the author of *Water in Darkness, The Names of Rivers,* and *Morning Dark.* His fourth novel, *Wet Trees,* is forthcoming in 2006. A former paratrooper and journalist, Buckman lives and works in Chicago.

Susannah Felts

TODD DILLS hails originally from Rock Hill, South Carolina, but desertion is sweet release: He has called Chicago his home for these past years. He is editor and publisher of *THE2NDHAND,* a broadsheet and online magazine (the2ndhand.com) for new writing. His stories, reviews, and erratta have appeared in numerous publications, including the *Chicago Reader,* where he also works.

Elivi Varga

ANDREW ERVIN lives in downstate Illinois. His stories have appeared in the *Prague Literary Review* and *Night Rally.* He has also contributed reviews, articles, and essays to the *New York Times Book Review, San Francisco Chronicle, Washington Post Book World, Chicago Tribune, The Believer,* and other places.

Andy Halpern

ALEXAI GALAVIZ-BUDZISZEWSKI was born and raised in Pilsen on the South Side of Chicago. He has published numerous stories in journals such as *Triquarterly, Ploughshares,* and the *Alaska Quarterly Review.* He still lives and works on the South Side of Chicago.

Wayne Geist

LUCIANO GUERRIERO, a contributor to Akashic's *Brooklyn Noir,* recently completed his first noir novel, *The Spin.* His fourth play, *Fireman's Dance,* will be produced in New York City in the fall of 2005. Luciano has acted in or directed seventy-five plays, and has appeared in twenty Hollywood and independent films, and in many television shows.

Bryan Bedell

KEVIN GUILFOILE'S first novel, *Cast of Shadows,* was published this year by Knopf. He lives in the Chicago area with his wife and son.

Andreas Von Lintel

ADAM LANGER is the author of the novels *Crossing California* and *The Washington Story.* He divides his time between New York City and Bloomington, Indiana.

Daniel Sinker

JOE MENO is a fiction writer from Chicago and winner of a Nelson Algren Literary Award. His latest novel, *Hairstyles of the Damned,* follows the exploits of adolescents as they struggle for belonging on Chicago's South Side. He is a contributing editor and columnist for *Punk Planet* magazine, another 2nd-city landmark.

MICHAEL K. MEYERS is a writer and performance artist. His fiction has been published in the *New Yorker*, and his performance work has been presented around the world, including at MoMA, Tel Aviv Museum, and Warsaw Institute of Contemporary Art. He teaches in the M.F.A. Writing Program at the School of the Art Institute in Chicago and lives in Evanston, Illinois. He is the recipient of numerous arts fellowships.

Philip Cantor

ACHY OBEJAS was born in Cuba and grew up in Indiana, looking across Lake Michigan at Chicago and thinking it was her own Emerald City. The author of three books, including the critically acclaimed *Days of Awe,* she currently lives in Kenwood, on the South Side, and teaches at the University of Chicago.

Ovie Carter

BAYO OJIKUTU was born and raised in greater Chicago. He is the son of folks who migrated to the city from West Africa (Lagos, Nigeria) and the Deep South (Shreveport, Louisiana). Ojikutu's first novel, *47th Street Black* (Three Rivers Press, 2003), won the Washington Prize for Fiction and the Great American Book Award. His second novel, *Free Burning,* will be released in 2006. Currently, Ojikutu teaches in the Department of English at DePaul University, Chicago.

Allan Landau

PETER ORNER was born at Michael Reece Hospital in Chicago. His first book, *Esther Stories* (Houghton Mifflin, 2001), was a *New York Times* Notable Book and won the Rome Prize from the American Academy of Arts and Letters and the Goldberg Prize for fiction. His novel, *The Second Coming of Mavala Shikongo,* will be published in 2006.

Simonetta Bogetti

NEAL POLLACK worked as a reporter for the *Chicago Reader* from 1993–2000, where he wrote the "Petty Crime" column, among many other assignments. He's the author of three books of satire, including the cult-classic *The Neal Pollack Anthology of American Literature* and the rock-n-roll novel *Never Mind the Pollacks.* He is a regular contributor to *Vanity Fair* and *Nerve.* He lives in Austin, Texas, with his family.

Niles Fuller

Brandon Roberts

AMY SAYRE-ROBERTS lives in Springfield, Illinois with one beautiful husband and two talented Malamutes (both born in Chicago). Her work has appeared in the *American Book Review* and the *Alchemist Review*.

Steve Goodman

C.J. SULLIVAN'S idol growing up was Chicago Cub legend Billy Williams. He works by day as a Court Clerk in Brooklyn Supreme and by night as a reporter for the *New York Post*. The two loves in his life are his twin girls: Luisa Marie and Olivia Kathleen Sullivan. He lives in New York City.

Janice Zulkey

CLAIRE ZULKEY was born in Evanston, Illinois, and lives in Chicago. She has contributed to the *Mississippi Review* and *Chicago Magazine,* and published a book of literary humor titled *Girls! Girls! Girls!* More of her writing can be found on her website, Zulkey.com. Whatever crimes she has committed are not very interesting.

Also available from Akashic Books

BROOKLYN NOIR
edited by Tim McLoughlin
350 pages, a trade paperback original, $15.95, ISBN: 1-888451-58-0
*Finalist stories for EDGAR AWARD, PUSHCART PRIZE, and SHAMUS AWARD

Twenty brand new crime stories from New York's punchiest borough. Contributors include: Pete Hamill, Arthur Nersesian, Maggie Estep, Nelson George, Neal Pollack, Sidney Offit, Ken Bruen, and others.

"*Brooklyn Noir* is such a stunningly perfect combination that you can't believe you haven't read an anthology like this before. But trust me—you haven't. Story after story is a revelation, filled with the requisite sense of place, but also the perfect twists that crime stories demand. The writing is flat-out superb, filled with lines that will sing in your head for a long time to come."
—Laura Lippman, winner of the Edgar, Agatha, and Shamus awards

BROOKLYN NOIR 2: THE CLASSICS
edited by Tim McLoughlin
309 pages, trade paperback, $15.95, ISBN: 1-888451-76-9

Brooklyn Noir is back with a vengeance, this time with masters of yore mixing with the young blood: H.P. Lovecraft, Lawrence Block, Donald Westlake, Pete Hamill, Jonathan Lethem, Colson Whitehead, Irwin Shaw, Carolyn Wheat, Thomas Wolfe, Hubert Selby, Stanley Ellin, Gilbert Sorrentino, Maggie Estep, and Salvatore La Puma.

SAN FRANCISCO NOIR
edited by Peter Maravelis
325 pages, a trade paperback original, $15.95, ISBN: 1-888451-91-2

Brand new stories by: Domenic Stansberry, Barry Gifford, Eddie Muller, Robert Mailer Anderson, Michelle Tea, Peter Plate, Kate Braverman, David Corbett, Alejandro Murguía, Sin Soracco, Alvin Lu, Jon Longhi, Will Christopher Baer, Jim Nesbit, and David Henry Sterry.

San Francisco Noir lashes out with hard-biting tales exploring the shadowy nether regions of scenic "Baghdad by the Bay." Desperation, transgression, and madness fuel these tales celebrating San Francisco's criminal heritage.

SOUTHLAND by Nina Revoyr
348 pages, a trade paperback original, $15.95, ISBN: 1-888451-41-6
*Winner of a LAMBDA LITERARY AWARD & FERRO-GRUMLEY AWARD
*EDGAR AWARD finalist

"If Oprah still had her book club, this novel likely would be at the top of her list . . . With prose that is beautiful, precise, but never pretentious . . ."
—*Booklist*

"*Southland* merges elements of literature and social history with the propulsive drive of a mystery, while evoking Southern California as a character, a key player in the tale. Such aesthetics have motivated other Southland writers, most notably Walter Mosley."
—*Los Angeles Times*

ADIOS MUCHACHOS by Daniel Chavarría
245 pages, a trade paperback original, $13.95, ISBN: 1-888451-16-5
*Winner of the EDGAR AWARD

"Out of the mystery wrapped in an enigma that, over the last forty years, has been Cuba for the U.S., comes a Uruguayan voice so cheerful, a face so laughing, and a mind so deviously optimistic that we can only hope this is but the beginning of a flood of Latin America's indomitable novelists, playwrights, storytellers. Welcome, Daniel Chavarría."
—Donald Westlake, author of *Trust Me on This*

HAIRSTYLES OF THE DAMNED
by Joe Meno
290 pages, a trade paperback original, $13.95, ISBN: 1-888451-70-X
*PUNK PLANET BOOKS, a BARNES & NOBLE DISCOVER PROGRAM selection

"Joe Meno writes with the energy, honesty, and emotional impact of the best punk rock. From the opening sentence to the very last word, *Hairstyles of the Damned* held me in his grip."
—Jim DeRogatis, pop music critic, *Chicago Sun-Times*

These books are available at local bookstores.
They can also be purchased with a credit card online through www.akashicbooks.com.
To order by mail send a check or money order to:

AKASHIC BOOKS
PO Box 1456, New York, NY 10009
www.akashicbooks.com, Akashic7@aol.com

(Prices include shipping. Outside the U.S., add $8 to each book ordered.)